DOCTOR WHO

EYE OF HEAVEN

JIM MORTIMORE

BBC BOOKS

Other BBC DOCTOR WHO books include:

THE EIGHT DOCTORS *by Terrance Dicks*

THE BODYSNATCHERS *by Mark Morris*

GENOCIDE *by Paul Leonard*

WAR OF THE DALEKS *by John Peel*

ALIEN BODIES *by Lawrence Miles*

OPTION LOCK *by Justin Richards*

THE DEVIL GOBLINS FROM NEPTUNE *by Keith Topping and Martin Day*

THE MURDER GAME *by Steve Lyons*

THE ULTIMATE TREASURE *by Christopher Bulis*

BUSINESS UNUSUAL *by Gary Russell*

ILLEGAL ALIEN *by Mike Tucker and Robert Perry*

THE ROUNDHEADS *by Mark Gatiss*

THE FACE OF THE ENEMY *by David A. McIntee*

THE BOOK OF LISTS *by Justin Richards and Andrew Martin*

A BOOK OF MONSTERS *by David J Howe*

DOCTOR WHO titles on BBC Video include:

THE WAR MACHINES *starring William Hartnell*	BBCV 6183
TIMELASH *starring Colin Baker*	BBCV 6329
THE E-SPACE TRILOGY BOXED SET *starring Tom Baker*	BBCV 6229

Published by BBC Worldwide Ltd,
Woodlands, 80 Wood Lane
London W12 0TT

First published 1998
Copyright © Jim Mortimore 1998
The moral right of the author has been asserted

Original series broadcast on the BBC
Format © BBC 1963
Doctor Who and TARDIS are trademarks of the BBC

ISBN 0 563 40567 8
Imaging by Black Sheep, copyright © BBC 1998

Printed and bound in Great Britain by Mackays of Chatham
Cover printed by Belmont Press Ltd, Northampton

For

Nick Walters, Liz Holliday, Finn Clarke, Meg Henderson, Sean Gaffney, Ruth Bell, Mark Healey, Ian Mond, Dave Golding, Raymond Sawaya, Ian Cooke, Mike Agate, Mike Morgan, Alex Pinfold, Daniel O'Connor, Alan Forrester, Martin Barclay, Martin Killeen, Alan Darlington, Carl R. DeSkauton, Brian Copeland, Alex Bacon, Stuart Vandal, Andrew Grisdale, John Carruthers, James Russell, James Middleditch, James Hawden, S. Resh, Andrew J. Muller, George Zahora, Ralph Burns, Fred Herman, Shona Macleod, Ron Plath, Robert E. Smith, Leighton James, Clive Banks, Geraint Wyn Williams, Peter Fitzgerald, Dom J. Cericola, Richard Holland, Joe Lidster, Chris Cotgrove, Michael Agate, Ed Watkinson, Steve Foster, Peter Robinson, Matthew Barclay, Iain Martin, Ian Smith, Rodney Cobb, Chris Orton, Mark Clapham, Paul Clarke, Keith Burton, Wilf Burton, Peter Ware, Simon Simmond, Alister Pearson, David Richards, Rhys Davis, Adrian Couper, Elisabeth White, Erik Pollit, Paul Castle, Julian White, Rob Maile, Tony Gardner, Graham Farquhar, Richard Styles, James Crowther, Carmen Martin, Brett Gabbatt, Adam Bansak, Alex Wilcock, Alan and Bridget Penman, Craig Hurnouth and Kristin Elisabeth Sanderson.

Ta peeps. I owe you one.

A big thank you to Brett, Ian, Brian and everyone else who offered thoughts for Dad.

Jim Mortimore
Earth, 1997

'Easter Island is the loneliest inhabited place in the world. The nearest the solid land the inhabitants can see is in the firmament, the moon and the planets. Therefore they live closest to the stars and know more names of stars than towns and countries in our own world.'

Thor Heyerdahl,
Aku Aku (pub. 1958)

'The shadows of the departed builders still possess the land. One cannot escape from them. They are more active and real than the living population.

Everywhere is the wind of heaven; around and above all are boundless sea and sky, infinite space and great silence. The dweller there feels unconsciously that he is in the antechamber to something yet more vast which is just beyond his ken.'

Katherine Routledge,
'On her expedition to Easter Island' (1914)

Contents

Prologue
Rongo-Rongo

October 1842

'In childhood, in boyhood, and in man's estate, I have been a rover; not a mere rambler among the woody glens and upon the hilltops of my own native land, but an enthusiastic rover throughout the length and breadth of the wide, wide world.'

R.M. Ballantyne,
Coral Island

The night. The night is moving, changing shape around me. The night is stone and the stones are hunting me. The great *moai* are walking. The stones are walking. The stones. The stones are hunting me. O God, help me, the stones are hunting me!

Blood. On my face. Blood and sweat. Fear made liquid by my straining body. My hands clutching wood made slippery by the same cold fear, a tablet, the *rongo-rongo*, its surface etched with ancient words, a secret history, the knowledge of a people that wants to kill me, to strip the life, the soul, the very humanity from me.

And so I am running. Running for my life across cliff tops softened by wind and sea spray and birdlime, softened to crumbling whiteness where the footing is more treacherous than the blackest swamp.

And they follow, patient, angry, unforgiving. I can hear them behind me, pattering upon the whitened rock, a soft rain of footfalls. The gulls answer their voices, sharp, impatient, angry. It is not hard to distinguish between the two. I keep running.

The cliffs end abruptly, white edges uncharacteristically sharp against the night, the southern moon, the lashing seascape below.

How far down? A tree's height? Two? High enough for the wind to lash at my face and hands, vanquishing the dirt and rock dust but burning the cuts in my skin with salt.

I look back. I see nothing but the night. The wind hides them from me, but oh, it brings me their voices. I can hear them. Hear them hunting me. I stand at the edge of the cliff. The wind takes me, sucks the breath from my mouth, the resolve from my heart. I know if I stand here for another second I am lost. I rip open my shirt, stuff the tablet inside, and fold my arms across it for protection. Even now I think to protect the tablet above my face. I lean forward, screaming into the wind.

Terror. Defiance. Joy.

I jump. I fall.

I fall.

I –

– hit the water as if it were solid ground. I scream in pain. What little breath the wind has left me is driven from my lungs and replaced by water. It is shockingly cold. My arms and legs move of their own accord, thrashing the dark waters into foam, all thought gone except the need to move, the need to rise, the need for –

– air! Sweet air! Cold air! Stinging air! It fills me and lifts me. I grasp it with a lover's desperation and cry aloud with my release.

I drift. Salt wetness cradles me roughly.

My lover, the air, is joined by the sea. Now we are three. A *ménage-à-trois* of nature. But my lovers are cold. I slow in their grasp. Controlled by them. Numbed by their attention. Driven by their passion. I struggle but cannot prevail. I have lost myself within them.

And then I hear it. Above the wind. Above the waves. The voice of stone. Stone, moving. Stone, grinding through ancient earth, pushing aside rock as if it were a carpet of leaves. Stone, walking.

I swim. I shout defiance and swim. I scream abuse at the night and my failing body and God himself, and I swim and swim and I crack my head against solid darkness. The night takes shape around me. The canoe. Thank God. Thank all the gods. I drag myself into the rough hollow of wood and collapse. My hands move without conscious volition, checking my shirt. The tablet is safe. The *rongo-rongo* nestles cold and sodden against my heart. I can feel its ancient hieroglyphics abrade my salt-swollen skin.

Safe. It is safe, the *rongo-rongo* is safe.

I grope within the craft for a paddle. I find it, jerk myself into a sitting position and dig the paddle into the waves. I tell myself the hardest battle is won, but I am lying: a quarter of a mile of water and ten miles of volcanic rock and a hundred furious voices in close pursuit tell me so.

Stone, walking, tells me so.

I dig with the paddle, flipping the canoe around and angling out into the choppy waters. Rapa Nui is a dark shape, lightless and comfortless, brooding upon the horizon. I dig again and again, and the jagged shape grows closer, towering above me with the sound of waves and gulls, the white cliffs glistening beneath a moon divided by umber clouds.

I break the paddle against rock before I realise the canoe has beached, thrust up on to land by the force of an angry sea. I scramble out, stagger on to the rocks. There is no light. The moon is shrinking, clothed in gathering clouds. I blink salt spray from my eyes, wipe stinging tears on the back of my

3

hand, the blood there diluted in my flight across the channel.

I do not look back. I cannot. No sound reaches me above the restless waves. Have they given up? Do they think me lost? Dear Lord, am I lost?

My heart answers that question by telling my legs to move. Lacking a clearer course to pursue, I obey, clambering across weed-slick rocks to a drier shore. There is no sand. The only sand here is at Anakena Bay, on the other side of the island. Ten miles across near-treeless fields of volcanic glass and jagged rock. I focus on the sand. It is a balm for my pain. Cool where my skin burns. Warm in the golden sunlight of these latitudes. It is safer to think of the sand then the ship laid at anchor there. The *Marco Polo* is my salvation. If I can reach it. But I dare not think of it, lest my hope bring even greater catastrophe than has already befallen me.

I scramble across the shore, searching for a way to ascend the cliffs, double the height of those from which fortune had barely granted me my life. There is a way but it is treacherous, a giant's ladder of jagged rock. My path is made even more difficult by the failing moonlight. It is as much as I can do to begin the ascent, let alone end it.

I am aware of the passing of time only as an apparently endless series of pain-filled steps. I will not say strides. I am a young man, having attained my twenty-fifth birthday while crossing the Equator, yet I feel as old as the earth itself as I struggle to reach the top of the cliffs before exhaustion claims me.

I have crossed half a world to hold that which I now cradle so near my heart. Pray God that same heart can provide me with the strength to cross another ten miles to safety.

I climb. The night grows old and I climb. The wind dries me and stiffens my clothing with encrustations of salt and makes my already painful steps even more laborious. I climb, hand over hand, foot before foot, abrading skin and shoes, eyes fastened upon the rock before my face as my mind is fastened upon the heights to which I must ascend. The night closes in around me; a bitter chill soaks into my bones. My limbs slow. I cannot control them. Sleep is close, but sleep is a fair-weather friend whose embrace, I know, would be filled with images of such bitterness and severity that to lie in her arms would be to die of shame.

Alexander. My dear friend, where are you? Have I become this obsessed that I can spare you no single thought in my desperate flight from capture? My mind tells me that guilt is a purposeless nonsense. Even dangerous. This is not some romantic adventure. My mind tells me this; my heart, more honest, tells me otherwise. My heart tells me I am a coward. My heart tells me to run, to forget my dearest friend and fellow explorer. My heart tells me to accept the truth.

I cannot, so I ignore my heart as I ignore my friend, the memory of his cries for help as I ran. I tell myself the cries I heard were the cries of gulls disturbed by our plundering, and then by our discovery and flight, nothing more than birds in the night. I tell my heart this but it will not be silenced. This is the nature of a heart, that it will not be stilled or silenced short of death.

So I climb to forget Alexander and the journey shrinks. In moments, it seems, I am standing atop the high cliffs, the wind tugging at my body, threatening to topple me backwards. I struggle for breath, ignoring the coldness spreading from the *rongo-rongo* to numb my heart and silence its cries for truth.

And then, passing exhaustion, judging my direction by luck, and by a meagre handful of stars, I begin to walk.

I do not know how I have the strength to place one foot before the next. On this desperate night I conclude there are many things I do not know. For a young man, cradled in the arrogance of wealth and position, this is a startling truth. But it is driven into me with every step, every jagged rock that slashes at my shoes and my feet, every time I stumble in the knife-edged darkness, every time I draw breath to announce my pain and yet dare not for fear of discovery. It is an intimate truth that after so much pain I can still be surprised by its application.

I am struck motionless at this thought and in the darkness around me I hear movement. Gulls? The whisper of grass? The rattle of volcanic pumice across harder rocks?

Or the patter of footsteps?

Patient, angry footsteps?

I remain motionless, crouched upon the ground in the lee of a slab of black rock, willing my breath to merge with the sigh of the wind.

The footsteps come nearer. I hold my breath. The footsteps cease. I hold my body motionless. The effort is even more painful than walking. I wait. My lungs are screaming for release. For a moment I am back in the water, drowning, choking on salt water, dizzy, thrashing, straining for life. I can wait no longer. I take a breath. The sound of it is like a summer storm slashing across an English forest. I cannot stop the breath. My limbs move, a combination of fear and panic. I fall against the rock. The sound is like thunder in the silence.

I wait for discovery, too exhausted to move. Too exhausted to beg for my life, even if I supposed the effort would do me any good.

I wait. Clouds cover the moon. Sweat freezes upon my face and hands. I wait.

Nothing.

Was I going mad? Had I heard footsteps? Had there in fact ever been anyone there at all?

I scramble to my feet and begin to walk. I am too tired to ask the questions, let alone answer them. The *Marco Polo* is a beacon in my head, rocking gently before my eyes on a watery cradle, its lights providing the warm glow of civilisation, of clean clothes, of brandy.

O Lord, of brandy.

The scream drives all thought of comfort from my mind.

I stagger, mind almost broken by the sudden noise. Is my punishment not complete even now? Is there more to endure?

There is.

My mind, numb with pain and cold, does not react to the sound as it should. I should turn away from the scream, flee from it, find another route to Anakena Bay. Instead my mind directs me *towards* the sound. It is an insane desire. I have to witness the source of the scream, even give myself to it. Anything, now, to end the pain, the cold, the dreadful fear of capture.

I stumble across the lip of the island's volcanic crater, origin of the stone from which the *moai* were supposedly carved. The caldera spreads out before me, a darkness upon the greater darkness of the night, one dappled with firelight.

Ranu Raraku.

The Navel of the World.

Luck or exhaustion brings me to my knees just beyond the lip of the crater. I collapse between black rocks, stare out across the depression in the ground. If God made the world, here was where He had pressed an experimental thumb into the still-malleable clay. Water collecting within the depression had formed a lake whose edges were peopled with outcroppings of stiff grass. Slots in the rocky ground had given birth to the *moai*. The stone giants, in various stages of completion, now stood guard over the place, their bulky faces and shoulders glimmering in the meagre starlight, and in the light of the many fires burning in the crater.

I look closer. Shapes move within the crater. Tiny by comparison with the *moai*, but many, so many, many shapes.

Islanders.

I watch them, captured by the flitting movements, mind numbed by the flickering torches; the chanting of many, the screams of one.

A voice I now recognise.

Tortorro.

Tortorro, who had greeted us upon our arrival at the island. Who had befriended us, shared his simple home with us. Whose family had made us welcome, their childlike curiosity unquenchable. And whose trust we repaid with guile, trading tobacco and a pipe for a guide to the Bird Men's Cave. The tablets. The *rongo-rongos*. Tortorro knew he was breaking the law of his people. We didn't care. That was his problem. There were more than a hundred tablets. Who would miss one?

Movement brings my attention back to the present. I watch the islanders. They surround Tortorro. They are waiting. For what? Tortorro is on his knees. He is begging. He is not bound. Why doesn't he run? What is he so afraid of?

My mind shies away from the answer to that question.

The islanders are watching Tortorro. Even the *moai* seem motionless, not transfixed geologically so much as in deliberate, ponderous attention.

Poor Tortorro is obviously about to pay for his indiscretion. But pay in what way? I watch, the anthropologist in me fascinated by the ritual. Tortorro is now standing. He is quite still, surrounded by other islanders, about fifty of them. The islanders do not appear to be threatening him. They are merely watching. As the *moai* are watching, expressionless eyes flecked with bronze in the firelight, great chiselled noses casting deep shadows across the high stone cheeks. Motionless. Or are they? I catch a movement, look away.

8

Nothing. Except… surely the statues were not all looking at the tableau that I myself was observing? Surely some had been facing in other directions just a moment before?

I listen for the sound of stone walking.

If I hear it once more I am lost, I know it.

The *moai* weigh more than a dozen horse and carriages. Surely they cannot have moved? I have no answer. No answer that I am prepared to acknowledge anyway. My heart might have had an answer but I am no longer listening to my heart. Ignoring the *moai,* I concentrate on the islanders. They are motionless now, and silent, as is Tortorro. It is totally silent here in the crater. So quiet I can hear them breathing. That and the distant cry of nesting gulls.

The quiet is broken suddenly as Tortorro begins to scream. He simply stands there, arms slightly outstretched from his sides, and screams. There is no movement from the islanders or the *moai.* Tortorro suddenly falls over. He convulses, writhing upon the ground. As I listen, horrified yet at the same time fascinated, his screams turn to words. He begins to invoke the gods of the island.

I am reminded of the legend attached to the *rongo-rongo*: that the tablets are forbidden to be touched by anyone but the island priests on pain of madness and death.

Tortorro convulses once more, clutching his head and screaming in pain and fear. I recognise many languages, including Spanish, which I am passingly familiar with. My mind cannot help but acknowledge the truth occurring here. Tortorro is speaking in tongues. I lean closer, trying to get a sense of what other languages he might be uttering. I'm too far away to hear properly. Then Tortorro convulses a final time, lying still upon the ground. His chest heaves once and he utters a strangled cry before becoming totally motionless.

None of the islanders have touched him; none have come

anywhere near him. His submission to madness and apparent death is inexplicable and terrifying. I wrap my arms about my sodden shirt, hugging myself, desperate for even that much human warmth.

For a moment there is no movement of any kind. Then another figure is brought into the firelight. I cannot believe my eyes. It is Alexander. My dear friend. He sees the fallen Tortorro. He begins to scream.

I cannot listen to his screams. I cannot. I scramble backwards over the lip of the crater. I try to keep silent but my foot slips on loose stones and I cry out. Alex looks up. He looks up at me. I know he cannot see me in the darkness but somehow he knows I am here. Perhaps he has sensed the change in the islanders' manner. There should be no interlopers present at this ritual. Alex's expression confirms my supposition: the hope on his face tells me he knows it can only be me. He calls to me. A plea for help.

I ignore him.

I run. His voice lifts in a despairing wail behind me. How can I bear this? He is more than my friend. My brother. And I am abandoning him. How can I justify this?

I cannot. There is no sense in me any more. No logic. No science. Just fear. Total fear. My mind is gone, my heart is dead and in its place instinct takes control.

And I stop running.

Instead I get down on my knees and begin to scramble about on the ground. Deep inside I know I have gone utterly mad, that in a few moments the islanders whom even now I can hear running after me will catch me and then Alexander and I will both suffer the same fate as poor Tortorro.

While my mind is busy screaming this information my hands are otherwise occupied. Rocks are scraped aside, similarly dirt and tough-bladed grass.

Underneath – a hole.

I scramble into the hole, keep on wriggling. I am packed tightly into the rocky passage. Dirt presses against my head, my shoulders; the weight of the island, the whole of Rapa Nui, bears down on me as if to prevent my escape with the tiny fragment of itself that I clutch so dearly, so close to my heart.

Footsteps pass by – less than a yard from my own feet. But I am safe – for the moment. Safe in this tunnel, one of many shown to me by Tortorro before our sacrilegious collusion caused the islanders to turn against us. I take a moment to catch my breath. It comes with dirt and roots and wriggling insects. I have taken refuge in one of a number of tunnels made by the islanders to conceal them from the unwanted attentions of acquisitive Portuguese slavers. Wide enough to permit only one person at a time – and generally speaking one with a frame considerably smaller than mine – the tunnels descend through the upper geological layers of the island, linking together at a depth of fifty or so feet to form a series of caves. The caves can be stocked with food and inhabited in times of crisis. Some perform the function of living quarters. Others double as temples to the islanders' gods.

I recognise the cave I now wriggle into immediately.

The Cave of the White Virgins.

It was here that young women were kept, often for months at a time, to bleach their skin in emulation of these same god-figures. Alexander and I both considered this a barbaric practice – even more so when we were presented with half a dozen not entirely uncomely girls upon our arrival on the island, apparently in honour of our own skin colour, and in particular my own hair colour, which, when not darkened by dirt and blood, and matted by immersion in salt water, is a bright copper-red.

I slither into the cave from an opening in its roof and come to an undignified halt among a shower of dirt and roots and crawling things. I sit up, my first thought for the *rongo-rongo*. Yes. It's still there. I breathe a sigh of relief. All I can hope for now is that I can remain undetected long enough to exit the cave through another tunnel.

Something moves to my left. There is no light here. I cannot see what is making the noise. An animal? Perhaps. I scramble away.

The noise comes again.

And with it a light.

It's a girl. She cannot be more than fifteen. Her skin is pale, even in the yellow torchlight.

'I am a friend.' I speak gently, as gently as I can. I know she won't understand the words but if I am lucky the tone of my voice will prevent her from calling out.

I am not lucky.

Her scream is piercing. I don't understand the words – it's not necessary. She jams herself back into the cave wall, seeming to melt into it. A moment and she is gone, the light with her. There must be an opening in the wall. I move quickly to investigate. Already I can hear scraping movement in the tunnel through which I entered the cave. I have only moments to escape.

I run my hands across the wall. I was right. There is an opening. I push my way inside. The new tunnel slopes downwards steeply. I can feel a breeze blowing against my face. There must be a way out. I crawl forward as fast as I can, all the while conscious of movement behind me in the darkness. I imagine the islanders coming upon me in the darkness, hands gripping obsidian knives, hacking at my feet and ankles, drawing blood, forcing me on until I collapse through blood loss or exhaustion. What will they do then? Drag me out to participate in the same ritual in which Tortorro died?

Or leave me here to die, jammed into a tunnel barely as wide as my shoulders, eventually to become part of the geological composition of the island itself?

Horror and fear drive me on. My shoulders ache abominably. My chest and stomach and hips are a confused mass of grazes. I am sure I can feel blood upon my skin. Several times I crack my head painfully against rocky protrusions, once bringing a small shower of dirt down on to my back. I scream then, claustrophobia propelling me onward in a panicky rush. Then my elbow twists sideways and jams. Now I can hear how close the islanders are behind me. I think of those knives and wrench my arm until I am sure my wrist will break. The arm comes loose and I move on – ever more slowly.

The passage steepens, narrowing even more as its angle increases. And now I can hear another sound above my pursuit and my own desperate gulps for air: a sound like thunder.

Surf.

A hand touches my foot, grasps my ankle. I kick out wildly, feel my foot hit something. A painful grunt sounds behind me. Something sharp digs into my calf. I scream, kicking and struggling madly within the confined space, my movements carrying me forward and down, faster and faster, steeper and steeper on a sliding carpet of dirt and roots and what feels like animal bones. My fall is totally beyond my control. The passage begins to widen. Soon I am tumbling, then rolling, then falling free through chill damp air.

I fall for much longer this time. I lack the strength even to wonder if jagged rock or booming surf will break my descent. It is as much as I can do to clamp my mouth shut against the sucking wind which seems intent on ripping the breath from my lungs for a second time in one night.

I have time enough to wonder why I don't faint when something smashes against my chest with incredible force. I faint then, for just a moment. I awake under water and kick madly for the surface.

When my head breaks the surface my first thought beyond getting air into my lungs is that I can see lights. Not the guttering orange flames of islanders' fires but the steady yellow glow of cabin lights. *The Pride of Hannay!* I am in Anakena Bay. My flight has brought me within moments of safety. All I have to do is swim towards the clipper and cry out for help.

I move my arm – and nearly faint again. The pain is so great, it is obvious my arm was broken in the fall. I offer a brief prayer of thanks not to have been knocked completely senseless and drowned.

Kicking weakly, I strike out for the clipper. I have no way of measuring my progress against the tide. My mouth is clamped shut, my eyes as well, my mind bent upon a prayer my mother had me learn more than two decades before.

The clipper is within calling distance when I hear the sound of paddles behind me. The islanders have canoes of course. Woven from bundles of reeds, the little vessels are virtually unsinkable. Propelled by broad paddles, they are capable of skimming across the waves like swans.

And now they're chasing me.

And the tide is driving me away from the clipper.

And I'm half dead with exhaustion, waterlogged, going under for what seems like the last time.

That's when I hear the bell. The clipper's bell. A longboat smacks into the water. Captain Farmer, bless his ears and his one good eye. First Mate Keable drags me into the boat, heedless of the moan when he grabs my broken arm. By now the islanders are close. I can see the light of burning torches. There are more than a dozen of them, three men to a canoe. Nearly forty enraged islanders, obsidian knives clutched between their teeth, murder in their eyes.

We make the clipper moments ahead of the lead canoe. Hands grasp me and pull me from the longboat. I stagger on to the deck and collapse, one arm useless, the other clutching the precious bundle within my shirt.

Captain Farmer is understandably annoyed. 'What the bloody hell are you playing at, Stockwood? Where's Richards?'

I level a cold glance at Farmer. 'Richards is dead. Tortorro is dead. Weigh the bloody anchor, man. Do it now before we join them!'

By this time islanders are climbing on to the clipper. The crew have turned out in force, half drunk on cheap rum and wielding whatever weapons come immediately to hand. Knives, cutlasses, belaying pins.

The first islander across the deck rail recoils from a cutlass blow, which more by luck than judgement takes off three fingers of his hand. Fingers and islander fall on opposite sides of the rail.

That's all it takes. The Captain calls his men to arms. First Mate Keable breaks out the pistols.

Another islander hoists himself over the rail. I kick him in the stomach. It's a weak blow, driven more by desperation than anger, but it does the job. The islander falls from the deck into the water with an angry yell.

Pistols discharge, the reports deafening in the night. I hear gulls screaming angrily with the islanders. And above it all the geological grind of stone moving upon stone. No, stone moving *through* stone, and my gaze lifts as, for the first time in ten miles and what seems like an eternity, I gather sufficient courage to look back, to see with my eyes and not just my fearful imagination the island I have robbed, the people I have betrayed, the friend I have abandoned.

And that's when I see them.

Ranged along the top of the cliffs, silhouetted against a

suddenly cloudless, star-filled sky: stones as big as houses where none had been before.

Moai, standing guard along the cliff top.

Motionless, they gaze out across the bay, their expressionless eyes directed towards the clipper. No – towards me. What I'm carrying.

And that's when I hear the scream. A single, fearful ululation lifted desperately against the night.

My name.

Alexander.

Oh, Alexander, my friend.

I sink to the deck, clutching the tablet to my chest, sobbing hysterically. Captain Farmer weighs anchor himself, the sails snap out at the touch of the wind, and the clipper moves slowly away from the island.

The blank eyes of the *moai* and the accusing screams of Alexander Richards follow me for months back to England and a lifetime beyond.

Part One
East of the Sun, West of the Moon

August–December 1872

'My Father told me it was for men of desperate fortunes on one hand, or of aspiring, superior fortunes on the other, who went abroad upon adventures, to rise by enterprise, and make themselves famous in undertakings of a nature out of the common road.'

Daniel Defoe,
Robinson Crusoe

1
Windjammer

I gripped the stern deck rail with one hand, whipped the other up and around, grabbed the flying fish behind its head. I hooked my fingers into its gill slits, yanked it down out of the sky, broke its back across my knee. I dropped the flopping animal to the deck. We'd been at sea for less than a week and I was sick of fish already – but food was food.

I looked up to the sound of applause. Jack Devitt was watching me from the ratlines below the spanker. His boy-thin legs were curled around the boom, dangling beside six head of fish, leaving both hands free to grasp the line with which he'd caught them. His grin was even brighter than the cloudless August sky from which I had made my catch. The spanker itself snapped with the wind above and behind him, a smaller version of the acre of sail set across *Tweed*'s three tall masts and bowsprit.

'Damn, gel, but you ain't 'aff good at that. You'll be 'aving me back on the slops as a waster if the Cap'n sees y're that good.'

'We must eat.' I felt the satisfaction of the hunter who has provided for the village. Even if this village was running before the wind at ten knots across the North Atlantic ocean towards the Equator.

I took out my knife, topped and tailed the fish, gutted it, threw the remains overboard to attract more prey for Jack, tucked the edible portion into a wooden bucket already more than half full. 'My name is not "gel". It's Leela. Use it or do not speak to me.' I allowed the sun to reflect off my knife blade into Jack's face as I spoke, and had the satisfaction of watching his almost permanent smile slip just a bit. 'I have spent many nine-days learning your way of speaking. Show me the same respect.'

'I take it the arm's working out all right?' The new voice belonged to James Royston. I heard him walking quietly along the deck, heard the quiet rasp of his skin across the rail and the still-unconfident tread of his shoes above the slap of water against the hull and the greedy screech of gulls. I did not look up. Royston's voice was like his face: gruff, confident, untrustworthy. 'I thought you might like this.' I felt rather than saw him reach a hand out towards me. I turned. He was holding a small metal ball no bigger than the end of my finger. It was squashed on one side. 'Little souvenir from our dockside tête-à-tête. You're lucky to be alive, you know.'

I took the metal and examined it, watching Royston out of the corner of my eye as I did so. This metal had been inside me. Inside my body. It might have killed me. How well did it know me? How dangerous was it now?

Royston said, 'I understand from the Doctor that your people believe possessing an enemy's weapon provides protection against further attack.'

'You say you understand. You do not.' I hefted the metal. 'This metal knows my blood. In the hands of an enemy it could do great harm. The tribe of Tesh can use my blood against me with their holy machines. I do not know what the other tribes of this land can do.' I threw the metal as far overboard as I could.

Royston frowned. 'I'm sorry. I just wanted to say you can trust me, you know.'

'I will decide when I can trust you.' I whipped around and took another flying fish from the sky, laid it down on the deck and gutted it. I said nothing more and, after a moment, Royston walked away. That was good. I did not want to talk to him. If the Doctor had not stopped me both he and the woman would be dead already, Stockwood would be safe, and I would be much happier.

I caught another fish. I filled the bucket but the satisfaction was gone.

A short while later Jack gave a triumphant cry and landed his fourth fish. He hung it beside the others and began to rebait his line. 'When I was a lad – nobbut four or five now, y'unnerstand – I used t'watch clouds when I could get away wiv it. *Tweed*'s like a cloud, I reckon. A cloud made o' teak an' canvas an' sweating boys like me.'

I scanned the sky for more fish. 'Clouds are silent. Like hunters. This ship would not make a good cloud. And you do not sweat, Jack Devitt, because you do not work.'

'Oh tha'ss right, go on an' ruin it. Me one chance t'get a bit o' daydreamin' in an' y' go all practical on me. You foreign types is all the same.'

'I am not foreign. I am alien. I am from the future. Many –' I hesitated, the word was still unfamiliar – '*generations* from now. The Doctor brought me here to see my… *ancestors*.' Another strange word.

'Oh yeah? The future, eh? An where's 'at when it's at 'ome then, the New World? I en't never 'eard of no country called the future.'

'I come from the Place of Land.'

'Dem, gel, you jes' said y'came from the future. You messin' about wiv me now, are yer?'

I did not know how to answer the boy. 'I don't know. I come from the Place of Land and the future.'

'Nah, get off. How can y' come from two places at once?'

I began to feel angry. 'I do not know. Now be quiet or the fish will not come.'

Jack had his mouth open for a smart reply when a voice yelled, 'Spanker! Spanker Jack! Haul away with the damn fish or there'll be no supper for the Cap'n an' you'll be food fer the fishes, I'll be bound.'

'It's Cook!' Like Captain Stuart, the cook hailed from a place called Scotland. Jack leapt off the boom and bounced barefoot on to the quarterdeck so close to the stern rail that one more yard would have seen him overboard. 'Comin' right now, I is!' He grabbed the bucket of fish and shot off with yet another grin. I smiled too. We were many nine-days into the voyage. Ship's stores were close to half used up, though there was still salted beef and fruit in the hold to feed the Tribe of Sevateem for a season in the Place of Land, besides the live poultry in the coop at the ship's waist and the half-dozen pigs penned in the hold. The fish were a way of making the real food last longer.

Jack vanished towards the mizzenmast and I sat cross-legged by the stern rail. I took some sailor's yarn and a needle from my pouch and began to stitch the pile of flying-fish fins together into a bracelet. Maybe the power of the fish would help me someday, when I needed it. In any case, with the sun scattering rainbows from the scales, they were by far the most beautiful things I had seen since the Doctor brought me to Earth more than a week before.

'They'll dry out, you know. And the smell. Oh my. You won't be very popular then.'

I looked up at Stockwood. 'I heard you coming.'

'I know.'

I stood. 'Old feet tell loud stories. You must be very excited.'

'I am now we've been let out of the hold. A week is a long time to spend in the same room with four other people.'

'Even if one of them is your best friend?'

Stockwood smiled. The lines on his face were a map to his feelings. I tried to imagine how old he was. More than fifty summers. It seemed incredible. The oldest man in our village had been barely thirty summers – and he was lame and had to be fed or he would have died. The smile did not last long. 'They've taken the *rongo-rongo*,' he said quietly. 'And my notes.'

I reassured Stockwood with a scowl. 'The last man to try to steal the *rongo-rongo* is dead. So will they be if I have anything to say of it. We must wait our chance and then strike.'

'I noticed they let you keep your knife.'

'You saw how many I drew blood from when they tried to take it from me.'

'But you haven't killed anyone yet.'

'The Doctor made me swear. On my honour. The Hunter's Promise. I cannot kill her now. Not while this village floats upon water. Everyone knows this.'

Stockwood nodded slowly, his grizzled head bouncing gently off the warm afternoon breeze. 'The Doctor seems to be very pally with her.'

I frowned. 'Do not accuse the Doctor of betraying us, Stockwood. I know him. He would rather die.'

'I wonder.'

A flying fish leapt the starboard rail at head height. Stockwood ducked, spry for a man of his age. I let the fish go. It hit the deck with a wet slap and slithered beneath the rail and back into the sea with a splash, disturbing on its way three gulls perched on the rail waiting for their next free meal. I considered making the gulls our next meal – but Jack had warned me they were bad eating, the meat stringy, the bones sharp, sometimes dangerous.

I put the flying-fish fins and the needle and yarn back into my pouch. Stockwood was still staring out from the stern rail, eyes fixed on some horizon only he could see. A horizon thirty summers old. I touched him on the shoulder, my fingers light; part comforting, part curious.

'Stockwood.'

'Yes, Leela?'

'In my tribe the old are revered for their wisdom and skill. You are nearly twice the age of anyone in the Sevateem.'

He did not turn, but his voice showed he was pleased with my words. 'Why, Leela, my dear, I do thank you. That's a very kind thought. But I fear I may not be as wise or skilled as you think.' He hesitated. 'Things are different in this world – in my Place of Land. So are people. We live longer and we make more mistakes. Most of these mistakes won't kill us. In some ways we are very lucky like that. But some mistakes – some errors – stay with us our whole lives. They can never be forgotten, and should never be forgiven.'

I nodded. 'You understand the way of the hunter. When you are responsible for the death of a fellow hunter you must make the atonement. For us the punishment is physical. For you it is inside your head. It does not matter: the pain is the same. Here. Give me your hand.'

Trusting, he did so. Quickly, so he could not pull away, I took out my knife and cut a deep slash into his forearm. I held him when he tried to pull away. 'Do not move!'

To his credit he did not utter a sound louder than a surprised gasp.

I muttered the words of invocation over the fresh wound: '"Reroute control from main to subsystem, confirm transfer, seal and lock."' I thrust my hands forward, fingers splayed in the Position of Transfer, and waved them across the cut I had made in Stockwood's arm. 'Now this wound carries your guilt so that you will not have to.' I looked into Stockwood's tear-filled eyes. 'Do you understand? The Doctor says everyone makes mistakes. He says it's how we learn. The wound carries your pain so that you do not have to feel the guilt any more.'

Stockwood wiped a hand across his face. He composed himself with an effort, bandaging his arm with a small cloth taken from his top pocket. I was amused. As a bandage the

24

cloth was hopelessly small. 'My dear, I –' He winced. 'I don't know what to say. I don't believe anyone since my late wife has offered me such – ah! – such a kindness.'

'Your wife was wise.' I took his eyes with my own. 'As I said, in my tribe age is respected.' I held his gaze for several moments. 'Wisdom and skill must be passed on or the tribe will die.'

His eyes widened – and not with pain. 'My dear, if you are saying what I think you are saying, then you may rest assured that I am most flattered, and indeed thankful but, more's the pity, completely unable to implement – er, that is, *perform* the – um, well, you see, it's been a very long time and, well, under the circumstances I feel it would be inappropriate to – well... you know. Don't you?' I said nothing. 'Oh dear. I suppose the truth of it is I'm simply not up to much these days.'

I stopped his words with a smile. 'You do not know yourself as well as you might, Horace Stockwood, my best friend. And you do not know your body half as well as I do.'

His face turned bright red. I had not seen such awkwardness since childhood.

'Oh. Um. Yes. Well. You know, I think that smells like cooking fish.' He moved away quickly, his feet, though shoe-clad, still familiar with the deck and its movement. I watched him go.

A movement from above caught my eye. I looked up at the Doctor, balanced casually on the spanker boom. His hair stuck out in all directions and his scarf was a plaything for the wind. His shoes barely touched the oiled teak of the boom. Anyone else would have fallen prey to the movement of the ship and been tossed overboard directly.

'They do things slightly differently here, you know.'

'Yes.' I agreed. 'They are stupid and guilty and old and do not see what is right in front of their faces!'

The Doctor laughed.

'Doctor. Stockwood says you have become friendly with the woman. Is this true?'

The Doctor twirled his scarf absently. He did that whenever he was trying to think of a way of avoiding answering a question.

'Stockwood. Yes. An intelligent man. You know, he was right. That skipjack does smell good. I wonder if the cook has any sauce tartare.' He leapt from the boom and, sure-footed as a webspinner on the tilting deck, wandered after the smell of cooking fish, leaving me to my thoughts and memories of our first meeting with Horace Stockwood, so many nine-days ago in the Land of Eng.

2
Expedition

I stood beside the Doctor and we both listened as Horace Stockwood finished his story.

'I'm not a coward. You have to know that about me. I'm not a coward and I'm not a thief. I don't slink around in the night like some archaeologists I could name, with a gun and the thought of personal gain uppermost in my mind. I don't. Truly I don't. You have to believe me. I was only running that night because... well, because I was in mortal fear for my life. The islanders were chasing me because they wanted my life... they wanted my soul. I saw what they did to Alexander. They thought we were gods – fulfilling some terrible prophecy. The *rongo-rongo* was incidental. I am sure of that. Well, I am sure of it now. Then, of course, well... things were very different.'

I watched the old man carefully. Old eyes in an old face. That didn't change anything. Nor conceal anything. Not from a hunter. Did Stockwood know he was lying? His body knew it, even if his mind did not. I looked at the Doctor, who was standing by a hole in the wall bordered by flat rocks with a fire in it. The Doctor's expression told me nothing. His body also told me nothing – beyond his interest in Stockwood's tale.

Stockwood rose, his grey hair tanned by the firelight. He opened the door to a shelf in another wall – this one made of wood – and took out a water bag. I watched the bag with interest. The only water bags I'd ever owned had been made out of horda stomachs. They were soft and, though tanned well, rarely lasted longer than a summer before rotting away. This water bag was different. It was hard and clear, like ice, but it did not melt in the warm room. I had seen such things before – but I did not understand them. Stockwood poured some of the contents of the bag into a cup, also made out of the same not-ice.

I felt the Doctor looking at me. 'It's called *glass*.'

'Not *cup*?'

'No. The cup is called a glass.'

That I understood. I pointed at the water bag. 'Glass.'

Stockwood looked up, shook his head in a gentle negative. 'Decanter. Bottle.'

I felt agitated. 'I don't understand. The glass is called glass. But the bottle is called glass too?'

Stockwood ventured a weak smile. 'It's what's inside that matters.' He continued to pour water from the glass to the glass.

I watched Stockwood for a moment, noting the set of his limbs, the angle of his head. I tried to catch his eye but he avoided my gaze. I looked instead at the Doctor. 'Stockwood is like an animal,' I said quietly. 'Trapped by hunters.'

The Doctor glanced distractedly at me. He nodded, curly hair bouncing around his face so that I wanted to giggle. 'You're right. Only this time the hunters are memories and we're here to rescue him.'

'We are?'

'Oh yes.' The Doctor beamed, grabbed a handful of his scarf and began to wiggle it distractedly. I knew this meant he was thinking so I said nothing. I just waited. Stockwood finished pouring his drink, gulped it down and returned to his throne. I watched him walk. He was so old. Oh, the Doctor once asked me to believe he was over seven hundred and fifty summers old but it was obvious he was playing a child's game of pretend. I told him I was a minion of the Evil One and he laughed. I got angry then and he changed the subject.

I felt Stockwood staring at me. I was used to that. Men in my tribe did it all the time. I drew my dagger and showed it to Stockwood. 'I am a hunter. I will choose a mate in my own time.' It was not an invitation to fight, more a gesture of respect. But I held the dagger in the killing grip, point up, just in case. With animals you could never tell.

A moment passed. I smelled Stockwood sweating. Fear. Then Stockwood showed me his teeth. The Doctor did that a lot. He called it a *smile*. He said it meant he was 'happy – sometimes sad, but generally happy'. I wondered how Stockwood could be happy when he was so badly haunted by memories of his friend.

Stockwood said, 'You're making me nervous, Leela, standing there like that. You're as still as a statue. Why don't you sit down?'

I glanced at the Doctor. He nodded. I picked a clean stretch of cloth covering the ground close to the fire and sat down. I sheathed my dagger, though I held myself in readiness for anything unexpected.

Stockwood showed me his teeth again. 'I meant on the sofa.'

What was a sofa? I looked around quickly. There were several thrones, some holes in the walls, lots of wooden shelves and flat stones with paintings on. Some hollow things made of… glass with flowers in. Even the cloth on the ground was painted. But there was nothing to tell me what a sofa was. And I did not like not knowing. I said carefully, 'We are in your temple. It would not be respectful.'

Stockwood's lined face creased in a way I did not understand. But he had stopped sweating. 'It's not a temple. It's a house.' Obviously the ritual of *sofa* was not that important. I felt myself begin to relax. The fire was warm. I was close to the Doctor. I felt safe here. I didn't need a *sofa*.

I kept watching Stockwood as he continued to talk to the

Doctor. I did not listen to the words. I found out everything I needed to know about Stockwood by using the Hunter's Eye. '*You must see the broken stem, the blood spilled on a turned leaf. You must see the set of the eyes, the quiver of the nose and ears. You must test the air for scent and judge it for fear or madness. You must let yourself become the prey, respect it, offer prayers to it; know it as you will one day know your mate, your child. Only then may you kill.*' When my father told me that I laughed aloud, set my crossbow and shot a web-tree spinner from its high cocoon. I set the bow again and killed its young when they came to nuzzle their dead parent. I was only ten summers old but the kills were clean. My family had meat for an entire passage of the lesser moon, but father did not speak to me for a long time. It was another full summer before I understood what he had been trying to teach me. '*Anyone can kill, Leela. The skill is in understanding. Understanding is a tool like the axe or the Janis thorn, only much more dangerous.*'

I understood Stockwood. He was an animal. A man, yes, but an animal too, in his desire for the trappings of this comfortable temple, his desperation, his lack of self-awareness. Stockwood was not confused. Animals never are. They do not understand enough to be confused, and they run away from whatever frightens them. Animals will run before fighting. And animals do not know when they are to die. I understood more about Stockwood from the story he had just told us than he did himself.

And it was clear to me that Stockwood would die soon.

I wriggled with satisfaction. I was clever and the fire was warm and that was good. The Doctor was still listening intently to Stockwood. I listened for a moment, then reached into my belt pouch and pulled out a square of fragile cloth. There were marks on the cloth. They were like the marks on the holy relics of the Sevateem. I couldn't understand them of course, but I knew what they meant. The Doctor had told me and I had memorised his words.

The holy marks meant, *The Times, London, 21 August 1872*. The Doctor had told me this cloth was a sheet from something called a *newspaper*. He said there was a different newspaper every day. I thought this was good: the cloth was so flimsy I could poke a hole in it with my fingers. I did so now to prove how strong I was. The hole joined others beside different marks, ones I had been told meant, *Noted Archaeologist Seeks Sponsorship for Expedition to South Seas*.

I had no idea what the words meant until the Doctor explained them to me earlier that day. Now it was clear: Stockwood wanted to return to Rapa Nui. The Doctor told me that Stockwood probably thought there was an important scientific truth there, waiting to be discovered. I heard the word *scientific* and shuddered. That word I knew. It was both the word uttered by the Tribe of Tesh whenever they captured members of the Sevateem and the god they invoked when torturing their prisoners.

The memory made me angry. I touched my neck, shoulder and hip briefly. The Doctor had once told me the gesture had special meaning. He said it was the *check sequence on a Starfall 7 spacesuit*. I didn't understand that. But he was right. The gesture was important. It gave me comfort. Just as holding this holy cloth gave me comfort. Comfort in knowing that I had a talisman of the Tesh. Knowing I had power over them. Even here, so far from the Land.

The Doctor spoke then, and I quickly put away the talisman. I could feel his voice through the floor. In the Land there had been those of the tribe who could touch the ground and know when a storm was coming. I could never do that. But now I knew what it must have felt like. To feel a thing and know that it had power to affect you, even kill you, before you even saw it coming. The feeling was frightening. But good-frightening. I shivered.

The Doctor said, 'I don't understand why you felt the need to advertise for financial backing. Surely there are establishments which would provide you with support?'

I listened to the Doctor's words and tried to understand them. What was *advertise*? What was *establishment*? I concluded that in this Land there must be high priests whose permission must be sought before any journey could be allowed.

Stockwood's answer told me I was right. 'My observations of the walking stones were made thirty years ago. Since publishing I have been treated as a scientific pariah. A lunatic. The scientific community has held me up to fifty different sorts of ridicule. I have even been expelled from the town library society. Such research as I have been able to conduct over the years has been funded by my family money. My father left me a thirty-room mansion in Kent when he died. I sold it twenty years ago. The money lasted less than five years. My own personal fortune has dwindled so much so that even this, my town house and only remaining home, dilapidated as it is, is under threat of repossession.'

'My dear Horace.' The Doctor *smiled*. 'It sounds to me as though you need a date with Lady Luck.'

'I need a date with a sympathetic banker.'

The Doctor reached a long arm across to Stockwood and pretended to pluck something from the older man's ear. 'Bankers are ten a penny if you know where to dine and what to order.' He handed Stockwood something that glittered, much like the bottle of glass had glittered in the firelight. I could have held three such things in my clenched fist.

Stockwood's expression changed. He began to sweat again.

He was obviously impressed by the Doctor's trick. I wasn't. I'd seen him do it many times before.

Stockwood sat up a little straighter. I could see the effort it cost him: not the movement, the trust. The Doctor was like that. He made you want to get up and take action. The trouble was that most people acted without thinking – something my father had demonstrated in the manner of his death.

Stockwood took the shiny object from the Doctor and stared at it in amazement. 'Do you have any idea what this is worth?'

'Name your price. There's only one like it on the planet – and you're holding it.'

Stockwood blinked. 'I certainly am.' Stockwood stood abruptly. I watched him carefully as he went to each of the three large French windows which looked out on to the grounds.

'What you have given him is precious?' I asked the Doctor. To Stockwood I added, 'You are frightened in case someone tries to steal it?'

Stockwood nodded, moved closer to the Doctor. Something about him made me nervous. 'Someone did break in here last night.'

The Doctor took the sparkly talisman from Stockwood and made it vanish. 'Now there's a coincidence.'

'Quite.' Stockwood poured himself another drink.

'The tablet?'

'No. I keep that safely locked away. But some of my notebooks were disturbed. And one was missing.'

'Let me guess. The notebook contained a translation of the inscription on the tablet.'

'More precisely, my notes on the structure of the language inscribed there. But with that knowledge anyone could decipher the inscription.'

'And has the tablet been sketched or displayed at all?'

'Briefly. About fifteen years ago. Oh, the British Museum contacted me and discussed a collection based on my findings. About five years ago, that was. I decided against it.'

'Too close to your own solution?'

'Age and public ridicule have made me a suspicious man, Doctor. It is hard to trust anyone when you have been declared a charlatan as many times as I.'

'I see. And do you have any idea who might want to steal the work of someone held in as much scientific disregard as yourself?'

Stockwood sighed wearily. 'I have no idea. Between ourselves I wondered briefly if my servant James might not have been persuaded to allow someone to enter the premises unseen in return for money. God knows, in all fairness I can't pay him anything like a reasonable wage.'

The Doctor began to pace. He seemed agitated but also happy. This was normal. He loved a mystery. 'So you're worried that a rival will steal your findings and claim them as his own?'

Stockwood nodded. 'I can't afford to return to Rapa Nui to prove my observations. If this… this nemesis can, then I will never have a chance to prove that I was right.'

'And you have absolutely no idea who this fellow could be?'

Stockwood shook his head. 'Nobody believes me – they think I'm mad. Who would want to steal secrets from a madman?'

'Another madman, perhaps?' The Doctor tapped a fingernail against his teeth thoughtfully. 'I imagine a man in your position knows of one or two reputable dealers of *objets personnels*.'

'You mean pawnbrokers?'

'If you will.' The Doctor took out a pocket watch and flipped open the lid. 'Eighteen seventy-two… half past August. Yes, there should be several appropriate establishments just off the Portobello Road.' He flipped the watch closed, slipped it back into his pocket. 'Leela, I have to see a man about some gold. In the meantime, I want you to stay with Stockwood. See what you can find out. And remember, you're his best friend, all right? No daggers!'

I frowned, but nodded. I hardly ever understood the Doctor but I trusted him.

'Good. I'll see you later on this afternoon.' Tipping his hat politely to Stockwood, the Doctor left.

3
Downhill Run

Another three nine-days had come and gone. We had passed the Equator amid strange, directionless winds and much singing by the men. Now I was perched on the cathead, my legs curled underneath beside the anchor ropes to keep me secure. The cathead was made of planks as wide as my leg and jutted out from the forecastle level with the deck but at an angle to the bowsprit. The anchor was tightly lashed to the deck beside me. I was watching large grey fish Jack called *dolphins* dive and swim all around the prow of the ship.

Stockwood clung to the port deck rail a few feet from me. Beyond him the men inhabited the rigging and the decks, going boisterously about the business of running the ship. Today the sun was hot and *Tweed* had made all the sail she could. The shrouds billowed above the ship, snapping and cracking in the wind. From the mainsail boom on the mizzenmast, twice a man's height above the deck, I could just see the Doctor leading the men in a chorus of a song he called 'Octopus's Garden'. Matthews, the ship's bosun, loved the Doctor. When he was on deck, *Tweed* easily made half again the average day's travel.

I hadn't realised the Doctor loved so much to sing. In the Tribe of Sevateem the only songs we sang were of victory in the hunt, of war against other tribes, or of celebration at a new birth or coming of age. Songs of death and life. The songs of this land were so different. I had never thought that there could be songs about so many things. Diamonds. Revolutions. Guitars. Meter Maids. Even an octopus. I asked Spanker Jack what an octopus was and he described it to me, laughing at my ignorance. It sounded like a very strange animal to sing songs about.

The dolphins I was watching seemed to appreciate the song, too – or perhaps it was the tones of the Doctor's voice, booming like the wind itself across the decks, that moved them. They leapt from the water in arcs that left miniature rainbows glimmering in the spray in their wakes. Somehow they seemed to be able to do this in time with the song.

Close by me Stockwood nodded, smiling. I noticed and was pleased. It had been many nine-days since I had seen him smile. Now at last, the anger he felt at our expedition being hijacked was beginning to fade. That was good. Anger is not beneficial to revenge.

'They're lovely when they play.' Stockwood pointed at the dolphins. 'They remind me of being a child.'

I changed position slightly on the cathead, shifting to keep my balance as *Tweed* cut through the water. 'When I was a child I learnt to hunt and kill. I could use a crossbow when I was seven summers old. I made my first kill at eight summers. I was a good hunter. I used to teach the other children of the tribe.'

Stockwood did not seem to know how to respond to my statement. After a short silence he said, 'You mean you never played? You had no games?'

'We had games. Whoever killed the most bark-skippers in a day had more food at mealtimes.'

'Oh.'

'I killed three in one day once. Bark-skippers are very fast.'

'I should think they probably were.' Stockwood drew attempted to relight his pipe, which had gone out. 'I would be too if I thought you were hunting me.'

'I would not hunt you, Stockwood. You are my –'

'– my best friend. Yes, I know.'

'Good.'

I went back to watching the dolphins, ignoring the odd tone in Stockwood's voice. Out of the corner of my eye, I saw that his attempts to relight his pipe had failed. The wind was too strong. And now I felt moisture on my face. It was beginning to rain. I looked up. Clouds had swept up across the sky. The sun was fading. The Doctor stopped singing as the bosun began to call for the sails to be furled. Some of the men began to fill wooden tubs with rainwater to wash in.

The Doctor climbed quickly down the rigging and swung on to the deck. Somehow he managed to do this without losing either his hat or his scarf. He was grinning broadly as he strode towards us. He stopped by the deck rail and reached into the pockets of his jacket, emerging with two pairs of unfamiliar objects. 'Presents,' he announced, handing us the objects.

'Lemons and soap.' Stockwood frowned. 'Can I take it you are implying something?'

The Doctor's grin widened even further. 'The ship's out of fresh fruit. Lemon juice is an excellent preventive for scurvy. As for the soap…' The Doctor looked sideways at me and winked. 'I rather imagine that speaks for itself.'

I looked at the lemon. Jack had told me he once saw someone go blind from scurvy. I bit deeply into the lemon, munched and swallowed. I did not want to go blind. At the same time I sniffed suspiciously at the soap, then tasted a piece. I spat it out immediately. 'You are trying to poison me!'

Stockwood roared with laughter. 'Not as nice as chocolate surprise, eh, Leela?'

The Doctor explained, 'We've been at sea for sixty-eight days. You haven't washed for three weeks.' The Doctor nodded back over his shoulder at the sailors splashing rainwater over their bodies. 'It's not ladylike.'

'I am not a lady! I am a –'

'– warrior of the Sevateem. Yes, I know. A hunter. You wash when the prey washes, or they smell you coming.' The doctor smiled a bit to take the edge off his words. 'Well, animals wash when it rains, Leela, and it's raining now. I suggest you take advantage of the weather and hunt down a bucket of clean water.'

I glared angrily at the Doctor. 'I thought you understood about the rituals of the Place of Land.'

'And I thought you wanted to learn about your ancestors.'

'I do!'

'Well, then, why not start with the Ritual of Carbolic?'

'Carbolic?'

'Yes. In this land Carbolic is the patron saint of sailors and hunters.'

'He is?' I was doubtful. I had never heard of this god.

'Oh yes.'

'Oh.'

'The bar of soap I just gave you is his holy symbol. It's even named after him.'

'It is?'

'Oh yes. Use this once a day with clean water and everyone will be your friend.'

'In that case I will do as you say.'

'Good. Now off you go while I have a little chat with young Horace here.'

Stockwood frowned. 'I'm hardly young, Doctor.'

'Believe me, Horace, by the standards of my people Methuselah was a babe in arms.'

I turned back, interested. 'Methuselah?'

'Soap, Leela!'

'All right, I'm going!'

'And don't forget to wash behind your ears.'

'I know!' Leaving the Doctor to his 'little chat' and chewing on the lemon, I took the soap and went in search of a bucket.

I found one easily enough in the galley, located beneath the forecastle where I had been sitting on the cathead. The cook was busy preparing food when I got there. He was a man of extremes, with massive arms, oddly spindly legs and a habit of either speaking very quietly or screaming loudly – usually at Jack, when the boy had not worked as hard or fast as the cook thought he should. He came from a place called Glasgow, and apparently saw no reason to make an effort to be understood when he spoke.

I moved quietly into the galley, stole a leg of chicken from the pot while Cook was shouting at someone, grabbed the nearest bucket and got out fast.

I had not been below decks much since being released from the hold, where we had been imprisoned. Though the upper decks were interesting enough, the inside of the ship made me nervous. I did not like the idea of being close to the water, or even beneath it, even though the ship was well caulked and did not leak except slightly in the bilges. The only thing that drew me to the lower decks was the pig pen.

Carrying the right sort of food was important on a long sea voyage. The Doctor had explained to me that lack of meat or fresh vegetables could result in a disease he called rickets. He said he once saw someone die blind from *rickets* on a ship called *Santa María*. Hence the pigs. For myself I found the old sow and her piglets to be an interesting diversion if I got bored or restless, which I did from time to time. A hunter runs often and becomes restless when confined. *Tweed* was a big ship – much bigger than my old village if you counted all her deck space – but, of course, it was impossible to get off her. Running on the decks was impossible because the men were working there. And in any case there was nothing to hunt. I was eating regularly and getting fat. This made me feel strange. I had never been fat before. That was a privilege of the village shamans – those who mind-worked and communed with the gods. Whenever I felt most restless I would come and talk to the pigs. The old sow had a reputation of being irritable and bad-tempered – anyone would if confined below decks and denied access to the sun and the sky – but I liked her. Shortly after being released I had come to the pig pen and climbed in. The smell was comfortingly familiar. I wanted to think. The old sow had grunted and shoved her huge body against me. I shoved her back as hard as I could, and kept shoving until she left me alone. Now we regarded each other with a kind of mutual respect. But the piglets seemed to like it when I was there. They nuzzled and jumped on me. I liked the piglets. I sometimes slipped the catch and let them out of the pen, just for the pleasure of helping to run them down. It was a good game. I found I did not like it when, every few nine-days, one was slaughtered for food – even though the meat of such well-fed animals was by far the best I had ever tasted.

Now I walked back along the mid-deck, planning to climb down the ladder to the orlop, the lowest deck on the ship – the place where the ballast and bilges were located – and home to the pigs. But as I came to the ship's waist, to the place where the main mast cut down through the deck head and passed through the ship to finally connect with the keel, I stopped.

Tweed was by no means a silent ship. At any time you could hear the sounds of men working and shouting, the hammering and sawing of running repairs, of food being prepared, of running feet, shouted orders, the crack of the sails and creak of the rigging. The sounds that stopped me now were not unfamiliar in themselves – only when taken together.

A hunter takes note of everything. The sound of a man and woman talking was not unusual. What was unusual was who was talking. Richards, obviously. She was the only other woman aboard the ship. But the man was Royston. Royston who had spent so much of the time since we had left England trying to convince me he was trustworthy.

What was he doing talking to the woman I had every intention of killing at the first opportunity?

I moved closer, keeping to the side of the companionway, and found the voices coming from inside Richards's cabin. I crouched beside the door and listened.

'I have money.' That was Royston. 'I can arrange to give you a banker's draft – or gold if you prefer. All I ask is that –'

'I know what you want of me. I have money of my own. You must realise that. If you want my co-operation you must forget about money. A more important consideration would be asking me to forget that you are his best friend.' Richards was angry – the emphasis on the word 'his' was very clear. Richards was obviously referring to Stockwood. By the tone of her voice she clearly hoped to see him dead. It was her good luck she had not made any serious attempt to do so while aboard ship.

But Royston was Stockwood's oldest friend. What was he doing trying to strike a bargain with the one who so obviously wanted Stockwood dead?

'If you want my help you must renounce your friendship with Stockwood. Do that and I will consider your offer.'

There was a long silence from the cabin. I wondered what Royston's response would be. I was not going to find out. In a moment or less conversation resumed – and quickly become an argument.

I moved away from the cabin and climbed through the hatch leading to the main deck a moment before the door banged open and Royston strode out.

I took the bucket to the quarterdeck and waited for it to fill with rain. I had just stripped my skins off and began the Ritual of Carbolic when the rain stopped. A moment later I heard cook screaming angrily that someone had stolen his slops bucket.

Ignoring looks and shouts from the sailors, I scraped the soap off my skin as effectively I could, got dressed, and went below to see the pigs. I needed to think.

4
Heresy

After the Doctor left Stockwood's temple – *house* – Stockwood and I watched each other for a while. Then he stood up. 'I have precious little in terms of provisions, but what I have is yours.'

I frowned again. Stockwood spoke politely enough but his words made no sense at all.

I stood up, trying to work out what he meant. What was a provision and why was he offering me one? Obviously it was an important ritual, but what did it mean? I decided it would be better to change the subject.

'I'm hungry. Do you have food?' He laughed. 'You are laughing at me!'

'No, no, of course not. It's just that… Oh dear… Come with me into the pantry. I'll see what we can scrape together.'

I followed him through the temple. 'Once I had to scrape the flesh and organs from a horda skin. The taste was foul but the meat kept me alive for a week. 'Have you ever eaten horda?'

'Not exactly. I have eaten python, though. And marmoset brain.'

'Our shaman said if you eat the brains of your enemy you take on their intelligence.'

'I wouldn't have thought that was much good if you were clever enough to defeat them in the first place.'

I felt myself frowning. 'I always thought it was a stupid thing to say.'

'Your shaman should have taken his own advice, by the sound of it.' Stockwood laughed. I wondered whether to join in.

Stockwood's pantry was as big as the room we had just left. It was full of shelves. The shelves were filled with jars and boxes.

I touched one of the shelves. 'How do you make the wood so straight and smooth?'

'I employ a carpenter.'

'I see.'

'Do you have carpenters where you come from?'

'I don't know.'

I felt Stockwood's eyes on me. 'You don't know where you come from or you don't know what a carpenter is?'

'I come from the Place of Land. I don't know what a carpenter is.' I tried to control a surge of anger. 'Why? Does it make you feel cleverer than me to know things I don't?'

'No, of course not.' Stockwood's tone was reassuring. I felt a bit better.

'Here. Have a sandwich.'

I sniffed the bread, peeled apart the layers. 'You are trying to poison me! This is covered in mould!'

'It's meant to be covered in mould. It's cheese. Blue cheese. You have heard of cheese?'

'Yes,' I lied defensively.

Stockwood did not seem convinced. 'Let's try again.' He brought me a bowl filled with a brown paste from a cupboard. I took the bowl. 'It's cold,' I said in surprise.

'It came from a cold place.'

'You are laughing at me again!'

'Try some.'

'It looks like –'

'Yes, well, I never could get the consistency right. Try some.'

I stuck my finger in the bowl, brought it to my lips and nervously licked off some of the brown paste. 'Oh!' I sat down suddenly on the floor. 'I've never tasted anything like it!' I scraped up a large handful and swallowed eagerly. Two more handfuls followed the first. Then another three. I handed the empty bowl back to Stockwood. 'It's good! Do you have any more of this... what do you call it?'

'Chocolate surprise.'

'What's the surprise?'

Before he could answer I retched. The sudden reappearance of the food I had eaten was as much of a shock to me as to him. I scrambled backwards from the steaming puddle, dagger drawn, and aimed without hesitation at Stockwood's heart. 'You *are* trying to poison me!'

'My dear, I assure you that –'

'Do not think that because you are old I will not cut out your heart and wash it down with your blood!'

Stockwood stood quite still.

I could smell him sweating.

I waited.

Stockwood didn't move.

My stomach rumbled.

'Uh... we are supposed to be best friends. You remember?'

'Yes.' I frowned. 'Then why should you wish to poison me?'

Stockwood spread his hands to show they were empty. 'I didn't. I suppose you were simply not used to the food. It was very rich.'

He seemed to be telling the truth. And I was beginning to feel better. And hungry again. I sheathed the dagger and eyed a few of the nearest jars. 'Do you have any more food?'

Stockwood showed me his teeth. Somehow I don't think it was a *smile*. 'I think a walk in the fresh air might be more appropriate.'

'Yes. We will hunt for food.'

'Yes. Of course. Whatever you wish.'

I glanced at Stockwood. His expression did not change. He showed me to the big entrance to his house. There he took a large skin from a hook and pulled it on. He offered me a similar skin. I felt the cloth. It was rough and had holes in, like pouches. 'This is a good skin,' I told him.

'It's a navy greatcoat. It belonged to my uncle. It'll keep the wolf from the door.'

I nodded. 'In the Land, the horda hunt in packs. Sometimes they take children that are too young to defend themselves.' I wrapped the greatcoat around my shoulders like a cape. 'My sister was killed by horda when she was three summers old.'

'I am sorry.'

'Do not be. Death is part of life. Ennia died and the horda ate her and then my family killed the horda and the whole tribe ate them. A summer later I was born. If Ennia had not died, I would not be here.'

'I see.'

I studied him closely. 'Yes. You do. Tell me, where we are going, the hunting is good? I would like to see the animal from which you make… chocolate surprise. To kill it would be a challenge.'

'That it would, Leela, that it would.' Stockwood laughed as he opened the big door. There was only a little sadness in his voice this time. I smiled too, though I was careful not to let him see. Many of the Sevateem thought it was dangerous to reveal your thoughts and intentions in this way. I had not made my mind up about the idea yet.

Stockwood continued, more sadly now, 'Perhaps we could leave the hunting until later.'

'If that is your wish.'

'Thank you.'

We walked in silence for a time. I listened carefully to the land around me. The land the Doctor had called London. I had already seen part of it but this part was different. It was very beautiful. There were trees and grass, and everything smelled nice. Not like the smoke and rot of London. Everyone I had seen wore skins all the time. Some of them were even clean. Keeping skins clean was normally impossible. You just wore it until it wore out and then killed something else to wear.

There were huts here, the big huts made out of stone, but they were much bigger than in London – and further apart, each set in its own piece of land. The huts were bigger here – bigger than trees. And like Stockwood's house they had holes in the walls that were filled with glass. I tried to look in through several as we walked but I could not. I wondered why I could see out from the inside and not in from the outside. This glass. You could only see through it one way, you could put water in it, you could put flowers in it. It was clever.

And there were animals. Huge animals whose shoulders stood higher than my head. Animals that snorted fiercely and stamped angrily upon the stony path. I thought I had seen one before – but I had been confused then, and most of the time fighting for my life, so I was not sure.

'What's that?' I asked, pointing at one of the animals.

'A horse.'

'Can you eat it?'

'Only if you're a dog.'

'What's a dog?'

'Why, Leela, a dog is a man's best friend.'

'The Doctor said I was your best friend.'

'Ah, yes, well, it's like this, you see… I… Oh look, there's a bicycle. No. You can't eat it.'

'Of course not. It's metal.'

'You know what metal is?'

'Of course I do! We have metal in the Land. Metal is holy.' I quoted the First Message. '"Metal brought the Sevateem from the Sky to the Land."' Stockwood seemed impressed. I said, rather cleverly, I thought, 'That man must be a priest to own so much metal. We should pay homage to him.'

'Actually he's a postman. The only thing we pay him for are stamps – and those are far too expensive, if you ask me.'

'I see.' I didn't of course. This land confused me. Much of it frightened me. The horses stamped and snorted because they were angry and they were angry because the tribes here made them walk on stone when it was clear to me their hooves were designed for walking on dirt. And although they were tied up, the things they were tied up to had wheels and moved around, dragged wherever the horses felt like going. What was the point? Letting animals roam free inside your village was dangerous and stupid. Someone would get hurt.

I had a sudden thought. Maybe they weren't animals. Maybe they were the people here. The Doctor was always telling me to try to see the other point of view. Yes. That was it.

Grinning at my own cleverness, I approached the nearest horse and prepared to make homage to it. The horse reared up immediately. It screamed at me. I made the sign of Xoanon – neck, left shoulder, left hip. Moving my arm just excited the horse even more. It began to squeal. I noticed a man on top, dressed much as Stockwood was, hat and coat. He had a whip. He whipped the horse and pulled on some leather thongs which it held in its mouth. The horse moved around me and stamped away, the wooden box to which it was tied rattling along after it.

I turned to Stockwood, puzzled. He held up a hand to stop my questions. I nodded. Rituals were strange and not to be questioned.

By now we had reached a high wall made of baked-clay bricks. Metal poles were set into the wall at intervals. I peered through the fence. Inside the enclosure were trees and grass and flowers. It smelled like summer.

Stockwood opened a gate and beckoned me inside.

I touched branches as we walked, pulled handfuls of grass,

sniffed at flowers. Then I stopped. How could I have been so foolish? 'Are there wild animals here that will attack?'

'No. You're thinking of the zoo.'

'Zoo?'

'Never mind.'

'What is this place? It is beautiful.'

'It's a graveyard.'

'And these stones? They serve no purpose that I can see. Why not have them removed to build more huts for your tribe?'

'They're headstones. Graves.' Stockwood led me to a small hut made of stone. Metal gates led into a dark interior. Holy marks were carved into the wall. I pointed to them. 'Does your shaman live here?'

'Nobody lives here.'

'Then why have walls and a gate?'

'To stop vandals.'

'Stop them from what?'

'Defacing the tombs.'

Stockwood took some flowers he had bartered for while we were walking and laid them at the foot of the wall. He pulled off a glove and touched the holy marks. 'I'm sorry, Alex. I should have gone back for you.'

'Why do you put flowers here?'

'To honour the dead.'

I sniffed impatiently. 'It is a waste. Are they not edible? Why waste flowers on the dead?' I shook my head. 'Why waste the dead by burying them? The meat will rot.'

Stockwood pulled his glove back on. His manner had changed. He seemed angry. I wondered why.

'Do you miss your sister?'

'No. I never knew her. But I respect her. And I pay homage to her memory. For without her I would not be.'

'I miss him, you know, Leela. He was my best friend. We went

51

through Eton together. It was hell. I know it's not the done thing to talk about one's schooldays in such a negative way but I am too old and too angry to ignore the truth now. The other boys were horrible. I was fat. Alexander was my only friend. He stuck by me. And I left him there to die. He cried out to me and I left him there. Oh, God, I'm such a bloody coward!'

'Be silent!' I said harshly. 'You do not honour your dead by squealing at them like a wounded animal. Show them pride. Show them respect. Show them you envy their position nearer the gods.'

Stockwood wiped the back of his gnarled hand across his face. The afternoon sunlight showed his tears clearly. They looked like glass too.

He continued to walk. After a moment I followed. 'He's not there, you know. I left him at Rapa Nui. We never went back for the body. I had the tomb erected in his memory. I suppose it was selfish. I needed him to be here. For me. Even in death I needed him to be here for me.'

I frowned. 'I do not understand. You lie to yourself and it makes you happy?'

'Oh yes.'

'Your tribe is strange.'

'That it is, Leela. That it is.' We walked in silence along the edge of a pond. Birds flapped and quacked on the pond. 'Tell me about yourself, Leela. And your friend the Doctor. Are you close? How did you meet? Why do you want to help me?'

I thought for a moment. 'We will help you because you need help. And because we can. That is what the Doctor does. He helps people. As for myself, I am a hunter. I come from the Place of Land. My tribe is called the Sevateem. My father's name was Sole, my mother Neela. My father taught me well of the ways of hunting and died to save my life when I was stupid.'

'What did you do that was stupid? If you don't mind my asking.'

52

'I do not mind. The Doctor says we learn from our mistakes but only if we –' I struggled with the half-familiar word – '*acknowledge* them.'

Stockwood groped in his pocket and pulled out some breadcrumbs, which he threw at the birds. They began to fight over them. Clever. Provoke them to fight and then kill the survivors. Twice as much food for the tribe. I held my hand out for some bread. 'I did a stupid thing. I told my shaman that there was no god. No Xoanon. I was tried for heresy. My father took the test of the horda in my place. He failed. He died. I was banished into the Beyond.'

'What is the Beyond?'

I threw bread at the birds and waited for them to kill each other over the scraps. The Beyond is… well, the Beyond. It's full of monsters. You cannot see them but they can kill ten warriors with a single blow. The Doctor said they *homed* in on *audible vibrations*. He defeated one with something he called an *egg-timer*.' I pointed at the birds, all of whom were still alive. 'Your hunting tricks are useless. These birds are not killing each other.'

Stockwood laughed. 'I should hope not. It's not the jungle here, you know.'

I looked around nervously. 'The Beyond was near a jungle.'

'Don't worry, Leela. There are no invisible monsters here.'

I studied him closely. 'How can you tell? Do you have an egg-timer?' He did not answer. 'I will kill a bird and we will eat it.'

Stockwood quickly placed a hand on my arm. I managed not to break his arm.

'Tell me about the Doctor.'

'He is good.'

'That's it?'

'He is very good. But odd as well. I do not understand him. But I know he is good.'

'How did you meet?'

I thought back to the Land, to my childhood. 'When I was old enough to train for the Hunt, I told my father I did not believe in Xoanon, our god. My father got angry and told me I had been born deformed; that something inside had been stillborn: the part inside every Sevateem that knew Xoanon and worshipped him was missing from me.

'For a long time I hated my father and I secretly turned against everything he and our Shaman taught. My father died for me. I never understood that. I hated my father even though he knew I was different from the rest of the tribe, and protected me for as long as he could.

'Then when the Doctor came to the Place of Land he told me that my father had been wrong. I hadn't been born with part of me dead. I had been born with part of me alive. A part which had been sleeping in the tribe for many times of fathers.

'My first thought was to hate the Doctor as I hated my father. He just wanted to change me, to make me do what he wanted. But I have come to know that what the Doctor wants for me, I always seem to want for myself, only I don't always know it when the Doctor does. He is a good man. Trust him and he will help you.'

Stockwood nodded sadly. 'Thank you for your kind words. But nobody can bring Alexander back from the dead.'

'That is not what you asked us to do.'

'True enough. Tell me, do you know where your friend obtained that diamond he showed me?'

'Diamond? Oh – you mean the talisman? The TARDIS has many such things. He got them from something he called *another planet* – whatever that is.'

Stockwood looked at me strangely then. I was just starting to feel threatened when he smiled. 'Come on. It's high time we had some tea. I'm starving.'

The walk back to Stockwood's large hut seemed to pass more

quickly than the outward journey. When we arrived Stockwood was shocked to discover someone had broken into his study for a second time.

I drew my dagger, moved ahead of Stockwood into the study. The room was panelled in wood. It had a table, a throne. Lots of shelves. Someone had disturbed the room. Talismans, sheets of paper, pieces of metal, glass tubes, all were scattered across the room. I asked Stockwood, 'What is missing?'

'Um… well… a notebook… here… these artefacts… my analysis of the composition of the tablet wood… and look here… the safe is open! The *rongo-rongo*! Oh my life! Where is the *rongo-rongo*?' The desperation in Stockwood's voice made him sound even more like an animal. It reminded me of the sound the infant web-tree spinners made when I killed their parent. I sniffed. There was a faint scent. 'Give me your… that pipe thing you put in your mouth to blow smoke.'

'My briar?'

'Yes! Quickly!'

Stockwood did as I asked. I took the briar and a pouch full of dried leaves he offered and sniffed them. No. The smell in the room was not either of these things. But it was similar. Very similar.

Stockwood took back the pipe and pouch. 'Someone was here?' he asked. 'Someone who smokes?' He began to tidy the mess, his movements slow, dispirited.

'They did not blow smoke while they were here. The smell is faint. But new. Made within the hour.' I leaned forward and sniffed Stockwood's jacket. It smelled like the briar, only not so strong. 'The smell was on his clothes.'

'Who?'

'Whoever was here.'

Stockwood stopped tidying abruptly. 'Fennel wears an old smoking jacket from time to time. I believe it was his father's.'

'Fennel?'

'The butler.'

I nodded. 'Do you have any more of his clothes?'

'His coat… the hall stand.'

Stockwood fetched the coat. I sniffed it. 'This is the smell.'

Stockwood uttered a short, annoyed sound. It was enough like a laugh to confuse me. 'Old Holborn. I should have guessed.'

'I will check the house. You stay here. If this Fennel is still here I will kill him.'

Stockwood began to say something. At that moment I heard a sound from nearby.

Fennel!

I would kill him now!

We rushed into the drawing room only to find the Doctor sitting cross-legged upon the dining table. A bucket full of ice rested on the table beside him. In the bucket was a bottle. Three clay mugs were arranged neatly on the table beside the bucket.

There was no sign of Fennel.

'I'm afraid the Butler did it.' The Doctor spotted us and sprang to his feet with a gleeful grin. 'You were right,' he said. 'The theft was down to Fennel – I caught him in the act and fired him on the spot. I let him go because I wanted to follow him but he was too quick for me. Still, never mind. At least I managed to retrieve this.' And he pulled a small slab of wood covered with holy marks from his pocket.

Stockwood let out a shocked sigh and leapt forward, snatching the wooden slab and cradling it to his chest. 'The tablet. How can I ever thank you!'

The Doctor smiled modestly. 'Oh, it was nothing. A mere frippery. This is much more important.' And, with an even larger grin, he dumped a huge bag of gold coins down on the table with a crash. 'You leave for Portsmouth at first light tomorrow morning. I suggest you begin packing immediately. And, Horace,' he added conspiratorially. 'Don't forget the provisions, will you? I'm rather partial to a nice chocolate surprise – only someone I could name seems to have wolfed it all.' The Doctor winked at me as he picked up the bottle and a mug. 'So. Anyone for champagne? Sorry about the mugs – I couldn't find the glasses.' His grin, already enormous, seemed now to swallow up his entire face. 'I think perhaps the butler stole them.'

The Doctor poured two mugs of champagne and was in the middle of a third when the doorbell rang.

'Horace,' the Doctor prompted Stockwood, still absorbed in his study of the *rongo-rongo*.

Stockwood looked up. 'Yes?'

'Doorbell. No butler, remember?'

'Oh. Oh yes, quite.' Stockwood glanced at the *rongo-rongo* again.

The Doctor looked at the window. 'I'll meet you in Portsmouth tomorrow. I'll arrange passage for us and book hotel rooms. You take care of the packing here. We'll need your notes, the tablet, instruments... all the usual stuff.'

'Yes... of course...' Stockwood finally put the tablet away and began to pay attention. 'Bless my soul, is that someone banging on the door? Did nobody hear?' And he went to answer the door.

I looked at the Doctor. He offered me a mug. I sipped champagne. It was disgusting. I spat it out. 'It tastes like poison!'

The Doctor grinned. 'It is.' He got up off the table and walked towards the window that opened on to the grounds. He unlatched the window and pushed the curved sheet of glass open. Beyond him I could see the ornamental fountain in which the TARDIS had landed. 'See you tomorrow.' He tipped his hat. 'Noon, at the George Hotel.' And he was gone.

At that moment Stockwood came back into the room with another man. They might have been brothers. They both had grey hair, though the newcomer had rather more than Stockwood, and it was neater, too. He also sported a short beard. They were even dressed similarly. I wondered about that. The skins the two men wore clearly came from animals so similar in shape and colour they must have been born twins.

Stockwood introduced his companion. 'Leela, this is James Royston, MD. James, this is Leela.'

I pointed at Stockwood. 'I am his best friend.'

'Indeed.' Royston made a strange face. It was almost a smile, but not quite. He looked puzzled but, when he spoke, he sounded almost amused. 'Well, Horace, for a man who roughly speaking makes a friend every decade your current choice seems about par for the course.'

Royston continued to look at me. I rested my hand on the hilt of my dagger. Was I going to have to show every man in this land that I was not his for the choosing?

Stockwood looked at Royston. 'Leela is more than she seems, James. I suggest you choose your words carefully in her presence.'

'Judging by the blade on that dagger, I certainly will.'

Stockwood looked around for the Doctor. 'Where is the Doctor, Leela?'

'Port… smouth.' I struggled over the unfamiliar word. He said we were to meet him tomorrow at noon. At the hotel named George.'

Stockwood nodded. He spoke to Royston. 'Well, James, if you've come to be social I'm afraid I must decline. Leela and I are going on a little trip.'

'I know. Rapa Nui via Portsmouth.' Royston said casually. 'And at your age you'll need a good physician. I'm coming with you and I don't want to hear any arguments. I've already packed.'

Stockwood seemed happy. But I didn't like this newcomer. He seemed too relaxed. Too confident. Too... well, I didn't know, but something about him made me suspicious.

'How did you know we were leaving so soon?'

'Why, the Doctor told me this very afternoon.'

I was not convinced. I leaned closer and sniffed his jacket. He seemed amused. 'My dear, you'd be a corker at parties.' He paused thoughtfully. 'They'd have to be the right sort of parties, though.'

I let him laugh. While he was off guard I took a leather pouch from his pocket. I sniffed it. 'Old Holborn,' I told him. 'The butler smoked Old Holborn and he tried to steal the *rongo-rongo*.'

Royston reached for the pouch with a strange look. He was pretending to be angry. But it was clear he wasn't. He just wasn't clever enough at lying with his body to trick me. I decided I didn't like Royston. I would watch him with the Hunter's Eye and if he tried to steal anything or hurt Stockwood I would cut out his heart so fast he would not even know he was dead.

5
Maps and Blood

Tweed had been running down the wind with all sails set, following sunrise for many days, and the weather had remained sunny and bright, if not quite as hot as it had been since we had left the Equator. I had been trying to find the Doctor – of all the people I have known he is the only one who could remain unseen for a nine-day on something the size of a sailing ship. I wanted to talk to him about my suspicions about Royston and Richards. I wanted him to take back the promise he had made me keep so far about not killing anyone.

When I finally found him and told him all this he simply suggested I was bored and restless.

'Of course I am bored and restless!' I said. 'And fat, too, I should not wonder. I am a hunter. There is nothing here to hunt. Except fish.'

The Doctor smiled. 'If the mind is willing there is always something to hunt.'

'I do not understand.'

'Then hunt that. Hunt understanding. Make it your enemy and track it to its lair. Grapple with it. Take it and make it your slave. Your tool. Use it. Feast upon it. Grow fat on it.'

'That is silly. Understanding is not an animal. It cannot fight.'

'Galileo wouldn't agree with you. Why don't you start by asking Captain Stuart about sailing around the world?'

I had done so, and to my surprise the Captain had agreed. This surprised me since he had not hesitated in accepting gold from our enemy – one who had tried to kill all of us before setting sail from Portsmouth so many nine-days ago.

Whatever I thought, the Doctor told me to listen to the Captain and I trusted the Doctor enough to do this. In fact the Captain was a man worth listening to, I had already decided. Had I not planned to kill him along with all those who betrayed us as soon as we reached dry land, I probably would have liked him very much.

When I told the Doctor this he chuckled. 'I'm not surprised you like him. Captain Stuart has Viking ancestors.' He smiled to himself. 'I wouldn't be surprised if you're related.'

I found Stuart a cheerful man with a Scots accent very much like that of the cook, only mild where the cook's was abrasive. He was tall, with a shock of red hair, thinning on top, which made him look like was wearing a bright cloth cap with a hole cut in it. He was not a particularly big fellow, but he was wiry and strong. The last time I let the pigs out for a bit of fun, he had been the one who helped me wrestle the old sow to the deck. As a captain, Stuart maintained the respect of his men not through violence or threat but by virtue of common sense and kindness. In this I found him confusing: after all, he had betrayed us by allowing himself to be bought by our enemy. I had talked to the Doctor about this. His advice was simply not to worry about things that you could not change. That was sensible enough.

This morning, Stuart took me to his cabin shortly after the bosun rang end of morning watch and Spanker Jack brought our breakfast to us, with compliments of the cook. The breakfast was accompanied by bread for the first time in a month. The Doctor had found some wheat seed in his pocket. While it was growing he showed the cook how to build a bread oven from metal scrap found in the bilges. Cook found this enterprise astonishing – and had promptly given the Doctor free run in the galley any time he liked. This was good. The Doctor was an excellent cook. And farmer, too, it seemed.

The bread was excellent.

Captain Stuart thanked Jack and dismissed him. He placed the two plates of food on a heavy wooden desk, whose legs were bolted to the floor. I glanced around the cabin. It was small, and, although the ceiling was one of the highest on the ship, I could still reach up and touch the deckhead without even trying. The cabin was beneath the quarterdeck, at the very stern of the ship. The walls curved with the curvature of the ship. A set of narrow windows looked out directly aft. The frames were thick wood, stained and polished – well made, like the desk, bunk, chairs and other small items of furniture. The walls held two pictures – one with writing I could not read and another showing a picture of *Tweed* herself, in which she looked very different.

Stuart saw me looking at the picture. '*Tweed* wasn't always a sailing ship, you know. She started life as a paddle-steamer. Built in the Bombay shipyards by the East India Company.'

'I have heard of that. The Doctor told me they made tea.'

'And ships. Fine ships too. She was called *Punjab* then. One of the last pair of frigates built by the Wadia family. She's known war and weather, Leela. War and weather. In 1854 she weathered a cyclone in the Bombay harbour which had her sister ship, *Assaye*, smashed against the castle walls. Five square riggers and three steamers were dismasted and hurled ashore that day. Not *Punjab*. She took what the wind could give, took it and laughed in the face of the storm. In 1855 she took two hundred and fifty horses and half the Tenth Hussars to Suez during the Crimea. In November of the same year she sailed for Bombay as a warship sent to fight in the Persian War. In 1857 she played her part in the Indian Mutiny. Four seamen were killed and twenty-one wounded. But Lieutenant Lewis and his detail received high commendations. And a young midshipman – Arthur Mayo – was awarded the Victoria Cross.'

I listened quietly. Know your enemies. Stuart was a good storyteller. I could smell the blood and hear the cannon fire and see the square riggers washed ashore to the sound of cracked masts and splintered timbers.

Stuart paused to eat part of his breakfast. I joined him. The piglet I had been playing with not a nine-day before tasted quite delicious.

'In 1862, after the old Indian Navy was merged with the Navy, *Punjab* and *Assaye* were sent to England for conversion to screw steamers. Both were sold to the present owner, John Willis. He sold the *Assaye* for more money than both had cost and then converted the *Punjab* to sail. He renamed her after the river he was born on. She's been a steamer and a warship, run cargo and passengers in luxury the Queen herself could wish for, and just three years ago outran the mail steamer between Hong Kong and Singapore. It's my pleasure to have her known as "Willis's Wonder".' Stuart was silent for a moment, chewing bacon. 'If I have my way I'll never lose a man under my command or damage so much as a spar or plank of her hull.'

Know your enemy indeed. Stuart was a man in love with a machine. He was like the Tesh. But still, somehow, different, in a way I could not quite work out.

'The Doctor said I was to ask you about sailing around the world.'

'So he did, so he did. And I promised him I would show you. Now look here.' Stuart set down his breakfast – I had eaten mine while listening to him speak – and moved to a smaller desk at one side of the cabin. On the desk were maps and unfamiliar objects made of finely carved wood and equally finely crafted holy metal. And something else. A thing like a ball made of wood and carved in intricate patterns, suspended in a circular wooden frame so it could spin freely when touched.

Stuart pointed out of the window. 'Do you see the ocean?'

'Yes.'

'What shape is it?'

I frowned. Was Stuart trying to trick me? 'Flat of course. All water is flat.'

He smiled. 'Have you ever thought about why you can't see the end of it then?'

'No.'

'I see.' He touched the wooden ball, set it spinning gracefully within its frame. 'The water is curved, Leela. So is the land. But they are very big. So big that they seem flat to us.'

'I do not understand.'

Stuart took the wooden ball from its stand and gave it to me. 'Look at this. You can see the curvature, yes?'

'Yes.'

'Now hold it up to your eye. That's right. Really close. And close the other eye. Get as close as you can. Look at just a little piece of the edge.'

I held the ball as he instructed, feeling very silly. 'Now what?'

'Now tell me, does it look so curved as before?'

'No.'

'Why not?'

'I do not know. It is magic. The ball changes shape when it is near my face.'

'No, Leela, it doesn't do that. What changes is the way your eye sees the ball. And it's called a globe, by the way.'

'Ball, globe. I do not understand. I can see, I am a hunter. How can I see things differently if they do not change?'

'Because you're only seeing a little bit of what you're looking at. You've been up in the crow's nest with Jack.'

'Yes.'

'What does the ocean look like from up there?'

'Why, it's round, like a –' I blinked. 'Like this globe.'

Stuart grinned. 'That's the first lesson. This world is round. Like a ball. Gravity holds us on it. And it seems flat because we are very, very close to the surface. Now look.' He took the globe from me and put it back on the stand. 'This globe is really a map of the Earth. Here's England, and Portsmouth, where we sailed from. And here's London, where you came from.'

'But they're so close together. It took us a whole day to travel from London to Portsmouth.'

Stuart nodded. 'And here's where we're going.' He spun the globe. 'Easter Island. In the Pacific Ocean.'

I compared the distances. 'No wonder we have been at sea for so long.' I studied the globe. 'If it took us a day to go this far, and we have been at sea for this many days, then we should be...' I stopped puzzled. 'We should have been there by now.' I frowned. 'It is a trick. Distances cannot change.'

Stuart grinned again. He moved the globe around, pointed to a spot on the underneath, almost half a world away from Easter Island. 'We are here. We rounded the Cape of Good Hope a week this Tuesday gone, travelling due east. God and icebergs willing, we'll see Australia in another month.'

'But we are sailing away from Rapa Nui!'

'At the moment, yes. But look what happens when you continue on from Australia into the Pacific.' He spun the globe again, tracing a route with one wind-gnarled finger.

'Oh.'

'Exactly. We reach Easter Island from the west.'

'That's clever.'

'Well, you couldn't do it if the world was flat, that's for sure. We'd all fall off the edge.'

'Hm.' I looked closely at Stuart. He was smiling faintly. Was he making fun of me? I couldn't tell, so decided to ignore it. Stuart finished eating his breakfast and then suggested that I go back to the crow's nest and keep an eye out for icebergs.

'What's an iceberg?'

'Ask Jack. He'll tell you. And make sure you shout if you see one. I've no wish for *Tweed* to go missing with all hands.'

'I will shout.'

'Good. Until later then.'

Stuart moved the globe and began to look at the pieces of paper on his desk.

I found the Doctor waiting for me as I left the cabin. He was lounging against the part of the mizzenmast that passed through this deck. 'How was the lesson?'

'Confusing. Captain Stuart told me the Earth was round like a ball but he had maps on his desk which were flat.'

The Doctor sighed. 'I told him. I told Columbus and told him. All you need is an orange and a biro. Nobody listens to me.' He wandered off, muttering to himself.

I walked through the central companionway towards the forward hatches and the galley. I was beginning to feel hemmed in below decks. I needed some fresh air. Whatever his ideas about the shape of the world, the Captain's instruction to climb to the crow's nest and watch out for icebergs was probably a very good one.

That was when I saw Royston emerging from one of the cabins on the port side. Richards was with him. Without really knowing why I ducked back behind the mizzenmast, using its bulk to hide myself. Royston and Richards walked the other way and did not see me. But I had seen something important. Royston was carrying was carrying some cloth. Bandages. They were stained with blood. And smelled of sickness. I crept towards the cabin they had come out of and tried to open the door. It was locked. But I could smell the sickness inside the cabin. I wondered what was in there.

And how I could find out.

6
Ticket to Ride

The Atmosphere Monitoring Subsystem didn't want to let me out of the TARDIS.

I gave the system a reassuring pat, told it the atmosphere was perfectly normal for Portsmouth Harbour *circa* 1872 and that such an important subsystem really shouldn't worry itself over so trivial a matter as my continued health. I had a respiratory bypass system, didn't I?

After a moment or two of gentle cajoling the AMS grudgingly consented to open the TARDIS doors and allow me to leave. I smiled, trying to seem grateful. The Old Thing is such a worriwort sometimes.

I took a good look around as I left the TARDIS. The docks had evolved somewhat since I had last visited, that being the occasion of breakfast with Nelson at the George. That had been in 1805, the day before his final contretemps with Napoleon at Trafalgar. Stalwart chap, Nelson. Good four-dimensional visualisation of events, for a human, though his grasp of the French tactic of 'advancing in a rearward direction' tended to leave him a little flat-footed on many occasions. Liked his eggs sunny side up, as I recall.

Putting aside my memories, I took in a little more of the present. The TARDIS had arrived on Victoria Pier, a new addition to the harbour landscape. The pier consisted of a rather attractive wooden jetty projecting out into the harbour, bordered to the west by the spit of land encompassing the inner and outer camber, along which Broad Street ran, and to the east by the Fortifications – a high wall encompassing the old town. The town itself nestled behind the wall, snug as the proverbial bug in the proverbial rug. Further to the east I saw the gently tilting movement of windmill sails. I smiled. I liked windmills. I seemed to remember there being a great many more on Portsea Island the last time I had visited. Ah, well. That was progress for you. Today the windmill, tomorrow geothermal energy and the electric toothbrush.

Beyond the pier, the harbour was clogged with boats of every description. I found my gaze drawn towards HMS *Victory* – and was saddened at the changes wreaked upon her since that day in 1805 when I had seen Nelson for the last time. Her bow had been built up and the cheerful yellow bands along her gun ports had now been replaced with a rather pedestrian coat of white paint. Beyond the dazzling array of masts and sails I could see the slopes of Wight, somewhat pert and attractively wrapped in the shawl of evening.

I closed and locked the TARDIS doors. The Old Thing sometimes gets nervous if I forget to secure the doors. I took several deep breaths just to prove the AMS wrong and then in very short order wished I hadn't. I stopped breathing for a minute or two, long enough to analyse the rather pungent cocktail I had just inhaled.

Fish.

Birds. Oil. Smoke. Rotting vegetable matter. Rotting animal matter. Burning wood. Hot pitch. Manganese. Rats. Dogs.

I concentrated.

The fish were a day old, the birds were tern, recently arrived on their yearly migration, the oil needed changing, the smoke was derived from cannabis, the rotting vegetable matter was carrot, the animal matter was dead rat (being eaten by several more live rats), the pitch was cooling upon the hull of a nearby ship, the dog was old, a canny purebreed turned to the wild (rather like myself, I fancied), and the burning wood was laced with human sweat and with teak oil, normally used to seal the decking of a ship.

All of which told me that somewhere nearby, a sailor had just thrown part of his lunch to a stray dog before grinding a strong toke out beneath his bare heel upon the deck of a ship recently arrived from the Indies, whose hull he was currently engaged in repairing. The Manganese I had detected came, no doubt, from tiny nodules lodged within the damaged section of hull. The nodules definitely originated on the sea bed and could only have been disturbed by a major storm. The fish go without saying, obviously. And the rats? Well… there are rats at the docks in any century.

Not all of them are animals.

I compressed my sensory input to human normal. This is something I do from time to time, a little game which keeps me entertained and alert, and I stepped away from the TARDIS.

The wooden dock creaked beneath my feet. Greasy water lapped at wooden supports. The sun was slipping away to westwards, leaving room in the sky for a wind. It was an interesting wind. The kind the French might refer to as *tu*, rather than *vous*. No familiar summer phantom, this, but a stranger of a breeze, a zephyr born in exotic latitudes, perhaps the offspring of some frightful hurricane or tornado, a wind of frightening and compelling potential, and one worthy of respect. It was a wind Columbus and Darwin and Phineas Fogg would have understood. I smiled up at it and waggled my fingers through it and twirled my scarf happily at the thought that such an apparently simple thing could provoke such wonder.

'Oi!' The voice was rough, and it was punctuated by a phlegmy tobacco-related cough. 'Wotcher doin' 'ere then? Passengers ain't allowed 'ere, are they?'

I turned. The dock handler was short, thick-set, with a brow that commanded attention as much for its obvious temporal proximity to his simian ancestors as for the thick mop of ginger hair that covered it. He wore the usual clothes one might expect of a dock worker, rough, smelly, dark. He was walking towards me self-importantly. Swaggering might be a better word. In one hand was a cargo manifest, in the other a hip flask from which I clearly detected the aroma of a rather dubious malt whisky.

I smiled. 'I was just admiring the wind.'

The man looked at me with an expression I had come to be quite familiar with in the last couple of centuries of dealings with humans. 'You can admire the boats from the other side of the harbour. Or buy yerself a whisky in the Three Tuns on the 'igh street.'

'That sounds rather splendid. Tell me, do they serve ginger beer?'

'Ginger...? Wa'ss at then? Some foreign muck, issit?'

I checked my watch. 'Ah yes. I was forgetting. It hasn't been discovered yet.'

The handler clearly lacked either the time or ability to be confused. 'Look, mate, it's easy. Move along or I'll dump y'in the dock and *then* you can move along. Only not so sweet smellin', if y'take me meaning.'

'Assuredly I do, Mr...?'

'Just do as yer told, afore Mr Harper takes it outta both our hides with a whaling 'poon.'

'And Mr Harper, he would be the Captain of this fine clipper here, the *Tweed*, would he?'

'No, that'd be Cap'n Stuart. Mr Harper is the harbour master. He's much worse. So y'best be getting along, like I said.'

'I shall certainly take your advice.' I started away from the dock handler with what I hoped he would consider a sprightly step. 'If you'd just be so kind as to direct me to his office...?'

Actually, I didn't need to be directed. There was only one place the harbour master's office would be located in a port such as this. 'No, never mind,' I added over my shoulder to the annoyed dock handler. 'I'll just follow the smell of corruption, shall I?'

I marched along the dockside, through a forest of packing crates, past several ships lying at anchor. At no time did I walk fast enough to quite lose the handler. I was relying on his presence to get me through the ranks. And very effective he was, too, because, as fit as he obviously was, I was fitter, and I moved at such a speed that he expended all his energy keeping up, with none left in reserve for protestation, which might have caused me some bother if many of the other workers had heard him.

The harbour master's office was set back from the inner camber, a hundred yards from the greasy swells lapping against the jetties. Gulls flapped indolently above the wooden building, a speckled cloud through which the town of Portsmouth could be seen rising in angular clumps towards a dusty sky. Dock handler in tow, I strode towards the office, knocked sharply on the door and, without waiting for an answer, opened it and strode inside. I closed the door behind me just in time to prevent the dock worker entering. I assume he decided business elsewhere was the better part of valour.

I turned from the door to find the harbour master looking at me with cold eyes. 'Mr Harper, I presume?' I beamed expansively to show him I was friendly, then made a mental note not to try this any more. It seemed to have the exact opposite effect from that desired. 'Smith. John Smith, at your service.'

Harper was a small man, and like small men throughout history seemed to have a disproportionately large opinion of himself. His clothes were immaculate, his cap so level you could set a foundation stone with it. 'Your business, sir?' he asked brusquely. 'I fear I am a busy man today, and indeed every day. And I take no pleasure in being interrupted so peremptorily, I can assure you.'

Well, he obviously had an education. One somewhat elevated above his station, I ventured. Interesting. 'Sir, I beg your indulgence for both my manner and my rather impromptu arrival. But there is a pressing matter of some urgency which requires our joint attention.'

The man's expression did not change. 'Indeed.'

'Yes. I wish to buy a ship.'

Harper sniffed, opened a ledger to a blank page, lifted a quill pen from the inkwell and prepared to make an entry. 'You mean you wish to buy *passage* on a ship,' he corrected smugly.

I extracted a large bag from my pocket and let it fall to the desk with just enough force for it to split, spilling coins across the ledger. The coins were of course gold. There were rather a lot of them.

'No,' I replied even more smugly. 'I wish to buy a ship.' Harper stared at the gold. 'There's a rather nice clipper berthed at dock two. I believe her Captain's name is Stuart.'

Harper continued to stare at the gold. He reached out a finger to touch one piece. I noticed that the finger was shaking.

'It's called *Tweed*,' I added helpfully.

Harper slowly pushed the gold pieces back into the bag and weighed it in his hand. 'I can get you a ship. But you'll need a captain, a crew, fuel, provisions, insurance, compensation for cancellation of cargo to previous contractor –'

I reached out, took the quill pen from his moneyless hand, put the pen back into the inkwell, opened his hand out flat and dumped a second bag of gold into it.

'To go where, sir?' Harper's voice held a slight quaver.

'East of the sun, west of the moon,' I told him with a smile. Then reached into my pocket and pulled out my favourite bag of all. 'Mint humbug?' I offered the bag to Harper, whose hands, of course, were full of gold. 'Ah. I dare say not.'

Harper took me, in something of a daze, I fear, back along the docks to the clipper that had caught my eye, the rather captivating *Tweed*. There he introduced me to Captain Stuart, a mild-featured Scot, and then retired to the Captain's cabin, presumably to talk business. While they were discussing my offer, I spent ten minutes exploring the ship. She was a fine vessel. Trim, efficient, with no excess weight on her anywhere that I could see. Her masts were firm, her decks showed no sign of rot, her hull displayed a satisfyingly odorous layer of bitumen. From stern to prow, crow's nest to keel, she was the very epitome of a mid-class sailing vessel. She was to sailing vessels what the Beatles would soon be to popular music.

On the subject of music, I could hear singing from below decks. The crew warming up for a night out on the town, I presumed. One of them noticed me right off, and soon I had a curious crowd watching me as I poked and prodded various parts of the ship's structure, ascertaining its quality – and qualities – as one might ascertain those of a horse by checking its teeth. The crew, two-thirds drunk by this time, watched with growing interest and some amusement. I let them. A crew this relaxed was one that got on well with its captain. A happy crew was a good crew, and that was the kind I wanted. Ten minutes later Stuart emerged on to the deck. Harper had already left. Stuart glanced at his crew, who at this particular moment were haphazardly arranged along the deck and rigging, and singing with enthusiasm, but less than wildly impressive talent, the chorus from 'Ticket to Ride'.

'Catchy song,' Stuart said quietly. I noticed he didn't smile.

I smiled for him. 'Talent borrows, genius steals. Lennon told me that shortly after he died. I never did work out whether he was being facetious or simply enigmatic.'

Stuart blinked. It was the only sign of hesitation I ever saw him make. Although he didn't smile, I could see him trying to work out if I had just made a joke and whether he should be laughing at it or not. 'Well, Mr – Doctor, I mean – you've got yourselves a ship, a captain, and a very happy crew by the looks of it.' Stuart added, shouting over my Beatles chorus, 'Well, lads, we got a new charter here. This here's the Doctor. Says his name is John Smith, but I don't hold there's much truth in that. Still, his money's good and that's what counts, am I right?'

A drunken cheer briefly interrupted the song.

'Glad t'hear it! Because we sail tomorrow on the midnight tide. So for tonight make as merry as y'like. Tomorrow we work fer our living. Are y'hearin' me, lads?'

A resounding '*Aye Aye, Captain Stuart!*' thundered across the deck and out into the docks, disturbing the gulls roosting on the harbour master's office roof.

'Bloody glad t'hear it, too! Now, Collins and Shaw, help Doctor Smith with his baggage and then you can all get royally quaffed on me!'

Another '*Aye Aye, Captain Stuart!*' boomed upward into the rigging as the man in question handed a gold coin to the first mate. 'As soon as the gentleman's cargo is secure, go to the Three Tuns and bring back enough ale to sink a man o' war!'

'*Aye Aye, Captain Stuart!*'

'And then sink it yourself, lads, are y'hearin' me?' Stuart roared, at least as loudly as his entire crew put together.

'*Aye Aye, Captain Stuart!*'

The mate smiled through a mouthful of less than perfect teeth. 'The pleasure, Captain,' he said, 'will be all mine.'

Stuart looked at me. 'It's a good crew y've bought with y'r gold and fair song.'

I nodded. 'My dear fellow, any crew that can remain as

intoxicated as this one and still co-ordinate more than three words more often than three times in the same three minutes is good enough for me.'

Stuart stared hard at me for a moment, then clapped me on the back. 'You have the luck o' the Irish about you', sir. That you do. For I like you. And better still, they like you. Now away with you, Collins and Shaw, to your cargo. The sooner we stow the baggage, the sooner the night will get interesting, am I right?'

'Aye Aye, Captain Stuart,' I said quietly. I smiled as the crewmen led me from the deck. But the smile was a sad one. For I liked Stuart. He was a good man. Well travelled, obviously, but not a braggadocio. And he had people skills. That was important. I hoped we would get a chance to talk properly before he died, though I suspected that my wish would remain unfulfilled. Such is the curse of the long-lived. It's one of the reasons Earth is my favourite planet. Somehow humans manage to cram so much into their butterfly lives – so much feeling and achievement that even I, who've accumulated a gnat's whisker shy of a millennium's experience, can scarcely articulate it.

I turned to Collins and Shaw. 'Gentlemen, I commend you, for you have the privilege to belong to one of the most heart-warming species it has been my very great fortune to encounter.'

'Oh aye?' said Collins.

'Z'at so?' added Shaw.

'Wanna drink?' they finished together.

They both proffered hip flasks. I grinned. This was going to be fun.

It stopped being fun about two minutes later, when I realised the TARDIS, which we were intending to load on to the *Tweed*, was not where I had left it. And that there was a conspicuous length of empty jetty where there had once been a somewhat down-at-heel sailing vessel.

The inference was obvious.

I grabbed the nearest dock handler. 'The boat. The one that was here. Where is it now?'

The man thought for a moment. 'Well, it's gone, ain't it?'

'And the blue box? There was a blue box here. About this high.' I gestured.

'Well, it ain't here now. All the crates that was here, we loaded 'em on to the ship. If your box was here it's halfway across the Channel b'now.'

'Going where?'

'India.'

I stared unblinkingly at the dock handler, as if that would change anything, as if I could bring the boat back by sheer force of will. The handler just shrugged unhelpfully.

I sighed. 'Oh well. The Old Thing always did have a hankering to travel.' I turned to Collins and Shaw. 'Gentlemen, my luggage will be travelling by a different route.'

'That right, then?'

'Changed y'r mind, have we?'

'Less work for us.'

'We'll be off for a drink, then.'

In a moment I was alone on the pier. I listened to the water lapping greasily against the wooden supports, then turned sharply on my heel towards town. Losing the TARDIS was inconvenient, but not a disaster. We'd run into each other again soon; it was a small enough planet. In the meantime I had other business to conduct. And two hotel rooms to book.

I left the docks and began to walk towards town. The buildings were low, mostly made of wood, and set close together on narrow streets. I could hear all manner of sounds. Dogs barking, women shouting, clothes flapping damply against walls. Once, several children ran past, giggling and yelling at each other. They all stopped and asked me for spare money. I gave them some humbugs.

One of the children – a girl with shadowed eyes and pale skin – looked up at me. 'Can't buy nuffink wiv sweets, mister. You sure you ain't got no brass?'

I stopped, crouched beside the little girl. I touched the hand she was holding out, the bioelectric field a fractal detail of her short life. Nine, maybe ten years old. Low to medium IQ. Rickets. I gave each child a gold piece. They ran off squealing with delight. The little girl looked at me solemnly for a moment. 'They're rude, that lot,' she said. 'Me mam allus told me ter say ta.' She grinned, exposing teeth that were already beyond hope. 'Ta, mister!' She bolted.

'Eat your greens!' I expect I sounded like her mother. She didn't look back.

I continued through town. By now afternoon was drawing to a close. The air was damp and a fog was drawing in. Moisture ran from nearby walls and made the road slippery. The sounds I could hear – which now included the clattering of horse-drawn carriages and the more distant cries of gulls – seemed to recede among the grey shadows. I imagined the sounds were playing hide-and-seek, visualising each as one of the children I had seen. The clatter of a carriage was a dirty boy, clothes flapping in the fog. The screech of a gull marked the impatience of the gang leader. The distant bark of dogs was the angry shout of a girl who'd been bullied. The slap of washing against walls was the hanger-on, trailing the rest in flapping shoes. The fog thickened. The sky swept down as if to grasp my hat. I watched it, noting the subtle shift of airborne particles, a cloying mixture of smoke and water vapour.

I started to look for an inn. Something small. Unobtrusive. With a good vintage lemonade.

I heard footsteps. Behind me. Pacing me. Muffled in the fog.

Soft. Deliberate. A hunter's footsteps.

I did not turn. Instead I increased my pace. Soon I was striding at what would be a fast trot for a human.

The footsteps faded. I slowed. Probably it had been nothing. But you can never tell. And in parts like these it made sense to play it safe. The local villains might have ambitions somewhat less grand than control of the universe but they would kill you just as quickly for your small change. I didn't want to risk being stabbed for the sake of a bag of mint humbugs, a yo-yo, a sextant, an African charm carved from an elephant tusk, a bottle of teak oil, a bottle of radish sauce, some penicillin and sulpha, some silicon chips, some grade-one diamonds, and a slightly soiled handkerchief with a knot in one corner. Among other things.

Breathing a sigh of relief that I hadn't had to resort to violence – even aggressive humans are more fragile than they realise – I turned a corner in the fog, and ran head first into someone running the other way.

I felt hands grasp at my shoulders, pulling me closer. No. This wasn't right. It was too controlled. An accidental collision would have provoked anger or apologies. Not silence. I showed the man that I knew more about his properties of balance than he did himself. He hit a nearby wall with a satisfying thump, slid to the ground, groaned and lay still.

Hm. The walls around here weren't that hard. Was he trying to trick me? To lure me closer?

Taking chance by the hand I bent over the man. I saw a narrow face with greasy hair and stringy musculature. His clothes were of very poor quality. His eyes were closed. He was barely breathing. Blood flecked his lips. I examined him more closely, distasteful though that was. The fellow had a knife, a short dagger. He had fallen on it.

I examined the wound. The smell of blood was clean and

pure beside the stink from his clothes. If I left him here he would have an infection in the wound by the time he awoke – if he awoke, and wasn't finished off and robbed by some other chancer. I hunted in my pockets. I thought might have some iodine or sulpha somewhere. That might help.

I found the sulpha, applied it to the wound, covered it with twenty or so Band-Aid plasters. The man was still unconscious. His breathing seemed better, though I doubted he could be moved. And he would still need medical attention. I took two diamonds and shoved them in his pocket. They just fitted. There. At least now he could afford the best medical care. The rest was in the hands of the universe.

I stood.

A man with a ginger mop of hair plastered over a thick brow was watching me. The dock handler I had first encountered on leaving the TARDIS some hours before.

'Come on, guv'nor.' The man's voice was as rough as I remembered, though not as drunk. He cast a quick glance at the unconscious cutthroat. 'You don't want to be discovered hanging round here, if you ask me. The peelers'll 'ave y'inside quicker'n blinkin' and Gawd knows what'll 'appen to yer then.'

'We should at least call for help.' I suddenly realised how remiss I had been in concentrating on my attacker. For he was not the man who had been following me at all.

'He was going to do fer yer.' The docker took a pistol from his pocket and pointed it at me. 'And I'll do fer yer if y' don't do as I say,' he added menacingly. 'Nah git along.'

7
The Screaming Sea

It is a hunter's job to be curious. But I did not get a chance to look inside the cabin that Royston had been to so many times for many days. My best chance came during the worst storm *Tweed* had yet encountered. By then I was desperate for something to kill. It was a feeling I found difficult to control – something the Doctor had been trying to convince me was not an attitude to take to a civilised world. It was hard, though. We had been at sea for so long now and I was *bored*. When the storm came I was almost grateful.

It began gently enough – what seemed likely to be another good day for washing. But as the rain continued and the skies darkened the men began talking of a demon they called *Cyclone*.

I was in the crow's nest again, with Jack, watching out for icebergs, waiting our turn to be called down from watch to wash. The sky, which until that morning had been as blue as the Doctor's eyes, had begun to change. Now it looked grey and greasy, like bad fat from old meat, left too long before eating. The sky coloured the ocean, too, as if the one was an infection, a poison, seeping down to taint the other.

The pigs and fowl seemed most affected by the change in the weather. They put up a tremendous racket. The wind dropped, gusting abruptly from different directions. The Bosun ordered the sails furled and everything that was movable, including the chickens, was lashed down or taken below decks.

Tweed sailed lazily for two days under two close-reefed topsails and two storm staysails. The weather did not improve.

On the morning of the third day I awoke from a fitful sleep to find the sky held a livid green tint – as if it had swapped places with the ocean, which was tossing fitfully beneath us, as restless by day as I had been by night. From the main hatch on the quarterdeck I could hear the pigs and chickens. If anything, being below decks had increased their fear.

I went looking for the Doctor and found him in the rigging to port of the foremast. He was sitting upon the fore lower topsail boom, and had tied himself there by his scarf. I ran lightly out along the spar and perched beside him. The tightly furled sail made a comfortable seat.

'Something is coming,' I said. He nodded. 'Invisible monsters, like those from the Beyond. The air has the same feel.'

'"By the pricking of my thumb, something wicked this way comes."' The Doctor frowned. 'Static electricity. It's filling the air with positive ions. It's like the dodgem cars at the fair. Only this will be a ride like no other you've experienced.'

I said nothing. I had a feeling the Doctor was right. We watched the sky together for a while, as the wind became more erratic, gusting harder and harder. I could not only feel this demon the men called Cyclone approaching, I could feel the men feeling it approach. Most of them were scared. I scented their sweat above the salt and the animal smell of the air. 'What can we do?'

'If I had the TARDIS we could at least take shelter. Or put up a force field.'

'But we do not have the TARDIS.'

'I know that. The Old Thing's probably halfway to India by now.'

'So what can we do? Can we kill this demon?'

'Kill a cyclone? No. But perhaps we can fight it off.'

'How? With prayer?'

'With good seamanship. Stuart's a good captain. He's not lost a man or passenger on any run yet. We must trust in him.'

'But he has taken gold from our enemy to betray us!'

'Leela, everyone wants to live. That's a basic tenet of human nature. Captain Stuart has an ego. It's humankind's most powerful driving force: the inability to conceive or accept the death of self.'

'You mean… if we die it will be because the Captain himself is dead?'

'And the ship is lost. Yes.'

I was about to answer when I stopped, listened. The air was moaning. 'Listen. The sea screams.'

The Doctor nodded slowly. His face was a thundercloud to match the sky. 'I've heard sailors speak of the wind as if it had a voice. Some say it whispers to them. Tells them to do things. Others say it moans with the desperation of a lost mariner. It can offer warning or threat, be joyful, or sad, or angry.'

All around us the rigging bent in the gusting wind, the ropes snapping taut and then slack, every rope a voice in an unholy chorus of demons.

Then a light shone in the gathering darkness. A dazzling thread connecting the sky to the ocean. I blinked. 'The sun! The cyclone has stretched it out thin and flung it into the sea.'

The Doctor seemed amused. 'It's lightning. You could call it a sun – a short-lived one, and very dangerous. We must hope that the Captain has secured everything made of metal.'

'I understand. Suns like this do not like holy relics. I have seen even the holy metal melted by the touch of a sun like this.'

'If it can melt metal imagine what it will do to the ship.'

'The Captain told me this ship once weathered a cyclone which smashed many other ships like it.'

'Good old *Tweed*. Let's hope she hasn't lost the knack.'

The wind rose even further. The Doctor urged me to tie myself to the boom but I would not. I did not like the idea of being trapped against the mast. Above our heads the sky changed colour again, this time with the appearance of great lumps of cloud. I had seen cloud like this only once before, as a child, when the *Xaust* wind had wiped out half of my village.

Men ran to obey the bosun as he called for the remaining sails to be furled. I did not hear the man's voice above the roar of the wind, the voice of the demon. The cloud dropped upon us, lower, lower, until it was scraping the crow's nest and the masthead had vanished into the murk.

The boat began to tilt before the wind. And it began to rain. Not the friendly, cleansing rain I had so far encountered but a dangerous rain which swept sideways off the ocean, slashing directly into our faces and threatening to blind us with spray, which stung more like sand or grit than water.

The mast swayed like a horn-runner I had once killed with a crossbow. Unlike the horn-runner, which simply did not know it was dead yet, the wind seemed to taunt us, to play with us. I felt it grip me and try to twist me off the spar. I wondered how long it would be before the ship fell like the horn-runner, to crash still against the waves and then slip beneath, as dead as my prey had been. I wondered what it would feel like to sink into the ocean. Would Cryuni be waiting for me there? I did not know. Perhaps there would be other gods, other demons, and they would fight for possession of my soul. I smiled. I liked the thought of the demons fighting and killing each other on my behalf, even after I was dead.

The Doctor glanced at me, eyes narrowed against the stinging rain. 'You seem to be enjoying yourself.'

I simply grinned.

We sat perched on the spar as the rain lashed at us and the wind drove *Tweed* further into the demon's arms. All day we ran before the wind, tipped first one way and then another. The sky darkened as night drew upon us. A burning glow on the horizon showed me where the real sun was setting. It ran from the false suns cracking down from the sky all around it. The ship's bell rang constantly until it was secured. It was only just audible above the voice of the storm and the demon's chorus sighing in the rigging all around us.

I was getting used to the motion of the ship, learning to anticipate the blows of the storm, when *Tweed* was caught in a gust which had her tipped so far to starboard that the crow's nest vanished into the waves. But for the fact that the sails had been furled we should have been dismasted and broken on the back of the sea. The Doctor and I allowed ourselves to move with the mast, trying to remain upright. The water was only three or four times a man's height beneath us now, the deck at an angle I felt sure would mean the end of us. Anything left loosely lashed down broke free and was carried off by the wind's soaking grasp. And then I heard the cry. Earlier that watch Spanker Jack had lashed himself to the crow's nest – now I realised he could not get free.

I began to crawl along the mast rigging towards him. The ship rocked beneath me. I wound my arms into the rigging to stop myself being blown away. It was as much as I could do to draw breath. I reached the crow's nest to find Jack, half drowned, lashed firmly to the mast. I cut him free and tied us together with what remained of the rope, then dragged him back along the mast. As we moved the ship tipped again. Jack slipped. The loss of his weight caused me to overbalance and we both fell – one each side of the mast. If either of us had touched the water we would both have drowned – for with one gone the other would surely have fallen. As it was I managed to grab the nearest rigging and scramble back to the mast, pulling Jack with me – in time to catch the next tilt of the ship as the wind died suddenly and she tipped back upright with enough force to launch both of us from the mast again, had I not deliberately entangled us with the rigging.

The movement of the ship did not stop with the dying of the wind. If anything it became worse.

The sea rose around us in inky mountains, a match for the clouds whirling above. These waves towered over the ship's deck, smashing against one another in torrents of foam.

Then out of the whirlpool of blackness overhead the moon appeared, full, yellow, like a demon's eye in the darkness, lighting the water and the ship with a dreadful light. The moonlight saw us tossed and whirled like a stick in a river, until the savage and unpredictable changes in direction had us flopping and sick. The waves washed regularly across the deck. I caught glimpses of men lashing themselves down. They had given up working and were simply trying to survive.

I do not know how long Jack and I hung in the rigging, clinging together against the storm. His scrawny arms wrapped tightly around me and, both of us tangled securely within the screaming ropes, we drew as much warmth from each other as we could.

There seemed no end to the terrible movement of the ship. I remember screaming at the storm, alternately defying the demon to take us and begging to be left alone. At one point I heard a terrible shriek – human or ship I could not tell. The next moment a wall of blackness rose above us. I remember seeing the shattered corpse of another ship like *Tweed*, sails flapping in ribbons like flayed flesh around the broken ribs of her body, hanging above us before the yellow moon, then bearing down upon us, driven like a stampeding animal by the black wall of water. I remember seeing the ghost-white specks of men clinging to her shattered timbers, and all of them screaming as they fell, a chorus of terror to match the demon wind that tried to drown them out. Then the ship flew across the masts and the water hit us and my scream was lost in the screaming of the sea.

8
Cryuni

I am small and the web trees are big. I watch the spinners making them. They are pretty. All different colours. I look around. Where is Mother? Where is Father? I am hungry now. I look at the big hut. Where is Father? I am hungry. I hurt. My stomach. And my arm. Something is moving on my arm! Something is hungry on my arm! I am frightened! Father! I am hungry! I am frightened! Mother! It hurts! It's hungry and it's hurting me, it's hurting my arm and

something woke me. What? I listened. Nothing. The room Stockwood gave me was bigger than my family's entire hut. Three people slept there for many seasons. Here there was only me.

Yet something woke me.

I got up from the floor. I took out my knife.

What woke me? What woke me up? I sniffed the air. Fabric, old, mildewed. Wood, dry, dusty. Nobody has slept in this room for many seasons. Nobody but me. I sniffed again, tasting the night beyond the walls.

Something...

Something woke me up.

I peered into the darkness. The eyes were the weakest of the hunter's senses but still a powerful weapon. I saw nothing beyond the walls and the floor and the glass windows. The curtains were open. So were the windows. The night looked in. I returned its cold stare. The night was an animal. It hunted you. There were things in the night. Things from the Beyond. Things that killed but not for food. I did not understand them. The

Doctor once told me the things from the Beyond were *mental projections*. That they were not really there. I thought I understood then, but really I did not. How can something that is not there be there?

And how can something else that is not there wake me up?

The windows opened on to a balcony which overlooked the grounds. I look down past a tree to the undergrowth. It was black down there. Black, green, the colours of night in this land. I looked up. Dark sky. Darker clouds. The wind was familiar but the city smells it brought were confusing. Smoke. Wood. Brick. Glass. Many different types of cloth. Animals. And people. So many different people. And metal. Metal everywhere, as if I were in a temple as big as the entire Place of Land. Metal knives, locks, bicycles, buckles, buttons; people wearing it, horses walking on it. It was too much, like... like looking at the sun. The smells were too bright. I closed my eyes, lapping up the dark, the familiar blurry patterns behind my eyelids. When I opened my eyes the clouds had parted. There was a moon in the sky. A small, cold, lonely-looking moon. I whispered a prayer to make it happy so that it would shine hard and make the night go away sooner and stay away longer.

I did not like the night in this land.

The prayer worked. I saw more light in the garden. The light was small, blinking quickly and moving fast, like many eyes in a cave of ice. I knew this light. Cryuni. Death spirit. The spell of winter. It was coming here. Coming for Stockwood. He was old and would die soon. I know this. Now the Cryuni knows it too. The death spirit was coming for him. But I liked Stockwood. The Doctor told me I was his best friend. I would protect him from the sleep of Cryuni, the sleep of death.

I whispered the spell of summer to keep me safe, held my knife in the killing grip and opened the door of my room.

Outside the house was dark and smelled like winter. I could

see nothing. No glimmer of light marked the spirit's presence. I listened. Something. I could hear something. Downstairs.

I moved down the stairs carefully. They were well built and did not creak. The material – *carpet* – covering the wood helped to muffle my footsteps. I am used to hunting prey in the Place of Land. To be silent in this place was easy.

Once downstairs I checked the study, the room directly below my own. That was where the light came from. That was where the Cryuni would enter the house. I pushed the door. It would not open. I pushed harder. Still no movement. Then my hand touched something cold – metal. A lump this big was worth a season's food for three people in the Land. This land was strange. So much precious stuff and yet no bars on the doors, or guards on the rooms.

I turned the handle. The door opened easily.

Inside the study I tasted the night. The big windows were open. I inhaled sharply, tasting grass, trees, the furry pelts of small night animals. I crouched to examine the floor. There was dirt on the carpet in the shape of a man's foot. I rose, confused. Spirits do not leave footprints. I checked the room against my memory of it from that afternoon. There was little difference. Anything of importance had already been packed. Had someone been here? Someone from outside? This afternoon Stockwood had been frightened that someone might have stolen his *rongo-rongo*. What if the *rongo-rongo* was a charm to ward off evil spirits? What if Cryuni had sent a human accomplice to steal it and remove Stockwood's magical protection?

And then I knew.

Royston.

Royston was in league with Cryuni.

The death spirit would get Stockwood's soul and Royston would take his possessions as a reward for helping the spirit.

I trembled. Without Stockwood I would not be able to find the

Doctor or the TARDIS. This land was strange. I did not know what was safe to eat or hunt. I did not understand why uniformed warriors with metal bicycles were not to be worshipped while empty tombs were. I did not understand anything. I was a stranger here. I needed the Doctor to explain. Somehow I understood when the Doctor explained things.

I got angry. If Royston had set Cryuni on Stockwood, then perhaps he had plans to kill Stockwood's friends and family. The Doctor was Stockwood's friend. I was his *best* friend, the Doctor told me so. If Cryuni was here for Stockwood's soul, perhaps it was here for mine and the Doctor's also!

I would not allow that while I lived.

There was obviously no one in the study now. I left, closing the door quietly behind me.

I crept back up the stairs and listened at the door of the room Royston was supposed to be sleeping in. Nothing. No snores. No breathing. No sounds of movement or dream-speech. Royston was not there.

I listened at Stockwood's door. Snores. Just one person. He was still safe.

Good. I would find Royston and kill him now. Cryuni was a cowardly spirit, attacking only when its intended victim was asleep. Without a human ally Cryuni would leave us alone.

I moved quietly back downstairs. I bared my teeth, anticipating the kill. I was aware of my body; every muscle, every movement, the relationships between my eyes and fingers, ears and feet. I felt like the air before a storm. A killing storm. I had been taught to respect the prey I hunted. Royston was not prey. I did not respect him. I knew him. His body betrayed itself to me with every breath and movement. I would take him like an animal – gut him like a horda. And then I would leave his entrails as an insult for Cryuni. It was no more than either of them deserved.

I tracked Royston by the smell of tobacco on his clothes,

crouched silently outside the laboratory. Inside the room I knew there were many packing cases containing Stockwood's talismans – his equipment and books. I could also hear voices.

I could not make out words. But I knew the tone. Anger. Fear. The sound a trapped animal makes. Did Royston know I planned to kill him? Was he even now conspiring with Cryuni to kill me before taking Stockwood's soul?

I gave him no chance to strike.

I eased the handle round and then kicked the door open. I went in rolling, screaming, making myself seem bigger than I was, more than I was. That is the way to take your enemy. If stealth will not work, then use surprise: screams and confusion and a strike to the heart.

Everything happened very fast.

I saw a candle flame guttering in the darkness, flickering shadows thrown against the wall. Attracted by the movement I turned, only realising my mistake when a shot rang out. There was a shout of pain, quickly stilled by death.

I crouched in the shadows cast by the moon shining in through the French windows and listened. Breathing. One man. I could smell blood and tobacco. A trace of the earth I had found in the study. There had been two men in here then. Royston and another. But which one had shot and which was dead?

I was not about to issue a challenge. I would remain silent. I would wait. Then I would kill.

I settled down to wait, controlling my breathing, making no noise in the darkness. Then footsteps sounded in the hallway. The door was thrown open and a light shone in. Stockwood. He carried a gun as if he were very familiar with it.

His voice was loud in the darkness. 'I'm armed. Come out with your hands up.'

I whispered a warning. 'It's Royston. He summoned the Cryuni and tried to steal the *rongo-rongo*. There is a dead man here. Get

93

out of the light before you are killed too.'

There was another noise. Royston. 'Horace. It's me.'

'James?' Stockwood lowered the gun. 'What the hell is going on here?'

I stood, prepared to throw my knife. 'I tell you he is in league with the Cryuni!'

'Don't move!' I saw Stockwood was pointing his gun at me. 'Leela. Now listen to me carefully. Put away your knife. Do it now, please.'

'You are bewitched by –'

'I am no such thing. James Royston is my oldest friend. He is not in league with anyone. Now put your knife away.'

'*Nobody tells me what to do!*'

'All right.' Stockwood sighed. He put down his gun. 'Now will you please do as I ask?'

I looked from Stockwood to Royston. The man's lip had curled in the tiniest of smiles. I sensed no fear from him. He was amused!

'Royston is not in league with Cryuni?'

'No, Leela. He's my friend.'

'And you are not bewitched?'

'Not since I was a slip of a boy.'

I put away my knife. 'Then I am sorry.'

Royston took a step forward, 'My dear, no apologies are necessary I assure you –'

I interrupted. 'Sorry I did not arrive in time to stop him killing *that* one.' I pointed behind the packing crate to the place I had heard the body fall.

Stockwood moved across the room and looked. His face creased in surprise. ''Pon my soul. It's the ruddy butler.'

Royston added, 'I couldn't sleep and I too heard a sound. I found this fellow creeping around, obviously intending to perpetrate some bit of mischief.'

I said angrily, 'You were talking to him.'

'I was *challenging* him.'

'You were angry with him! You knew him! And you shot him when I challenged you to hide that knowledge from us.'

'Well, you are right, I did shoot him,' Royston said simply. 'But not for the reason you think. And now if you'll excuse me I'll call the police. You might as well stay up. None of us are going to get any sleep tonight. And I expect you'll have to cancel your expedition. I don't suppose the police will want any of us out of their sight until their investigation is complete.'

Stockwood began to get agitated. 'That's simply not acceptable. It's a waste of resources. Yes, quite outrageous. It's clear what happened. Of course, you weren't to know, James, but Fennel here has tried to steal the *rongo-rongo* twice already. What happened to him is no more than he deserved.'

Royston looked interested. 'Then it seems justice is done.'

The two men looked at each other. I watched both of them.

Stockwood licked his lips. He smelled sweaty and nervous. 'As far as I know the man has no family. His only apparent allegiance is to a criminal.' Stockwood hesitated, then spoke his next words in a rush. 'We could just bury him in the grounds.'

Royston smiled. 'That's immoral.'

Stockwood began to pace. 'I know, James. Oh, Lord, I know. But thirty years, James. Thirty years. And now I'm so close. So close to *finding out*. I have the money. A ship is booked. If the police are involved now… it'll mean cancellations… delays… I cannot possibly countenance that, James. You must understand!'

Royston stopped smiling. He moved to the French windows and stared thoughtfully into the gardens, stepping over the dead butler to do so. 'Horace, your obsession has always been a mystery to me. To return to Rapa Nui seems such a trivial matter when placed against the pressing matters extant in our own time and place.' He paused. 'But then this never seemed like your time and place…' Abruptly he straightened. 'We are friends and as such I am prepared to indulge your head of steam.' He turned. 'I only wish you would put this much effort into maintaining the diets I prescribe for you.'

Stockwood seemed to collapse inwardly with relief. His sweat dried quickly.

I was getting impatient. I could smell the corpse already. It would not be long before the rest of the land could smell it. I glared at Stockwood. 'Bury him, eat him, it does not matter. But do it quickly! The gun made a noise a child of the Sevateem would have heard half the land away.'

Royston glanced at me. For the first time I noted surprise in his body language. 'Your tribe eat their dead?'

I answered quickly, impatiently. 'Only our friends and family. The honoured among us. Their spirit nurtures and strengthens our own.'

Stockwood said, 'You mustn't be surprised, James. She's not from England.'

Royston pursed his lips. 'Manifestly.' To me he added, 'If you eat your friends what do you do with your enemies?'

I laughed. 'A child knows that. If it's winter we skin them and wear them. If it's summer we use their bodies to feed the animals. Animals are much better to eat than enemies. Animals do not hate you.' Before Royston could react, I pointed at the dead butler. 'Now help me take this one into the gardens. We will need to bury him deep to prevent the smell of decay reaching those who would stop us.'

Royston and Stockwood exchanged glances. Stockwood put down his gun. 'I'll get some shovels,' he said.

I took hold of the corpse and began to drag it across the room. 'He is big. You will have many good crops this season.'

9
Rage of Ice

The storm lasted three days. At the end of it one boat was missing, swept overboard in the storm; both the remaining boats were stove in; the planking of the bulwarks was gone, burst outwards by the weight of water on the deck; the poop was ruined and the cabin gutted by the wind.

The galley had collapsed and lay bottom up in the scuppers. A few boards and bits of a pie which the cook had been preparing floated there, together with a few rather dazed chickens. We searched for the cook, fearing he had been carried away, and found him unconscious in the galley wreckage, thick fingers still tightly clutching the leg of pig he had been preparing when the wind struck us.

I managed to get Jack below decks. He'd broken an arm, which Royston set. He was the only casualty. There were no deaths. Captain Stuart thought it was a miracle and said so by leading the men in a prayer, before taking apart the remaining boats to repair the bulwark planking.

While the damage was being assessed and the repairs begun, the Captain began to work out our position. It turned out we had been blown several hundred miles off course to the south during the storm. The weather here was much colder – the decks were invariably scummed with ice and a sharp, continuous lookout was kept for bergs.

The worst news of all was that the ship's supplies of fresh water were gone, drained into the sea when the galley collapsed.

Tweed limped like a wounded animal across the sea for two

days before we saw the first berg. The sun was low in the sky, and cast a clear, cold light across the drifting mass. The berg was big – half again as high as the ship and twice as big. It was a jagged blue-white mass, capped with snow and mottled with deep indigo and aquamarine streaks. Waves pounded against it as we drew closer, and the wind whipped a thin drizzle of sleet from the upper slopes.

The Captain ordered us close in by the lee of the berg, using the protection from the biting wind to carry out repairs, and at the same time place a number of men on the berg to chip off ice to melt for water.

I took this opportunity to slip below decks and investigate the cabin that I had seen Royston go to and from so many times. I thought that if there was someone in the cabin, someone who had been injured and needed medical treatment, then surely the door would have been unlocked in the storm. Surely nobody would have let themselves be locked in during a time when they may have needed to escape on to deck at a moment's notice?

I moved silently through the companionway to the port mid-cabin. I listened outside the door. I could hear nothing. But that did not mean there was nobody inside.

I tried to decide what to do. I had waited for many days for this opportunity: Royston was busy setting Jack's arm and the men were busy making running repairs to the ship. I would not get a better chance to look inside the cabin.

I tried the door. It was locked.

I uttered a hunter's curse. How could I get inside now? I could break the lock easily – but that would get me noticed. Then I remembered the keys I had seen hanging on a peg in the Captain's cabin while Stuart had been explaining about sailing around the world. There had been many keys on the great ring hanging from that peg. One of them must surely fit the cabin lock.

Quickly I moved down the companionway, past the main mast and the mizzenmast, towards the stern of the ship and the Captain's cabin.

The door was closed but not locked. Of course. Who would steal anything while at sea? Where would they run to?

Inside the cabin I looked around for the keys. They had fallen from the peg and lay, along with many loose items, scattered across the cabin floor. I scooped them up, checked at the door to make sure no one was outside, and left the cabin.

Back along the main companionway I crept. My heart was pounding now, an unfamiliar sensation. I felt like I was on the hunt again for the first time in many nine-days.

I stopped outside the cabin. I listened. Still no noise from inside.

Wait – was that breathing I heard? The sound of a breath deliberately held in check?

Was someone hiding in there?

I put the key in the lock. Waited. Nothing. No breathing. No sound at all except those made by the ship itself. I turned the key. Still nothing. Removing the key I reached for the handle.

I heard the shot and felt the bullet graze my shoulder at the same time.

I turned. It was her. The woman. Richards. She was covering me with a pistol similar to the one Stump had injured me with as we left Portsmouth.

I cursed.

'The next shot will be the last thing you hear.' Her voice was quiet. Everything about her was quiet. But I should have heard her approaching. I should have heard the gun being cocked.

'I am old and stupid and deserve to die. You should kill me now.'

'Make no mistake. I will kill you if you open that door.'

'Then you will have to kill me.' I began to turn the handle.

'No, Leela!' A new voice. Stockwood. He was in the companionway, the other end from the woman.

'Do you agree with *her*?'

'No. But I do not want to see you killed.' He waited for me to take my hand off the door handle. I did not. 'You are my best friend. Who will look after me if you are dead?'

I felt anger surge up within me. I was caught between these two, as I was caught between a desire to kill and a desire to protect. But for now I was helpless. My own desire had allowed me to become trapped.

'Royston knows who is in here,' I said. I saw him come out. Many times. Once with bloody bandages.'

'James Royston is my oldest friend. I trust him implicitly. You should too.' I listened to Stockwood's tone, not his words. He believed them. Fool. He did not know what I knew. How could I convince him that we must overpower the woman together and then see what was inside the cabin?

I was not to get the opportunity. A new voice said, 'Leela, I brought you to Earth to learn about your ancestors not to steal things from their cabins. Now put the keys back and let's go on deck and help with the repairs.'

I scowled at the Doctor. 'Are you on her side as well?'

'I'm on the side of the angels, Leela. The side of the angels. Miss Richards, if you would be so kind?'

The woman lowered her pistol. I glared at the Doctor. He said nothing. I relocked the door. Then I threw down the keys and pushed past Richards, heading towards the mid-deck hatch leading to the orlop. 'I do not understand any of you. If you want me I will be with the pigs. They have not yet tried to kill or betray me.'

I had my hand on the hatch cover when the ship rocked. At the same moment the cries of several men lifted on deck. The bell clanged madly.

'*Ice! Ice away off the port bow!*'

'*She's cleaving!*'

'*Make sail – and jump to it or we're all food for the fishes!*'

The Doctor jumped on to deck as fast as any man aboard. Richards followed. After a moment Stockwood took the keys from me and joined them. I did not move. I was alone in the companionway. I looked at the cabin door, now safely locked again.

Then I smashed the palm of my hand against the lock plate and the door burst open.

I meant to move into the cabin slowly, blade at the ready. But the ship lurched again at that moment, and a terrible screech like all the demons from the Beyond made me shudder. I stumbled into the cabin and sprawled on the deck, just managing to snatch a glimpse of my surroundings as I fell.

The cabin was in darkness, the small porthole blocked by a cloth. It was small, barely large enough to contain a chest, a bunk and a rail for hanging clothes. I smelled medicine. *Antiseptic*. I smelled clean linen and traces of food. But underneath were smells impossible to remove, or ignore. Sweat. Blood. Sickness.

As I got up a shape rose from the darkness on the top bunk. I heard a cry, whirled to meet the shape. Two pistol shots cracked in the gloom. I slashed upwards, dagger searching for flesh, felt myself enfolded in a blanket. To anyone else it would have been clean. To me it stank of infection. By the time I had disentangled myself and retrieved my knife the figure – whoever had thrown the blanket – was gone.

I moved out of the cabin fast and low, rolling across the companionway. I was just in time to see a pair of heavy work boots vanish up the ladder leading to the mid-deck.

I followed warily. On deck the light dazzled me for a moment

– long enough for whoever was fleeing to try to slam the hatch cover down on my head. I ducked, waited a heartbeat, pushed the hatch cover up and leapt out on to deck.

I recognised the man in a heartbeat. Stump. He was loading a pistol. The berg loomed behind him, directly off the port side. Wreathed in fog, it loomed above the topsail booms. And it seemed to be shaking.

I reversed my blade and threw it – just as the ship shuddered again. Stump slipped on the deck and fell. My dagger flashed over his shoulder and embedded itself in the main mast. I was moving in an instant, no thought for words. The promise I had made not to kill did not apply to one who had shot me twice. I ducked to avoid a pistol shot, then reached for my dagger. By the time I had freed it from the mast Stump had ducked beneath the boom and was making for the port deck rail.

I drew back my arm to throw and then stopped. If I missed my blade would be lost overboard. It had been the one my mother used on the horda when they had attacked my sister. I did not want to lose it now, no matter how much I wanted to kill Stump.

I ran after Stump, just in time to see him vault the deck rail and vanish into a foggy gloom. I listened for a splash. Instead I heard a thud and a man's voice cursing. Without thought I stepped over the deck rail and lowered myself off the ship.

Behind me I was aware of voices shouting, running footsteps, but I was not in the mood to listen. I ignored them, let go of the deck rail, and fell feet first into the fog.

I landed on ice, packed hard and freezing to my skin. The surface was wet and slippery. Everything was wreathed in white. My breath hung in clouds around me. My skin was white with frost and already turning numb. I blinked away tears – only to find my eyelids wanted to remain stuck together. I unglued them, listening. Ice rose around me in smooth, irregular clumps. Fog rolled between them. The ice beneath my feet was shaking steadily. I listened for footsteps, breathing, a voice, anything.

I heard a scuffling sound, then a fall of snow and another curse. Stump. I moved after the sound. In moments I found Stump. He had slipped and fallen, fetching up against a spar of ice with one leg twisted beneath him. His face, already coated with frost, was also twisted with pain.

I approached. He saw me and began to crawl even harder, dragging himself through the snow, still trying to escape.

'Demons. Oh, demons. I hear y' coming fer me in the white darkness. I hear y' but y'll no get me today. No, fer the demon here'll get me first, this demon shaped like a woman, but no woman this, she'll gut me and leave old Stump's innards to glaze on this chunk o' white hell like ropes o' window glass stained red wi' me life blood now, will she not?'

I took three steps and drew level with the man. His voice was a continuous drone, the words, interrupted only by shuddering breaths, unbroken in the fog. I knew that sound. The sound of sickness. Of delirium. When he breathed his lungs spoke to me. They spoke of sickness and approaching death.

'It is fit that you will die here. The servant of Cryuni killed by his master's hand at his master's Place.'

At once Stump began to crawl even faster. I do not know where he found the strength. His limbs blurred in the snow but he moved hardly any distance from me. I paced him easily.

'Let me die, no, no, I don' wanna die, not here on this wretched stretch o' hell's white shore, lemme die at home in the sun, no I don' wanna die, I don' wanna, not here, not slow like this, I wanna die quick, make it quick, demon, or I'll haunt y'till me bones melt come day o' judgement.' And then, incredibly, he began to laugh. 'I'll haunt y'. Me, a man and a dead 'un at that, I'll haunt y', demon. Y'll never escape from the

Stump.'

I listened to him laugh and sheathed my blade.

I listened to him laugh as the ice beneath us cracked.

I listened to him laugh as I turned to run. Back to the ship. Off the ice. Now. Before I joined him in death.

The ground split as I moved, splitting beneath me, breathing frozen screams into the air as I ran, slipped, finally slid down the last slopes and–

– scrambled to a halt just short of falling into the water, where I surely would have frozen to death.

Hands grabbed me and hauled me upright. The men cutting ice for water. Ropes were thrown from the ship, its hull a welcome shadow looming through the fog.

We scrambled up the ropes, hands sticking to the frozen hemp, every arm-wrenching pull a struggle.

We made it on to deck just in time to see the mountain of ice cleave along one foggy peak and split in two. Balance disturbed, the smaller section rolled beneath the water, producing a huge wave which smashed against the side of the ship. The larger section, far bigger than the ship, trembled, hesitated, then simply flipped over. The noise was indescribable, at least as loud as the storm had been. A wave of sea water broke across the port side of the ship, which rocked as if slapped by a giant's hand. I knew then for certain that we had found the lair of Cryuni on this world and now the demon would stop short of nothing to take us all, as it had taken its servant, Stump.

As if to show I was right, the smaller part of the berg now rose again, tilting with slow but deadly force. One mass of green-grey ice after another smacked into the waves, giving rise to huge fountains, which soaked the already shivering crew, and then immediately began to freeze. Ice and snow swept from the tilting berg swirled around the decks and masts until sight, already fogged, was impossible. The bosun was already shouting orders. The sails unfurled, snapping into the wind and showering us with dislodged ice.

The last sounds I heard as the crash and roar of the berg rumbled into watery silence were the foggy echoes of Stump's cracked laughter, following us as, repairs unfinished, *Tweed* made all possible speed for safer waters.

10
Hunted

Early the following afternoon I stood in the foyer of the George Hotel in Portsmouth and listened to Stockwood argue with a uniformed desk clerk about whether the Doctor had booked our rooms or not. The clerk told Stockwood he had never heard of the Doctor. I felt cold. Something was wrong. The Doctor never failed to do something he said he would do. So why had he now? Unless someone had stopped him. Perhaps Cryuni had other agents apart from Stockwood's butler. Perhaps the death spirit still wanted Stockwood's soul. Perhaps Fennel's death had not satisfied it.

So many questions. The Doctor would be proud. He told me to question everything. He told me it was the sign of a healthy mind.

Very well, then, I would question everything. I would question his disappearance.

I walked out of the hotel, leaving Stockwood and Royston arguing with the desk clerk, who now claimed there were no rooms available. The uniformed man standing at the door looked at me strangely as I passed him. I had seen him open the door for other people entering or leaving the hotel. He hesitated as I approached. Did he sense I was a hunter and needed no special privileges? He probably did, for he did not open the door for me. I opened it for myself with a smile to show him I returned his respect. He scowled. 'We don' want your sort here,' he whispered as I passed him.

Puzzled, I took one of the gold coins given to me by Stockwood and gave it to him. His expression became one of disgust. I thought about killing him, then simply walked past. I had more important things to do. The Doctor was in trouble. I knew it. He needed my help.

Outside the hotel I paused. Which way to go? Portsmouth was a big village. Not as big as London but big enough. I knew I could hunt until sunset and not cover half of it. And the Doctor could be anywhere.

The journey from London had been by carriage. It had taken half a day and at every step I had to listen to the horse complaining about the roads it was forced to travel. Stockwood had constantly urged the driver to greater speed, a stupid and dangerous thing to do considering how much baggage there was strapped to the roof. Now, that baggage was outside the hotel, still beside the carriage, while the driver waited impatiently to be told whether he could feed and water his horses.

He stared at me as I left the hotel.

'Made their minds up what they're doing yet, 'ave they?'

I shook my head. 'The Doctor is missing. No rooms have been booked.'

'Well, if you think I'm going to take you back to the Smoke you've got another ruddy think coming.' The driver sat despondently on the step of the carriage. He reached around to stroke the flank of one of the horses and his voice softened. 'Never mind. Nice stable soon. And water. You wait.' He turned back to me. 'I want my money, you know. You can tell your husband that from me.'

I scowled. 'Stockwood is not my husband!'

'That so, is it?' The driver looked at me in much the same way as the doorman. 'In that case he can definitely afford to pay me.'

I ignored the driver, walking quickly away from the hotel. I was angry. I was beginning to think I would have to kill every man in this land. No one so far had shown the respect due to a hunter. Were there any hunters here? Or was this land so rich that nobody wanted for anything?

I looked around me as I walked. Portsmouth was full of beautiful buildings made of stone and wood. I felt like I was in a holy place. I tried to make as little noise as possible. The people I saw were all obviously priests. Their skins were well made, they wore hats and carried many objects of metal. I wondered what they thought of me. They all stared at me. I exaggerated my hunter's stride, displaying my knife prominently on my hip so that they would know who I was but keeping it sheathed so they would know I intended no harm.

The hotel was located on a street leading to the harbour. I could see huge wooden vessels, like the canoes I had used to hunt fish but many times bigger, with poles sticking out of the tops that held up sheets of cloth that would have covered half my village. I stared at the distant vessels in awe. They were so big and yet somehow they floated. Were these the *sailing ships* the Doctor had spoken of? Were we to travel on one of these to the Place of Rapa Nui?

I thought I would like to explore one of these vessels. I began to walk towards the harbour, then remembered I was supposed to be looking for the Doctor. I stopped. I had no way of knowing where the Doctor was. Portsmouth was full of noise and movement. There were birds, dogs, children running about. The priests were everywhere. I couldn't believe there were so many. Some of them stopped to look at me. I returned their stares arrogantly and most of them turned away. I sniffed the air, but it told me nothing. I crouched to examine the ground but all I could find were dirt and animal spoor and what were obviously temple offerings of fruit and vegetables which had been left in the sun for too long.

Then I caught the smell of blood. It seemed to come from the direction of the harbour. I followed the scent, stooping now and then to lift handfuls of dirt and check I was still moving in the right direction.

I moved quietly and quickly between the huts – *buildings* – following the scent, wondering if it would belong to the Doctor or some other. Maybe even an animal. There were those in my tribe who could tell the difference between animal and human blood. They were the most respected hunters. They ate the best of the kills and chose the best mates. I was not one of them.

I found the source of the scent in a dingy street walled in by buildings like sheer cliff faces. The place smelled old. Forgotten. The small windows that opened on to the street were closed. One opened just long enough for someone to throw a bucketful of foul-smelling water on to the cobbles almost at my feet before slamming shut again. I blinked. It wasn't that the smell was bad, it just masked the blood spoor.

Then I saw a place where the ground was stained reddish brown and I didn't need the scent any more.

I drew my knife, moving forward and crouching to examine the ground. There was nothing except the blood. And a few scuff marks in the dirt. One clear print seemed to be about the size of the Doctor's shoe. I lifted some dirt and sniffed it. Dirt. Blood. It told me nothing more than I already knew. What had happened here? The ground was so hard it had not taken an impression of footprints. I could not even tell how many people had been involved in the struggle. I stood up. There was more blood on a nearby wall. I examined it. It too was less than a day old. It smelled like that on the ground. Then I noticed something. On the ground nearby was a sweet. I picked it up. A mint humbug, still in its wrapper.

The Doctor had been here.

Running footsteps sounded behind me. I turned, knife at

110

the ready.

A child

(*Mother Father it's hurting me it's*)

skidded to a halt a short distance from me and was staring at me.

No. She was staring at the sweet I held.

I offered it to her. 'I won't hurt you.'

The child said nothing.

'Unless you are a servant of the Evil One,' I added, just to make sure the gods knew I was alert.

Suddenly the child ran forward and snatched at the sweet. She was very fast. I was faster. She grabbed the sweet but I grabbed her wrist, spun her round and threw her on to the ground. 'Show respect!' I hissed through clenched teeth. I could have gutted her.

The child looked up at me, silent, obviously frightened. I frowned. She was no servant of Cryuni. I sheathed my knife but held on to her wrist. A grown man would have opened his fingers and cried with pain at that grip. Her hand remained a fist, fingers clamped tightly about the sweet. Was it so important to her?

I prised open her fingers. 'You have seen one like this before?'

She said nothing, though her face showed the pain I knew she felt.

'Tell me and I will let you go.'

She said nothing. I considered what to do. I could break her wrist easily. That didn't seem right. She had not hurt me. But she might know what had happened to the Doctor. What would he do in this situation?

'All right. I'm going to let you go. I won't hurt you. I am your best friend.'

I let go of her wrist. Immediately she scrambled away, began to run. I started after her, but almost immediately she stopped. I stopped too. She turned. We stared at each other.

She held out the humbug. 'The last bloke I saw wot 'ad a sweet like this 'un had gold too. He gave me some. You got any gold, 'ave yer?'

I had the gold that Stockwood gave me. I showed it to her. 'Tell me what the man you saw looked like.'

The child came closer, small, hesitant steps, greedy eyes fixed on the gold piece I held.

"'E was tall. Like you. Loads of 'air. Bloomin' great scarf, 'e 'ad. An' 'e smiled a lot. George Fern said he must've bin mad t'give us gold. You mad too, are yer?'

I pointed at the blood on the ground nearby. 'You see that? Someone was hurt here. Did you see what happened?'

The child shrugged. 'Wot if I did?'

I flicked the gold piece up into the air and caught it again. I watched her watching the money. Her face was like a hunting web-tree spinner, total concentration, total focus.

She unwrapped the humbug and put it in her mouth. 'Gi's the gold an' I'll tell yer wot 'appened t'yer bloke.'

'Tell me what happened and I'll give you the gold.'

The child frowned. 'Awright. But you got to promise.'

'I promise.'

'On your mother's grave.'

'I will promise on my sister's grave.'

'You got a sister?'

'Not any more. Now tell me what happened here.'

The child thought for a moment, then said. 'Well, I was out, right, wiv Georgie an' the others. We was dossin' about, yeah? George was supposed t'be runnin' an errand fer Bleggs, the butcher. But we sees this bloke, right, the bloke what's tall, like you, an' we says to 'im, we says, "Got any money, guv?" like that, and he gives us a sweet like what you had, an' then he gives us some gold each and then we ran off, but I stayed back, right, 'cos, I was brung up proper and I was gonna say ta, like, and so I did, and then I ran off, but I followed 'im, see, to see if he had any more gold, like, and so I sees him get attacked by this cutthroat, an' a right nasty bit o' stuff 'e was, so I hid, like, and watched, and your bloke, he did sommat an' the cutthroat fell on his own knife, like, and then while he was trying t'save 'is life, not that I'da bovvered like, I'da just scarpered, but 'e was awright, your bloke, an' tried t'save the cutthroat, an' anyway while he was tryin' t'do this another bloke pulled a pistol on 'im and marched 'im off towards the docks, like, and that's when I thought it was time t'be gettin' back t'work, like, where I shoulda bin t'start wiv, see?'

I stared suspiciously at the child. 'How do I know you're telling the truth?' She was, I could see it in the set of her limbs, the jut of her chin, the unblinking stare. I wanted to make sure. I gained nothing by taking a chance. Hunters who took chances rarely lived long enough to use them.

The child rummaged in her pocket and held out a humbug. The wrapping was identical to the one I had let her keep. It was enough for me. 'And you say the Doctor went to the docks with this other?'

"'Sright. There's a tavern there. The Three Tuns.'

'And what did he look like, this man who took the Doctor?'

'Well, 'e was short, and mean-lookin'. His face was all pinched up, like 'e was angry or summat. An' he smelled of whisky. An' his hair was red.'

'Thank you.' I gave the child the gold piece. She grabbed it and ran off, turning once to call, 'Ta, missus!' before vanishing round the corner.

So I began to walk towards the docks. As I walked, I thought. The Doctor had been captured. Why? For his gold? His knowledge? His humbugs? This was a strange land – any of these could be true. I had a feeling it was something to do with Stockwood. Stockwood and our journey to Rapa Nui. What if Royston had told Cryuni we were coming here to Portsmouth on the first part of the journey to Rapa Nui? Cryuni could be lying in wait for us. For the Doctor. The red-haired docker could have been another servant, like Royston. Now I was in a quandary. I had left Stockwood alone with Royston. Both he and now the Doctor were in danger. Which should I try to save first? It took only a moment to work out that saving the Doctor was more important – if only because he could probably save Stockwood if Royston tried something before I got back from the docks. But what if Royston killed Stockwood? Even the Doctor couldn't bring a man back from the dead, could he? And worse – what if Cryuni claimed his soul? Then what would I do?

I became aware someone was following me. The child, after more gold, or humbugs? I looked back. Nothing. The road was empty. I listened. Nothing. I continued to walk. Still nothing. Then I heard footsteps again, soft, stealthy, deliberately trying to match mine so as not to be detected. I broke into a run. I could run very fast. But my aim was not to lose my follower but to tire him out. Then I would attack. I ran through the backstreets, pacing myself, occasionally leaning against a wall and feigning exhaustion if I thought my follower was falling too far behind. Gradually I let my pace falter, my pauses lengthen, drawing my pursuer out and making him overconfident. I looked back once or twice, but whoever was following – hunting – me was very good at concealing himself. Then, as I stopped and leaned gasping against a wooden fence, I caught my first glimpse of the man hunting me. He seemed short and powerful, but the only real detail I managed to get was his hair – it was red. The way the child had described the Doctor's attacker. All right then. I had seen him. He was getting confident, sure I was nearly exhausted. One more sprint and I would be ready for him. I staggered to my feet and stumbled on. There was a corner ahead of me. I would stop just round it and lay my ambush there. I staggered around the corner – and found myself in a backstreet marketplace.

There were many people. Stalls full of goods. And animals. Some of the animals were obviously being bartered, some were running wild, hunting for scraps and barking at anyone who tried to stop them. People shouted and laughed and argued about prices. Some were singing. Children and dogs ran underfoot. I smelled smoke, cooking meat, dirty clothing, the spoor of animals. I stopped. The crowd simply washed around me like fog in the forest. I moved into the crowd, listening carefully, trying to separate the footsteps of my pursuer from those of the rest of the market-goers. For he would surely follow me here; here where the advantage of anonymity was his. Here he would be concealed, one face among many. A face I did not know. But I knew his hair and I could look for that. Then I saw that many of the people were wearing cloth caps or hats. All my pursuer had to do was conceal his hair and I would not be able to recognise him among the crowd.

I kept moving, ignoring people who shouted at me and tried to get me to buy things, food, clothes, animals. I tried to ignore the mass of people around me but everything was too intense. There were too many smells, too many sounds. Everything was too much. It was like being in a storm. A storm of people.

I stopped, spun around, tried to get my bearings. I could not see the edge of the marketplace. All I could see were distant buildings rising beyond the crowds. And above them the masts of ships. I headed for the masts, then stopped. The footsteps. They were –

No, it was a child. A dog. A man chasing someone who had stolen from his stall.

I closed my eyes, shut out the confusing world of sight. Instead I listened. Shouting. Laughing. Bargaining. Arguing. Singing. The sound of a fight. The sound of tools. The wet slap of fish. The screech of a bird as its neck was broken.

And footsteps. Many footsteps. Running. Jumping. Jostling. Stamping.

And one set whose deliberate pace was familiar. Behind me. Close! Now! I drew my knife, spun round and lunged. I kept my eyes closed. I didn't need them. I knew where my pursuer was, knew he was closing for the kill. Only when I felt a body smash into me did I open my eyes.

'Bring that chop back 'ere you misbegotten bastard son o' the devil!'

A child bounced off my legs, fell, the meat he had stolen falling to the ground. I stepped over the child, trying to keep my balance. A huge man with a ruddy face and arms as thick as the child's leg elbowed me aside as he ran past in pursuit. I ignored man and child. They were not important. Only my pursuer. By now people had seen I was holding a knife. Some were pointing.

Then one shouted, *'Cutthroat! Take her down!'* It was him. My pursuer.

I turned to run, this time for real, and crashed into the burly man who had been chasing the child. I picked him up and threw him at a fruit stall. The stall owners took his place in front of me. They too had knives.

I stopped. The crowd hemmed me in. Someone threw some fruit. Soggy flesh spattered the side of my face. I blinked. The crowd was closer now.

I shifted my knife to the killing grip. *'One more step and I'll make a necklace of your entrails!'*

A lump of wood hurled from the crowd flew towards me. I ducked. Something smashed against my head. I whirled, felt my knife arm strike something warm and yielding. There was a scream. I screamed too. A hunter's scream – for all the good it did me.

Someone grabbed my leg. I kicked them away. More hands were all around me now. Screaming faces, fists, bits of wood, kicking feet. Pain bit at me like the

(*hurting me eating me it's*)

teeth of starving horda. The last thing I saw before the crowd took me down was his smile. A killer's smile. He hadn't moved at all.

He hadn't needed to.

11
Nightmares of the Sea

That night, bothered for the first time by the motion of the ship upon the chill water, I dreamed of Ennia, my sister.

In my dream I am a child, too young even to play. I know nothing of the hunt, or the rituals, the People, the Place of Land. All I know is that I am. And I am hungry. I am starving.

Mother's milk is gone now. She feeds me water from her fingers and grazer juice. It is not enough. I am growing. I am hungry. It is all I know. I cry out my selfish demands until Mother puts me outside in a crib made of branches and loose woven moss cloth. The crib hangs from the hut roof. The motion interests me. For a while I forget I am hungry. I stare up at the clouds. Then I remember I am hungry. It hurts. I cry again.

Mother is sharpening blades for Sole, my father, to use during the next day's hunt. Outside the hut a clay pot steams: yesterday's bark moss still boiling down into soup. The smell makes me even hungrier.

I reach up for the clouds. They look soft, like flesh, like meat running with fat and protein. I think, if I can only catch one I can pull it down and eat it, stuff it into my mouth and appease the howling demands of my infant's belly.

Mother works hard at the grindstone, pumping the pedal that turns the stone. Sparks fall hissing into the water trough, which keeps them from setting light to the hut or nearby undergrowth.

I almost reach a cloud. It slips through my fingers, staying obstinately out of reach. I wail. Mother scolds me. Her voice and the grind of stone against metal become one. My fingers flap angrily at the cloud.

Then the white cloud turns dark.

Something hangs from the roof of the hut.

It drops into the crib.

I am frightened. I wail louder. Mother just scolds me.

Another darkly glistening thing drops into the crib. I feel them crawling on me. I see them move, see the scaly backs and glittering eyes watching me.

They are horda.

They are hungry too.

I feel the crib begin to rock. More are coming. One is on my arm. I feel pain that makes my hunger seem insignificant. I scream. Mother scolds me. Another horda attaches itself to my leg. Another to my face. The crib rocks. I scream.

All I ever know in my short life is pain.

In my dream I am also my mother. Neela. Home-maker. Hearth-tender. Lover of Sole, my father. And I am hungry too. The hunt has returned for the last nine-day with nothing but scratchings: tree-skippers and bark moss for boiling into soup. The Sevateem are starving.

Now mother watches horrified: the crib is wriggling. No. The crib is not wriggling – the horda. The horda are wriggling, they're wriggling and feeding, they're eating they're eating the child –

And then I am moving, reaching for Sole's knife, slashing at the first layer of glistening beasts, grabbing them and peeling them away from the crib and stamping them flat or throwing them on to the fire. They scream and die at the touch of flame, and I scream with them. I scream in bloodlust, in horror at the feel of their bodies crunching beneath my feet, in guilt because

I did not respond sooner; I scream to drown out the sound of my dying child.

The horda are on me now. How many? I cannot tell. More than I have ever seen. I can feel their many legs and clinging teeth. I have no thought for my own death. The knife blurs until I am running with horda juice and blood. The stink of dead horda and the worse stink of live horda fills my nose, my head.

I go mad.

I become the knife.

When I wake from the madness Sole is holding me. His arm is slashed where I have cut him with his own knife. I drop the knife. I wail. The child. The child. I look into the crib. Dead horda carpet the basket, the cloth is running with blood. More horda lie stamped, crushed into the ground around the hut. Hundreds of them. I have killed hundreds of them. But there were more. And they took the child. They took the meat of her, the life of her, and they left only bones and scraps.

Sole says nothing. That afternoon the hunt sets out again, this time with fire. They do not come back for a nine-day. The stench of burning lasts for days.

All I know for the rest of my life is pain.

I awoke curled into a tight ball on the quarterdeck. I had taken to sleeping outside since the weather had become warmer. I liked the feel of the air on my face as I slept. I could smell everything – and I had room to fight or run if I was threatened.

I woke instantly, the dream banished to the place where night demons go. I knew straight away that something was wrong. The motion of the deck was wrong. A moment later a cry from the crow's nest told me I was right.

'*Thar she blows!*'

A second cry rose to join the first. '*Where away?*'

'*Two points off the starb'd bow!*'

I ran to the rail, ducking beneath the spanker to reach the other side of the deck. I stared out to sea. This land had only one moon but it was big and bright, and it lit the water like many candles. I grabbed the rail, straining to look out from the ship. Something moved nearby in the water.

Something broke the surface with a gush of spray. It was huge and the spray stank of salt and the inside of animals, and stung where it touched me. I fell backwards. An animal! But I had never seen one so large. It was nearly a third as long as *Tweed* and I could not tell how deep. The ship tilted, the spanker snapped its lanyard and whirled out of control. I ducked just enough to allow the boom to pass over my head and stood again. I heard men running on to the decks to secure the boom but I ignored them. I wanted to watch this living island.

For I realised it was not one creature but two, and they were locked in a fight to the death.

I felt a presence beside me. Royston. 'Sailors call them the nightmares of the sea.' There was admiration in his voice. He braced himself against the motion of the deck and held his hat down against his head. I felt his gaze on me for a brief moment. 'Bad dreams?'

'I dream of death and now death visits itself upon us.'

'They're not interested in us. When Captain Stuart gets us under way we'll have a magnificent view.'

Ignoring Royston, I watched the animals. One seemed to be a mass of writhing tentacles which had all but engulfed the massive head of the other. In return the first had an enormous mouth clamped firmly about part of the tentacled animal and seemed to be intent on eating as much of it as it could. Huge fountains of water burst into the air. I saw many smaller animals cutting the water with black fins circling the fighters, repeatedly approaching, biting, retreating, torn streamers of flesh gripped in wide mouths. The water, already alive with glowing plankton, now dimmed with a stain of blood.

'What are they?'

'The big black animal is a sperm whale. The one with tentacles is called a squid. The smaller fish are called sharks.'

'Why do they fight?'

'Why does anything fight?'

I remembered my dream. 'To eat. To survive.'

Royston said nothing. He seemed content to merely observe, and I watched with him. Behind me the ship's bell clanged, a call to decks. The entire crew swarmed into the rigging at the Captain's orders. The sails were set. *Tweed* hauled to port, straining into the wind to gain distance from the creatures.

'Why did you help Richards? Why did you save Stump's life?' I made sure Royston could hear my voice above the clamour on decks and the commotion of the creatures locked in their death embrace.

I knew Royston had heard my question. For a moment he did not reply. I turned to look at him. 'I could force you to answer.'

'I know.'

'I do not understand. You say you are Stockwood's friend and yet you skulk around below decks like a rat with his enemies!'

Royston turned to me, temporarily ignoring the commotion to sea. 'I am a doctor, Leela. My job is to preserve life.' He thought for a moment. 'You and I, we are not like animals, not like the whale and the squid. They come into each other's ambit and they attack. The fight is to the death, no quarter asked and none given. Animals. Animal behaviour. We are people. More sophisticated, more intelligent. We have morals and duties and choices. We can change our minds, we can balance judgements, weigh up greater and lesser evils.'

I scowled angrily. 'I think the animal way is better. You kill your enemies or your enemies kill you. Either way there are no questions or judgements or choices. Life is simple.'

'Life is *not* simple, Leela. Surely you see that?'

'I do not.'

Royston sighed. 'Then understand this: I offered Richards money to put us ashore. I did this to save Horace's life. The situation is not as black and white as you perceive. She refused to put us ashore. Now, I have no loyalty to Richards. But I thought to buy her co-operation by attempting to heal her man. Stump was injured as we left Portsmouth. He was shot. He took three bullets. The wounds were deep and became infected. The men spotted him clinging to a rope. He'd been dragged into the ship's wake. He'd tied himself on to stop from drowning. He was in the water for ten hours. He was close to death for many days. I treated him as best I could. I healed his body but his mind… that was another thing. It was broken by his experience. I hoped to heal that too, in time, but now… I do not know where he got the pistol from. I suppose Richards supplied him with it. We kept him locked in his cabin to protect him from you. Do you understand *that*?'

I felt anger move inside me. I gripped the rail so I would not gut this annoyance where he stood and pitch him over the side to be food for the sharks. 'I understand death. Death comes when there is no food or medicines. Death comes when you are stupid or careless, or when you are unlucky. Stump was lucky to live so long. And you – you wasted your time and medicines on a man who did not deserve them.'

Royston was about to reply when the ship gave a sudden heave. Despite all sails, the whale and squid had breached even closer to the ship. A huge wave smacked against the hull, drenching both of us. I could hear the animals now. A noise I had never heard before. A sigh. A scream. The sound of tearing flesh as a severed tentacle flopped back into the water. Waves beat against the animals. Sharks beat against the waves. More than I could count, their backs and bellies and fins gleaming like metal in the moonlight.

The ship gave another lurch. This time there was a terrible crunching noise as the whale scraped along the hull. The ship tipped to port. Royston fell against me and we both slid across the sopping deck, beneath the spanker boom. Royston gave a shout as he fetched up against the port deck rail. A moment later I hit him and grabbed the rail.

'Be still! Hold the rail or we will both go overboard!'

He gasped something I didn't hear. I didn't hear it because at that moment the ship righted itself and we were hurled back across the deck to fetch up with a shout against the starboard deck rail. A hatch cover broke loose and surged across the wet deck towards us. I grabbed Royston and threw him aside, then jumped as the hatch cover smashed into the deck rail. The rail snapped with a terrible screech of torn wood and then I was falling. I caught a glimpse of someone falling beside me. A moment later there was the sensation of being kicked hard by something very large and angry. And wet.

I was in the water, with Royston.

And the sharks.

My breath went as I hit the water. I tasted salty blood and the wet stink of predators. For a moment I was back in my dream, suffocating under a mass of horda. Then the freezing water slapped me to my senses. I clamped my mouth shut and struck out for the surface. I surfaced only a few arms' lengths from Royston. A black fin made metal by the moonlight cut through the waves between Royston and myself. The water was constantly being churned into a terrible froth by the thrashing bodies of the nearby giants.

The ship was nowhere in sight.

I swam towards Royston, hoping the movement of my body would go unnoticed by the sharks as they concentrated their feeding frenzy on the whale and the squid.

'Leela! Help!' Royston was thrashing in the water, gulping and spitting salt water in gobbets, trying to stay on the surface. 'I can't ruddy well swim!'

I came alongside Royston. 'Be still! Be calm! You are making more waves than those two together!'

'But I can't –'

'I have watched these sharks – they hunt movement and blood.' I dragged a breath from the wet air. 'We are not bleeding so they cannot scent us. Be still or I will kill you myself. If they attack us we are dead!'

A huge wave smashed into us at that moment. I felt myself dragged under the surface. When I came up for air, Royston was gone. I dived again, found him splashing feebly a man's height beneath the surface. I grabbed him and towed him upward.

We broke surface among a whirlpool of fins.

I tried to think. This was dangerous. There was no way we could escape from the sharks now.

Even as I thought this, one shark nosed closer and butted against my side. I struck out instinctively, smashing my fist against the front of its face. It turned away but another took its place. And another. I stopped moving. Would the sharks be glutted enough not to bother with us? Or were they like horda in that they would eat whether they were hungry or not?

Their continued attention suggested they fed like horda – whenever and wherever they could.

I drew my dagger. It wasn't much but it would stop at least one of these beasts. When the next shark approached it did so much faster than the others, and from below. I caught a glimpse of belly and the mouth opening wide, then I let go of Royston, who promptly sank, held my breath, turned in the water and dived to meet the monster.

More by luck than judgement, I twisted aside as it bit down

on the space where I had been. I grabbed the fin as the animal surged by, held on tightly and repeatedly stabbed it as deeply as I could. Blood pumped out into the water.

I was running out of breath but I did not dare let go. Yet the animal did not seem to want to die. I could not reach the head. My chest burned with the need for air. I was close to unconsciousness. I thought I could see Cryuni, swimming patiently in the depths just beyond the limits of my vision, waiting. Waiting for me.

I was on the point of letting go and striking out for the surface when the shark jack-knifed, turning almost double to try to get at me. Acting almost without thought, I struck out at the head and was lucky enough to feel my knife plunge into the creature's unblinking eye.

The shark jerked immediately, thrashing, dying. I let go and struck out for the surface in a cloud of blood. Other sharks were arrowing downward, homing in on the wounded creature. I broke surface, looked around for Royston. I found him clinging feebly to the shattered remains of the deck rail. The rail was covered in a tangle of rope and life buoys, and the smashed remains of the hatch cover.

I regained my breath quickly. My skin was freezing, my eyes stinging from the salt and blood in the water. The moon had moved further across the sky. How much time had passed? Where was the ship? Had anyone noticed we were missing?

Then I saw a sail black against the horizon, moving intermittently between the thrashing waves churned up by the whale and the squid.

Tweed was too far away to help us. We were on our own.

If we stayed in the water the sharks would make a meal of us. We needed some way of getting out of the water. But how? The deck rail was awash and would not support our combined weight. The life buoys were a help but only so far. The rope might be useful, if we had anything to tie ourselves to.

At that moment a wave larger than most hurled us through the air. A black wall rose nearby, cutting off my view of *Tweed*. A breath of stinking water shot into the air with a wet scream. Blood-caked tentacles rose like a writhing forest against the moon, to fall, slapping toothed suckers against the black wall that was the whale's flank.

I slapped Royston. I needed him awake.

'Leela – what –?'

'Shut up. Listen to me –' I spat out a mouthful of water – trying to speak in this sea was to risk drowning. 'We have to swim to the whale. Can you do that?'

'I can't swim!'

'It's that or die. Now go!'

I pulled Royston away from the deck rail, looped a life buoy around his shoulders and pushed him towards the whale. Then I grabbed hold of two pieces of splintered wood – one of which still held a deck cleat – and as much rope as I could cut free from the wreckage, and swam after him.

I roped my salvage to Royston's life buoy then, leaving the man himself to survive as well as he could, I dived towards the head of the whale.

The head – and the squid.

If my plan was to work I would need to separate these giants. That meant that one of them would have to die. I needed the whale, so it was the squid that I planned to kill.

I fought my way through the churning currents, felt my heart pounding against my lungs, squeezing the air in them with every hammer blow. I grabbed a tentacle, pulled my way along it towards the head. The squid must have felt me pulling myself closer. The tentacles writhed, thrashing the water. I tried to move faster. If the animal accidentally squashed me against the side of the whale I would be dead and Cryuni would feast on my soul.

I found myself scraping against a sharp beak. I wrenched my arm aside just as the beak slammed shut with the power of a falling tree. But now I was as close to the head as I could be. I sought the eye – it wasn't hard to find. It was as big as my head. And black. Deepest black. Without thinking I pushed my knife repeatedly into the eye. My arm went in as well, up to the elbow, until I felt the blade scrape against something a little harder than flesh. The animal convulsed. Fresh jets of black fluid spurted from the animal, mingling with the blood. A tentacle caught me and I was wrenched away. I felt myself sinking then rising. I shot into the air. There was a moment's dizziness, then I landed on something hard which drove what little breath I had left from my lungs. A moment passed and I sucked in air. I knew immediately what had happened. The squid had died and the whale had sounded briefly, then had risen to the surface, tossing the dead remains away into the sea. The tentacle that had hold of me had flopped over on to the whale's back. I was safe – until the whale sounded again – but what of Royston?

I saw him nearby, still lashed to the life buoys and the wreckage I had salvaged. Was he alive? I could not tell. But I could not see any sharks – they had followed the corpse of the squid as it glided slowly into the depths, trailing black ink and blood.

With the fight between the giants over the sea calmed considerably. The whale was breathing – snorting air in huge fountains into the sky. Its breath stank, and burned my skin wherever it touched. But I could not escape from it. I did not know how long we had until the whale dived again, so I tried to stand. I could not get my footing on the slippery hide of the whale so, clutching the tall fin, I called out to Royston. 'Throw me the rope! I will pull you out!'

It took him five attempts. Even then I thought he would die first, slip exhausted beneath the water one final time. I looped the rope around the fin for safety and pulled him from the water. Then together we slumped against the whale's wet back and the three of us together drew breath – the whale in huge stinging clouds, myself and Royston in slightly smaller, pain-filled gasps – while the moon sailed across the sky and *Tweed* sailed ever further away from us across the black ocean.

12
Three Tuns

It was some while before I even noticed Leela was missing. There was so much for James and myself to see to and I was so excited, trying to explain it to him as we stood there beside a mountain of boxes and crates upon the pier, supervising the men loading them into the hold of the *Tweed*.

James and I had known each other for some years, in fact since fate had washed me up into his Harley Street waiting room with a bad case the vapours. James had worked out very quickly what the problem was and had recommended I see a friend of his, a psychologist, who would be able to help me with the terrible nightmares I had experienced in the aftermath of my ill-fated expedition to Rapa Nui. Over the years James and I had become fast friends. It had been a slow process, as much due to professional curiosity on his part as anything else. As he always said, I was carrying enough guilt to sink a man o' war. The casual drinking partnership blossomed when I realised what an amateur archaeologist James was. As I had explained to him on many occasions, the worst part of the tragic affair had been my expulsion from the Geographical Society, and the resulting scientific void I was abruptly plunged into. I subscribed to magazines and kept up with the journals for as long as the money lasted, but that only served to reinforce my sense of isolation, for, with my former peer group still ridiculing me for my honesty, I had no one with whom to discuss the matters most dear to my heart. For many years my life remained devoid of stimulation. James changed that with his naive but boundlessly enthusiastic view of the earth sciences.

Now James stared at the luggage we had brought with us and the extra materials I had acquired while here in Portsmouth, and modified his usual comment: 'Horace, there's enough stuff here to sink a man o' war.'

I regarded the cargo with a frown, wondering if I'd forgotten anything. Sea voyages had a nasty habit of going wrong if you were not careful. The last voyage I had been on had been many years before, and it had most definitely gone horribly wrong. I was determined the same thing wasn't going to happen this time. With the Doctor's help, I prayed silently, it wouldn't.

I gestured to the crates and boxes as they were taken one by one across the gangplank and on to the clipper. 'The danger lies in the unforeseen,' I explained. 'Suppose we found a skeleton under water? Have we the right chemicals to preserve it? Have we the correct means of safely reaching inaccessible ledges or cliffs? What if bad weather marooned us on the island while the ship sought calmer waters? Would there be sufficient supplies? What if the cook burned a hole in the saucepan, the hull was damaged by coral, a sailor put his foot on a poisoned urchin? We must be prepared to meet all conceivable reverses, for, as the Captain has pointed out, we sail on the midnight tide.'

James frowned. 'All very sound and reassuring thinking,' he uttered, stroking his short beard with a customary gesture of interest and concentration. 'But according to the manifest, we are loading two hundred pounds of fishhooks. Surely our diet will be more varied than that?'

I smiled. 'They are not for fishing. They are for trading with the natives. They can supply food in the form of vegetables, repair damaged clothing and so forth.'

'I see. And the three tons of dental plaster that has just been delivered?'

'For taking a cast of one of the statues.'

I felt a shudder run through me as I remembered how the

(*walking they were walking hunting the great* moai *were*)
statues had haunted my last hours on the island. Despite the great distance and many years, the images were sharp enough to cause great pain. I saw the cliffs, etched against the night sky, I heard Alexander's cry, I felt the sting of salt in the wet air and the crack of my fist against a native face.

'Horace.' James's voice was a quiet whisper.

I blinked, realised I was standing quite still, my gaze fixed on the slow swell of the waves lapping against the jetty. 'James. Was I –?'

'Yes. Don't worry, it was just a short one. But it's probably not something you want to advertise.'

'I… suppose you are right.'

From time to time, more so in recent years than immediately prior to my earlier expedition, I had been plagued by momentary lapses, moments when for me the world simply ceased to exist. The spell never lasted longer than five minutes and had happened so rarely in the last few days that I had thought the problem all but cured. I shook my head as if waking from a restless sleep. 'It must be the excitement.'

James nodded. He took out a hip flask. 'Drop o' the hard stuff, Horace?'

I accepted thankfully. But as I drank I felt something nagging at the back of my mind. 'I wonder where Leela's got to.'

James affected little concern. 'Same place as her friend the Doctor, I shouldn't wonder. Why?'

I gulped another mouthful of whisky and capped the bottle. 'I just worry, that's all.'

My friend scowled. 'Horace, I sometimes feel you're altogether too trusting. If you ask me, Leela and her friend the Doctor are a rum pair. They turn up, out of the blue, and next thing we know your house is being burgled, then the Doctor finances an expedition to a level I doubt even a magnet could sustain and then vanishes, closely followed by his companion – herself one of the most peculiar young women it has ever been my pleasure or fortune to meet. No. There's something dark about all this, Horace. You mark my words.'

I handed James back the flask, shouted a warning to be careful at two boys loading a crate containing my scientific apparatus, turned back to James and sighed. 'Damn, but I am a man of mixed feelings. On the one hand I cannot deny all you have said is true. And yet, on the other… I am drawn to this woman and her generous partner.'

'They're playing games with us, Horace. I warn you.'

'Games… well, that may be true enough, my friend. But with us? I don't know.'

James sighed. 'If this Doctor is so rich, where are his servants? His estate? Why have we never heard of him or his family? And how did he get to Portsmouth so fast? Captain Stuart tells me he bought – not booked, mark you, *bought* – the *Tweed* last evening, a matter of an hour or so after he left us!'

'I do not know. Yet I have a feeling. A sense of… great benevolence about him. They say some wear their hearts on their sleeves. The Doctor is a man who wears his good intentions for all to see.'

'And a very palpable air of mystery which he draws around him like a cloak!'

'James, my friend. I do not wish to argue. Not on the eve of what may be the most important months of my life.'

My friend frowned. 'As a man of medicine I cannot but agree that the ills caused by bad temper and ill disposition will bring you naught but harm. Yet this situation must be addressed. And before we sail.'

I drew James aside from the sweating crew. 'Are you suggesting we leave our friends behind?'

He considered. 'I feel it may be prudent to consider this

134

course of action, yes.'

'But why? Without them we would not even be going.'

It was James's turn to frown. I knew him well, sensed the dilemma within him. And I was puzzled too. Why was James so ardently set against my friends? I put the question to him.

'Rather, I would have you consider just how many good friends you have made over the last years, Horace.'

I felt myself blush, for I knew my friend was right. I made friends about as easily as a dog that has tasted blood. I was a dog, the blood I had tasted, the past. 'James, that was unnecessary.'

He sighed. 'It brought me no pleasure, Horace. Your family are dead. You have driven the few friends you had from your side long ago with your wild tales and guilt. You must listen to me. I am the voice of reason within you. I am the one chance you have to see the truth.'

I considered. He was right. I knew that. At least he had been... until tonight. Now things were different. I had seen myself through other eyes. Her eyes. Leela was honest, forthright, as wise as a mystic yet as unsophisticated as the basest serving wench. A woman of extremes. A violent woman. A woman who felt her emotions passionately and expressed them with equal passion. Someone who cared for others and saw through their screens, who read them like a book, even though I knew she had never read a book, indeed, couldn't read a word. She had seen me and, in seeing, had known me. But where others had condemned, she had believed. Or at least, kept an open mind. Yes. Leela was my friend. How could I make James see this? He had never experienced my isolation, my loneliness, except at second hand. He did not know, did not understand, what it was like to be me. Leela did. And now she was missing.

'My friend, I respect your counsel as always, but for the first time in my life, I have something other than my own self-obsessed, indeed selfish, concerns to worry about. The Doctor knows we are to sail in less than three hours. He has vanished. Leela went to look for him and now she has vanished. Something tells me there's foul play here. Perpetrated, perhaps, by the very person who paid Fennel to steal my research.'

James snorted with minor amusement. 'A mysterious nemesis out to bedevil you? My dear fellow, you hardly have a career to ruin. No. If there's an enemy here I'll wager it is the Doctor himself.'

I clenched my teeth. His words angered me. 'Why are you so set against my friends?'

'They are no friends. Leave them. Sail and resolve your pain by all means – but do it alone, while you are still able.'

'You do not understand. If I leave her now I will simply be repeating the mistakes of the past. I left Alexander to die and the knowledge shall dog the remainder of my life. I will not let it happen again.'

James threw up his hands in a tired gesture. 'Very well, I can see you are set on this foolhardy course. It being three hours until midnight, how much of the town do you think we can cover? And where will you look first?'

'I have heard the mate talk of a tavern at the end of the docks called the Three Tuns, which the dock hands are known to frequent. Perhaps we can find someone there who met the Doctor and might be able to tell us where he is to be found now.'

James shrugged. The town clock rang nine. I began to walk along the jetty to the land side of the dock, and he followed. The docks were wet. A light fog was rolling in off the sea, gathering strength, blurring the lights from nearby windows. One by one the stars above us went out, obscured by a thickening blanket of cloud. I was concerned. If this fog held we would not be sailing tonight – maybe not for several days. I continued to walk, James beside me, our footsteps ringing dully on the road. Dim yellow lights guttered along nearby streets and up the hill towards town. Sounds of distant revelry drifted on the night air.

I heard laughter. A door banged open, spilling light into the street. Several drunken sailors stumbled past. They called a cheerful if beer-sodden greeting to us, before stumbling past. The door banged shut and the light and sounds from within faded.

James said quietly, 'A tavern.'

I shook my head. 'Not the one. We go on.'

A few minutes later we found the Three Tun,. It was a two-storey building which in the fog seemed to squat like some hulking animal upon the pier. It was a ramshackle affair, with boards peeling from the outside and guttering and a rain barrel clogged with moss. But light shone strongly from inside, blurred by the damp air collecting around the slatted windows.

I hesitated. Beside me, James stopped as well. I don't think either of us really knew what to do now we were here. A place like this was outside my experience – it was almost certainly outside James's as well.

I thought it looked like an animal. It smelled like one, too. Beer and tobacco and sweat. And I could hear the noise it made from the far side of the road. A guttural, angry noise, like an animal about to kill. The noise was a composite of crashes, angry shouts, gleeful taunts.

James and I exchanged glances. We had taken but one step towards the establishment when the window nearest us shattered, burst asunder by a wooden table which flew through the air and shattered on the ground before us. Smashed bits of wood and glass scattered across the pier.

Wreckage skittered along the wooden boards and dropped over the edge. I heard distant splashes, muffled by the fog.

That's when I saw it.

I grabbed the object, held it up to James.

'A boot. Horace, this is the mother of all bar fights. I really think we ought to think twice before –'

I waved the boot excitedly. 'Look at it! It's leather, hand-stitched, crude but very tough. A hunter's boot. Leela's boot!'

'You're clutching at straws –'

'No. I'm right. She's in there. Or was in there. Maybe she's involved in the fight. We have to help her!'

'Horace, you're fifty-five years old! What in the world do you think you can –'

I ignored James, ran towards the tavern, pushed the door open.

Inside was chaos. At least thirty men, all seemingly hell-bent on killing each other with whatever weapons were to be found at hand. Bits of wood, chair legs, chairs, tankards, jugs both full and empty filled the air in a continuous rain of projectiles. I counted three barmaids standing on tables – what was left of them – screaming as they bashed whatever head found itself nearest with whatever they happened to be holding. Mainly thick earthenware jugs by the look of it.

I glanced at James, who had entered the tavern and was standing before me. His eyes widened suddenly. We both ducked in time to avoid a body hurled out of the mêlée. The body – that of a medium-sized sailor – flew over our heads and crashed into the door, collapsing with a groan into insensibility.

James tried to speak, and only then did I register the volume of noise.

'– the wench, get her –'

'– she's got a –'

'– you fool, not with that, with –'

'– cut me, she –'

'– out of the way then you –'

'– bleeding, I'm –'

'– devil take you for a –'

I stood helplessly by and watched the throng. I dared not approach. At that moment there came the sound of a gunshot. I jumped with surprise. The noise had come from right beside me, and it cut through the confusion, bringing silence in its wake.

'That will be quite enough of that, thank you, gentlemen.' James's voice – and his pistol – brooked no argument.

The fight lost some of its momentum. I saw the barman – a squat figure belted with muscle – crack heads with a nasty-looking cosh and that ended it permanently. The barmaids began to clear up the mess as we pushed through the sullen-looking crowd to a hunched figure crouched defiantly on the floor. I stopped as the figure turned to threaten me with a knife.

A woman, yes. But not Leela.

Her face was scratched and bleeding, her hair and clothes in rags. A man lay bleeding on the floor beside her. As I watched, he got painfully to his feet and aimed a kick at the woman. The barman grabbed his leg, dragged him shouting to the door and tossed him out into the night.

The barman then returned, pushed back past us, grabbed the girl by the arm and dragged her towards the door. 'I told you before about this. You pay me and you can work all the men you want. But you pull a knife in my tavern and you deserve everything you get.'

The woman began to scream – a stream of abuse levelled at every man in sight. The barman slapped her hard, picked her up while she was reeling from the blow, and threw her out of the bar after the man on whom she had, presumably, just used the knife.

Someone banged loudly on the remains of a table. 'Ale. I want ale here!'

And in the blink of an eye everything was raucous laughter and tuneless, drunken singing.

I looked at James, who was still holding his pistol. He scowled.

'It was her boot, James. I am sure of it.'

I turned to leave, face red with embarrassment, and that was when I caught a glimpse of a red-haired man in dock worker's clothes for half a second before the cosh he was wielding struck the side of my head an agonising blow, and I fell insensible to the ale-sodden floor.

13
Sidewinder

We had been adrift the rest of the night and the sun had risen when I had the idea. 'Perhaps we can steer it.'

Royston roused from his exhausted stupor long enough to say, 'It's a *whale*. How can we possibly steer it?'

I shrugged; my skins, still wet, chafed my salt-sore shoulders. 'You steer horses, don't you? You use rope and kick them. We have rope. I am strong enough to kick this beast if it will not go where I want.'

'Leela, that's nonsense. Our only chance is to hope someone will find us. And hope the whale will not sound, or die. Either way we'll be food for sharks. If you want to hope for something, hope for that, not that we can drive this thing through the ocean like a coach and nine.'

'It is good that the men of your land are not all as weak as you or there would *be* no men in your land.'

Royston did not have the strength to reply. That or he could not be bothered. Either way I did not care. Royston could languish in his despair and die here on this swimming island if he wanted. I was going to live – or die trying.

I thought hard. It was true the whale had dipped beneath the sea many times since we had climbed aboard. Each time I thought we were to die. But the animal did not stay under water long, and did not go very deep, either. And I noticed that the spume from its blowhole was now darker, flecked with evil-smelling blood. I had mentioned this to Royston. He thought the whale was staying on the surface because it was no longer able to effectively oxygenate its blood. I did not understand that.

He explained. 'To live we must breathe. The air has many things in it but only one of the things keeps us alive. That is called oxygen. The more oxygen the whale has in its blood, the longer it can hold its breath beneath the water. It's bleeding copiously. Maybe it cannot dive.'

I had thought about that. The idea that the air was full of things we breathed in and out was nonsense. If there were things in the air I would see them. I ignored Royston after that. He was obviously delirious.

Nonetheless, the whale stayed on the surface. And it was swimming fairly quickly, so it was still strong. I hoped it would not die before I managed to make it take us to the ship.

I gathered together the rope we had. Horses were steered by rope in their mouths. Somehow I had to get the rope in the whale's mouth. I made a lasso and hurled it forward, nearly slipping into the sea as I did so. The lasso landed square in the jaws of the whale. I pulled the makeshift reins tight. The whale, irritated, slapped the water with its tail. It bit down. The rope snapped. I now had two pieces of rope and the whale had not changed course.

I thought about what to do next. The animal had eyes and ears and flippers. The flippers were motionless – obviously it did not use them to steer itself. Then I had another idea. The whale had not responded to force. Maybe it would respond to reason.

I crawled along the head of the beast and leaned over until my face was as close as I could get to one ear.

'Hear me, whale,' I cried as loudly as I could manage. 'I am the one who killed the squid and saved your life. Swim towards the sun. Do this and I will –' I stopped. What could I offer a whale? What did I have that it might want? 'And I live.'

The whale showed no sign of having heard me. I certainly was not going to beg this beast to do my bidding. I crawled back on to the top of the head. Royston was waiting for me there. He was laughing. Actually he was laughing and crying at the same time.

I showed him my knife. 'If you have a death wish I am sure the sharks will be very happy to indulge it.'

He stopped laughing. 'Blind,' he called. His salt-encrusted lips barely moved. 'You're as blind as a bat. Quite clearly we're both going to –'

I stopped listening. I had another idea. I remembered that the horses I had seen in London were also guided by putting covers over their eyes. I sat Royston upright, took off his jacket and let him slump back on to the whale again.

I took the jacket, crawled back across the head and found one of the whale's eyes. It was small – a lot smaller than the squid's had been. And it was curious. It looked everywhere. But mostly it seemed to look sideways, straight out from the head. The shape of the head meant the whale probably could not see directly forward. Wondering what might happen, I got as good a grip as I could on the slippery hide and draped the jacket over the whale's eye.

A moment passed. Had it made any difference? I could not tell from looking at the water so I looked up at the sky instead. The sun was in a different position. Now it was more directly ahead than to the side, as it had been.

I grinned. The whale snorted wet air from its blowhole.

'Thank you,' I whispered respectfully.

The sun climbed further up into the sky. After a while it grew very hot. The whale still dipped beneath the waves, though less frequently as time wore on. As the sun approached its highest point Royston aroused himself enough to join me on the head. He removed his shirt and positioned himself beside the whale's other eye. Shouting instructions to each other, we managed to keep the whale on a course heading east. I did not know if we were travelling as fast as *Tweed*, if they would stop and wait for us, if we would catch them up before we died of hunger or thirst.

As the sun began to move behind us I left Royston to guide the whale, tied myself to the great beast's fin and lowered myself back into the water. A short time later we had fish to eat. I squeezed fluid from the fish, which was close to fresh, and we drank that. Fish and water tasted foul, but I had eaten and drunk a lot worse as a child. They would keep us alive for another day – if the sun did not kill us. My skin was burning with exposure – I was in considerable pain, though I knew how to ignore it. Royston was different. He was more susceptible to the sun and the water. And he was still seasick. After eating the fish I had caught he was so sick I thought he would lose his grip on the whale's hide and fall into the water. I had to tie him to the fin and risk his drowning when the whale dipped without warning beneath the surface. I caught another fish for him. This one he nibbled – and managed to keep down.

By now the whale had veered off the direction I wanted it to take. I crawled back to the whale's head and put it back on course. I studied the water and the sky, wondering how much of Royston's improved health was due to the reduction in speed of the whale – which, it seemed clear to me now, would die soon. The squid had left many wounds in the whale's body, large circular bite marks which ran in curving lines across its back and flanks and head. I tried to see into the huge mouth; there was blood there. Had the squid damaged the whale's tongue?

The whale seemed unaffected by its condition. Apart from the gush of stinking breath from its blowhole and the slap of its tail against the water, the whale was able to produce an astonishing range of clicks and whistles, pops and other noises.

I wondered if it was trying to talk to me. I couldn't understand it so I stopped thinking about it. I was more worried about catching the ship up and getting some real food. Almost a whole day had passed by now – and I was very hungry.

I caught some more fish, gutting a trailing shark to distract the others from bothering me. We ate, and then took turns to try to sleep, roped to the whale's fin, awoken every so often by the stinging gush of the whale's breath, or an unexpected dipping beneath the now much colder waves.

So the night passed, the moon rose and set once more, and the sun rose once again – this time on to a much changed sea.

It was as we ate a breakfast of more fish and fish juice that I noticed that the sea had become very smooth. Blood trailing from the whale's wounds into the water during the night had attracted a few sharks but they had now vanished. The whale, though, seemed rather more agitated than normal. Its attempts to dive were becoming more frequent – although its success at remaining submerged longer than a few seconds remained unchanged. I had the impression the whale wanted to get beneath the surface. And in truth I found the slow oily swell which the surface had adopted was making me nervous as well. That or I was reacting to the whale's agitation. I wondered how close the whale was to death. I looked around for Cryuni but could not see him. Very well. We were safe for a while yet.

The sun was close to its highest point when Royston spotted the black column inching above the eastern horizon towards which we were moving. 'The ship,' he gasped through cracked lips. 'I can see masts.'

I looked more closely at the black line. 'That's not a ship,' I said quietly. 'It moves like an animal.'

Royston forced his eyes to work against the glare of the sun skipping off the lazy water. 'Oh damn. It's not a ship. What is it, a cloud?'

I looked more closely. Something about this thing was making me very wary. I had to keep the whale's eye covered all the time to hold our course. The animal seemed to want to swim away from this cloud – whatever it was.

And then Royston gasped. 'God save us, it's a tornado.'

'What is a tornado?'

'Bad news. I suggest you let the whale have its head. He'll swim away. If we get caught in that it'll kill us.'

'If we let the whale swim where it wants we will lose the ship and die anyway.'

'Talk about being caught between the devil and the deep blue sea.' Royston tried a laugh but it came out cracked and husky. There was no humour in it to start with. It was a horrible sound, full of despair and resignation. I knew the sound. Royston thought he was facing death.

The cloud was nearer now. I could see it clearly. It was a black column stretching from the surface of the sea to the sky. Where it touched the sea, the water rose in a large hill. I could see the sunlight reflecting off the surface. The water was spinning, snatched up into the air by a terrible force lurking like a web-tree spinner, somewhere out of sight among the clouds. I thought of the *Xaust* wind I'd been caught in as a child and shuddered. Not again.

Something hit me on the head and bounced into the water. I jerked with surprise. Another object landed on the whale's back in front of me. It was a fish. Fish were falling from the sky. Many dead fish.

'Makes a change from cats and dogs,' Royston mumbled. I did not understand him. I was more concerned about the fish. If this tornado had sucked the very fish out of the water, what chance did we have?

I uncovered the whale's eye but even as the animal began to change course I knew the truth. The whale was so close to death I don't think it could have swum faster than a floating stick. Its breath was coming more and more slowly, and was almost entirely blood-filled now. Both Royston and I looked as if we had been slaughtering tribal enemies for a nine-day.

And then it happened. With a final wheeze, a feeble muttering of clicks and pops, the whale glided to a halt and turned belly up. By the time I freed Royston from the ropes that had secured him to the fin, the storm was upon us.

We floated beside the whale's carcass and tried to breathe. The cloud sucked the air from around us. It sucked spray off the water and turned the surface into choppy hillocks around us. It was raining upwards. The sky was entirely black overhead now, though I could see blue sky and the gleam of sunlight at either horizon. But that might have been a world away for all our chances of reaching it.

And now the sea itself was curving upward, away from us, but dragging us with it, up the lower slopes of the hill beneath the whirling cloud. Breathing was even more difficult.

I grabbed Royston. 'We must dive. Try to swim away from it.'

Royston did not even have the strength to reply. It was all he could do to cling to the whale's carcass to keep from drowning. Not that that would do him any good for much longer: the amount of water being sucked into the air meant we would drown just as surely above the surface as below it.

Unless…

Perhaps the whale could save us again, even though it was dead.

Even as I thought this, I saw a black shape carried further up the column of water. It was a shark that had been following us, attracted by the whale's blood. Now it was carried thrashing into the sky, where I lost sight of it among the clouds.

If we wanted to live we had to move now.

Grabbing Royston, I dragged him around to the head of the

whale. The huge mouth was gaping wide, flapping open and closed in the currents of water, the lower jaw dragged upward repeatedly by the suck of the wind. Timing my actions, I shoved Royston into the mouth.

Another shark surged past me as I did so. Absurdly it seemed to be swimming backwards. The water was becoming steeper and getting breath was almost impossible. The whale was beginning to move up the hill now, sucked ever higher by the greedy currents.

I dragged myself into the whale's mouth. There were no teeth but the gums were hard and the tongue – a limp mass of flesh rocking from side to side with the motion of the dead animal – was heavy enough to crush or smother either of us. I felt around for Royston, hoping he had not already been crushed or smothered or drowned, and tried to avoid the heavy tongue. I found Royston and grabbed him tightly. I hoped enough air would filter in so that we could breathe.

Even though we were now inside the whale I could feel the current dragging us even further upward. And then the battering from the water stopped and we began to spin. The mouth flapped open and shut with terrible force. I wanted to close my eyes but found I could not. I locked my arms around the whale's strange teeth and prayed to the gods of the Place of Land that I would live through this nightmare.

'*Collision alert, collision alert,*

'*Prim sys fail reroute aux pow to grav null sys –*'

I repeated the Prayer of Landing until my throat screamed in protest. Beyond the whale's flapping mouth I could see glimpses of sky and sun, cloud and sea. None of them were in the right places. We were flying. Through the air. I remembered the shark dragged upwards by the sky and the rain of fish that had fallen upon us, and prayed even harder.

'*Lock standby sys lock cry uni sys lock all sys and,*

'*Strap in this is going to hurt like a bas –*'

Then my stomach lurched. I was flattened against the whale's cheek, the tongue came down upon me with crushing force and I knew that, like the gods before me, we were falling towards a new Place of Land.

14
Nemesis

I awoke freezing cold and paralysed. My first thought was that someone had stabbed me with a Janis thorn and now I was waiting to die. Then I realised the sensation was different. I could move, I was just restrained. Tied up. The cold pressure at my chest was water. A tide. The foul smell and scummy water told me exactly where I was: in a sewer running beneath the harbour.

Beside me in the darkness I heard a muttered curse. I recognised the voice instantly. 'Royston,' I said, 'when I get out of here I am going to make a present of your innards for the gulls.'

'I think it highly doubtful that any of us will see the tomorrow's dawn, let alone live beyond it.'

The second voice was familiar too. 'Stockwood, are you all right?'

'No, my dear, I have a terrible headache, caused no doubt by the fellow who coshed me.'

'A dock worker?'

'Yes.'

'Red hair?'

'Yes.'

I nodded, forgetting for a moment that I was tied up and banging the back of my head against the slimy wooden post. 'The same man who captured me.'

'Who captured all of us.' I wriggled around in the darkness. The Doctor! 'I'm afraid we've all been rather slow tonight.'

I felt for my knife. I could not even tell if it was sheathed at my side or had been taken. The water was so cold my skin was beginning to tingle.

Now Royston said in an angry voice, 'Do I understand that you blame me for what has happened here tonight?'

'If it were not for you the Cryuni would not have sent Fennel to steal the *rongo-rongo* and Stockwood's life! You killed Fennel to conceal your involvement.'

'My good woman, I said I knew nothing of that damn butler's involvement and I told you the truth!'

'With your words. But not with your body!'

'If you think that, you are quite mad. I pray you seek help before you cause injury to yourself or others.'

'I will injure you if I can just get out of these ropes!'

'Leela.' The single word from the Doctor was quiet, only just rising above the sound of the waves. It had a calming effect on me. I struggled hard and kept my temper in check. The Doctor was right. Anger wasted on futile gestures would help no one.

Stockwood spluttered nearby. 'How long do you think we have before the tide comes in?'

'Captain Stuart told us that *Tweed* was due to sail on the midnight tide. We've probably got less than half an hour until high tide.'

I looked around, allowing my eyes to collect what little light filtered beneath the pier. 'There are watermarks here. The weed grows high above my head.'

'That's it then.' Stockwood's voice was weary. 'I cannot possibly free myself. If none of you can either we will be dead in less than half an hour.'

His words were interrupted by more splashes as he tried to keep his head above water. I felt the waves lapping gently around my own chin. One wave splashed my face and made me gasp.

'What can we do?' No one replied. 'Doctor?'

'I'm thinking.'

'I'm drowning!' That was Royston, the anger in his voice giving the lie to his frightened words.

The Doctor said, still quietly, 'No you're not. Now be quiet. I'm concentrating on a little trick I know.'

I felt a sullen silence from Royston, and promised myself I would teach him some manners at the first possible opportunity – before we died if I could, but afterwards if not.

'I don't wish to criticise, Doctor, but the present moment hardly seems appropriate for tricks.'

'Oh, you'll like this one, Horace. It's a little trick I learnt from… my old friend Harry Houdini. A matter of concentrating on the muscles… controlling the flow of blood to the tendons… changing the shape of the limb by dislocation until it can slip through the restraints… Of course, Harry always worked with handcuffs, not wet ropes – and he did maintain that this trick was the most painful of his repertoire… though I never really understood why until now. Of course, I have an advantage over him… I can place chemical blocks at my synaptic gaps… prevent the conduction of specific nerve impulses… I can stop the pain Harry felt every time he performed this trick… Of course, I haven't actually done it for a while… so it's not quite… one hundred per cent… *effective*… Nonetheless, I think… I'm… almost… *there*!' His last word was punctuated by the cracking of muscle, a triumphant gasp and a splash of foul-smelling water.

By now the water was up to my lips. I tilted my head back, trying to get a clear channel to the air. Stockwood hadn't said anything for some moments. I hoped he hadn't drowned.

Royston said, 'So you have one arm free. Can you untie yourself?'

The Doctor's voice was filled with embarrassment. 'I can't reach the knots.'

By now the rope holding my arms was contracting in the water, biting tighter into my skin. I relaxed, letting it tighten even further. When I felt it was tight enough, I flexed my arms against the post. I was very strong. The rope now had little or no play in it. If there was even the slightest flaw in the cord, I would be able to break it.

Waves splashed into my face. I closed my eyes, tilting my head back as far as possible for air. I pressed my heels and shoulders against the post and

(the post was a web-tree spinner which caught me while hunting because I had been arrogant and stupid and now I was trapped between its web and its tree waiting to die but I would not die because if I died then my sister's death would have been for nothing and I would not waste her death so I)

set my mind against the pain and

(arched my back against the web and shouted my defiance and)

pushed and

(screamed my refusal to bow to nature and)

ignored the water splashing into

(the stinging web filling)

my mouth and

(pushed and)

screamed but

(the web held and)

the rope held

(and I knew)

I was going to die.

(I was going to die!)

That was the moment when, like the tree in my youth, part of the post I was tied to broke, and I found there was enough room to wriggle free.

I trod water for a moment, trying to ignore the pain that

coursed through my body.

Impatient words mixed with wet spluttering noises from Royston brought me to my senses. 'Here. Over here!' I pushed my way towards him, found a lump of wood that might have been a chair or table leg floating on the water. 'Be careful!' He was right. Pieces of thick window glass were embedded in the wood. 'Wreckage from the bar fight,' he said. I ignored him, grabbed the wood, swam to Stockwood, who still hadn't spoken a word, and slashed at the ropes binding him to the wooden post. He was alive. I left him clinging to the post and freed the Doctor. By now, Royston was forced to keep his mouth shut because of the water level.

I trod water beside the Doctor. 'What do we do now?'

'Free Royston,' he suggested pointedly.

'He is in league with Cryuni,' I said simply.

The Doctor sighed, treading water with both legs while he used one hand to realign the joints in his other arm. 'Cryuni is a construct invented by your shamans. It's a linguistic corruption, like Sevateem or Tesh. Cryuni is a corrupted version of cryogenic units.'

'I don't understand.'

'Your people came to the Place of Land in a starship. The journey was many lifetimes long. Cryogenic suspension kept your ancestors alive – but asleep – during the voyage.'

'Alive?'

'Yes.'

'Asleep?'

'Yes. You should be calling Cryuni the giver of life, not the taker of it. Now, are you going to release Royston before he drowns or would you rather become a servant of your own death icon?'

I freed Royston, not being particularly careful to spare his flesh when I cut the ropes that bound him. He burst to the surface, too near death even to show the anger I knew he felt. I did not care. He could do nothing to me. If he tried I would kill him. The Doctor might be right. I would have to think about that. In the meantime, I knew what I knew. And I still did not trust Royston.

The Doctor unravelled his scarf and handed it to me. 'My arm's still a little tender,' he said with a rueful smile. 'I wonder if you'd be kind enough to throw that over the pier supports. Then we can all climb out of here.'

'Why not just swim ashore?' Royston asked. There was a roughness to his voice caused by his near-drowning which made me smile.

'You and Stockwood must certainly do that,' the Doctor replied. 'Leela and I are going back to the Three Tuns. I want to find out who's behind this.'

'Doctor, why bother?' Stockwood's voice was also roughened by the sea. 'In fifteen minutes we will be on the *Tweed* and weighing anchor. We can forget about it then.'

'I'm not so sure. There is a force at work here and I must get to the bottom of it.'

'Cryuni.' I said matter-of-factly.

'Oh, it's something far more dangerous than a semi-mythical religious icon. Something – or someone – willing to kill all of us to ensure the success of their own objectives.'

'I do not understand.'

'That's why you're coming with me. I brought you here to learn about your ancestors. Never look a gift horse in the mouth.'

'You speak of learning and horses and you force me to leave my best friend alone with a man I do not trust! Sometimes I wonder if you are not touched by madness.'

'Good.' The Doctor beamed. 'I like an inquiring mind. Now throw the scarf, will you, and let's get down to business.'

I threw the scarf. It took three attempts because my back was in some pain and the scarf was heavy with water, but eventually I managed to loop the scarf around a pier support high above our heads.

As the scarf finally caught, Stockwood called out to the Doctor. 'Should I instruct Captain Stuart to delay sailing until the morning?'

'By no means,' the Doctor called back. 'We'll be there on time. Come hell or high water.'

Then, leaving Stockwood and Royston to swim ashore against my better judgement, I climbed the pier supports, following the Doctor upward, away from the foul water, towards the moonlit night. And the Three Tuns. And, I hoped, towards the red-haired dock worker who had nearly been the death of me.

We continued climbing, reaching the top of the pier supports, moving back along the underside of the pier and eventually breaking into the tavern through a hatch leading into a brick-lined tunnel.

We moved slowly through the tunnel. The smell of damp and alcohol was almost overpowering. The Doctor paused every now and then to touch the stone walls. I copied him. The bricks were drying out as we moved forward. We were approaching land. The tunnel ended at a thick wooden door fastened by a large iron lock.

The Doctor bent to examine the lock. 'Angus Bolton, 1856. A good year.'

'Why?'

'Because,' said the Doctor, rummaging in his pockets and eventually emerging with a bunch of keys as big as a grapefruit, 'they hadn't got round to inventing the double mortise yet. Now then,' he added, thumbing the keys quickly round the ring, 'spare TARDIS key, Venusian landcruiser dock

157

key, Ford Granada ignition key, key to the Bank of England vault, key to the Exchange, key to the city of Iskenderun, key to – ah! Here we are. Key to Angus Bolton's family fortune.' And with a grin, the Doctor chose a key, inserted it into the lock and turned. Nothing. The key did not move. The Doctor began to mutter. 'TARDIS, landcruiser, Granada, Bank, Exchange… ah. I see, now. Kublai Khan's Key to the World, *then* the key to the city of Iskenderun… Here we are.' He tried a second key.

Still nothing happened.

I frowned. 'Perhaps it's open.' I pushed lightly against the door.

It swung open.

The Doctor muttered something I couldn't hear and tucked the keys quickly back into his pocket.

'After you.'

I nodded, moved warily into the darkness.

The door opened into what was obviously part of the tavern's cellars. Kegs of ale were stacked everywhere. The smell of alcohol was as thick as that of blood at a hunter's kill. The floor underfoot was now rough brick, as were the walls. The ground was dry, with no signs of the damp mould that had accompanied us along the tunnel from the pier.

The stench of scavenger animals drifted through the cellars.

'Rats,' the Doctor said solemnly.

'And that's not all, Doctor.' I recognised the voice straight away. The red-haired man.

I grinned in anticipation. 'I can hear you. I tell you now you will not leave here alive.'

'So.' The voice came again out of the darkness. 'Y've got yer pet wi' yer. Where d'yer find her then? Dredge 'er up from Bedlam, did ya? Or did you tread 'er in from the sewers wiv the rest o' the muck on y'boots?'

'Very good.' The Doctor's voice was quiet, but carried

nonetheless. 'Must remember that one.'

'Fer about the next two minutes.' I heard the anticipation in the redheaded man's voice change to excitement, and shoved the Doctor aside as the gun fired. A muzzle flash lit the darkness. Something tugged at my tunic. I ignored it. A miss.

The Doctor hissed, 'He'll need to reload. Ten, maybe fifteen seconds.'

I nodded, moved away into the darkness. Another shot. Another miss. 'He has two guns.'

'I know. Be careful.'

'I will. And I will bring you his head as a trophy.' I moved off before the Doctor could argue. I moved silently, skirting the barrels of ale. I sniffed quietly, tasting the air, remembering with no difficulty the body odour of the red-haired man. I could track him with my eyes shut. The ale and smell of gunpowder complicated things only a little.

I heard the Doctor speak. 'Listen to me. I know you stayed here to make sure we were dead. But ask yourself why we came back. We could have just left.'

'Y'came back 'cause you was stupid or 'cause y'wanted t'find sommat out. Either way 'syer last mistake. I been well paid to take care o' you an' I'm goin' t'make sure the job's done right this time.'

The Doctor said, 'I have gold. I can pay you to leave us alone. All I want to know is who's out to sabotage Stockwood's expedition.'

Good, I thought. Keep him talking. He'll have had time to reload by now but in another moment I'll know where he is.

'I bet y'do. But y'll not get an answer from me and I'll have as much gold as I want when I pry it from y'cold, dead hands.'

There! Ten yards away behind a stack of barrels. That was where the voice came from. I moved quietly, scooping a handful of dirt from the floor as I did. As a weapon the dirt was a poor substitute for my knife – but I did not have a choice. I rounded the barrels ready to leap – but the red-haired man was not there.

That was when I heard the Doctor say 'Ah' in the tones he normally used when he realised he'd made a mistake. That and the distinct sound made by two pistols being cocked.

I ran around the corner, bumping my shoulder in the darkness, drawn to the sounds of confrontation. I found the Doctor with his back to the red-haired man, who had both pistols levelled at his back.

I stopped. If I attacked now the pistols would fire – and the Doctor would be dead. The red-haired man turned slightly. I could sense him grinning, the same smile I had seen when he outwitted me earlier. In a moment he swung around one pistol. Now he covered both of us.

I quickly took in the set of his body, the determination on his face, and I knew he was simply going to fire. He was going to shoot both of us like animals. But which would he shoot first? He smiled at me, teeth yellow in the dim glow from an overhead hatchway. Me then. I grinned back – and *moved*.

I heard the gunshot, felt the ball tug at my hair, threw myself at the floor, rolled, sprang upright, grabbed a barrel of ale and threw it as hard as I could at the place where he had been standing.

A shout of pain, the crash of wood, a splash of liquid.

And another shot. Aimed at me? I was already moving, following up the barrel. It wasn't necessary. The red-haired man was slumped in a puddle of ale, groaning, only just conscious.

The Doctor approached as I searched the man, taking his pistols and crowing triumphantly when I found my knife tucked into his belt. The Doctor bent to examine the mess on the floor.

'Theakston's Old Peculiar. Good year, too. Shame.'

'It will be a shame if we do not get out of here now. He might have friends waiting to avenge his death.'

'You're not going to kill him, Leela, so put those pistols down and come with me.'

Angrily I did as I was told. 'I do not understand you! He tried to kill you. Tried to kill both of us. Why do you not take revenge on him?'

'It's simply not the done thing. Spare an enemy, make a friend.'

'You are wrong. An enemy you spare just becomes a worse enemy. You have shamed him and he will try all the harder to kill you.'

'I don't think so. Now help me with this trapdoor. We've only got a few minutes to reach the ship before she sails. And we don't want to miss the boat, now do we?'

The ship's bell sounded as we scrambled out of the cellar and through the delivery hatch. There was no time now to find out who was behind the attempts to kill us. We only just had time to reach the ship before she sailed. The Doctor began to run. I ran after him, discarding my other boot as I ran. I hated to see that boot go, but having only the one unbalanced me. The docks were shrouded in fog. Lights glimmered in the night. I smelled fish and gas and smoke.

The bell sounded again, dull and distant in the fog.

'How far is it to the ship?' I shouted.

The Doctor, a few yards ahead of me, yelled, without turning back, 'I'll tell you when we get there.'

I straightened up, turned to run – and then fell over, a scalding pain running the length of my arm.

Only then did I realise that the sound I had heard was a gunshot.

The red-headed man.

I must have yelled. The Doctor turned.

Another figure stumbled from the tavern behind me. I heard the footsteps. I felt blood on my arm. I remembered what the Doctor said. Ten or fifteen seconds to reload.

But did he still have two guns?

I struggled to rise, my balance gone, lurched to my feet. Another shot. The Doctor threw himself to the ground.

Now we had ten or fifteen seconds.

I ran to meet him.

Running footsteps followed. Another gunshot. I fell again, this time with a terrible pain in my foot.

The Doctor didn't say anything. He scooped me up in his arms, slung me over his shoulder and began to run. I scrabbled for my knife with my good hand, but couldn't reach the scabbard. The Doctor's shoulder jammed into my stomach. I gasped. The running footsteps drew nearer. A shape appeared out of the fog. Another gunshot cracked in the night. A muzzle flash lit up the red-haired man's face. It was twisted in anger and pleasure. Something tugged at the Doctor's hat. He clamped one hand on it to keep it in place and ran even faster.

'Leave me,' I told the Doctor breathlessly. 'I am injured! I am a liability! If you respect me, then leave me here and save yourself!'

The Doctor dodged to one side, vaulted a wooden rail and began to run along the dock. 'Did I ever tell you… the story of the three musketeers… well, there were four of them really, but the point I'm trying to make is –'

Another gunshot cut him off. He stumbled, recovered, grabbed his hat and ran on.

'"All for one and –"'

The ship's bell sounded again, much nearer this time. Ahead of us I could make out the hull of *Tweed*, lamps blazing in the night. Sails reached up from her decks to the sky, vanished into the fog. The bell sounded again, a constant rhythm. She was already moving away from the jetty.

'"– one for all and –"'

The Doctor ran for the edge of the jetty. There was a moment of calm as he leapt into the air. He was mad. A web-tree spinner could not leap as high as the deck of *Tweed* even if it could cover the distance between the jetty and the ship.

'– all that – *ooofff!'*

The moment ended with an agonising thump as we smashed against the side of the ship. I waited to fall into the water. A moment passed. We did not fall. I looked up. A rope dangled off the stern of the ship. The Doctor was clinging to it with one hand, his feet fighting for purchase on the smooth wooden planking of the hull. The water beat against the hull twice a man's height below us. The deck rail was half that distance again above my head.

I craned my neck to look back at a familiar sound.

The cocking of a pistol.

The red-haired man was smiling at me from the docks. One pistol was aimed at the Doctor, the other at me.

The Doctor couldn't climb with one hand. If we fell we would probably drown.

I stared at the pistols.

'Thank you,' I told the Doctor, 'for trying.'

The moment stretched out.

Then I heard the sound of whistles and running feet. A loud voice cried. 'Oi! You with the pistol! Put it down at once! This is the police! Fire one more shot and we'll skin you alive!'

The red-haired man caught my eye and dived into the water amid a volley of pistol fire. I saw him swimming strongly away from the dock, bullets peppering the water all around him. I thought I heard a yell of pain, then the fog closed in, hiding everything from view.

The Doctor said, 'You're welcome. Do you think you can hold

on to this rope while I climb up and pull you aboard?'

I grabbed the rope with my good hand. A moment later I was being hoisted over the stern rail.

'Where is Stockwood? Why did he not try to help us?' I was angry. And my arm hung uselessly at my side, the skin running with blood. I was in severe pain and I wanted to kill something – anything – very badly.

The Doctor said quietly. 'I think you'll find they didn't have any choice.' I looked up from the deck – to face Stockwood and Royston, both being held at gunpoint by a cloaked figure, flanked by several seamen.

'It seems very much,' the Doctor said, 'as if our nemesis has beaten us to the ship.

'And hijacked it.'

Part Two
Across the Sea of Night

December 1872

'I approached that island in my fancy from every possible direction; but in all my fancies nothing occurred to me so strange and tragic as our actual adventures.'

Robert Louis Stevenson,
Treasure Island

15
Vortex

I first experienced the power of the *Xaust* wind when I was eight summers old. I remember how it moved through the jungle, disturbing the web-tree spinners in their high nests, pushing between branches and undergrowth, unrolling the ground in thin strips of earth and leaves and small animals.

I had been practising with father's crossbow near the edge of the village, the common land between the furthest huts and bordering the nearest edge of the Beyond. Now I dropped the weapon, laughing and clapping, jumping into the air and clutching at the whirling stuff, feeling the prickle of webs brushing against my hands and face, the spindly jab of wriggling spinner limbs. Then I saw a medium-sized webspinner whirl up into the sky trailing webstuff and the unravelling skin of a bark-skipper which it had caught only moments before and was in the process of disembowelling.

I remember being amazed that such a vast change could happen so quickly. It was as if the world had changed for my amusement.

At first the *Xaust* wind was gentle. It played with me, whirling branches and the lighter web-tree spinners into the air, peeling them away from the jungle like pollen, a gossamer rain that fell upwards into the darkening sky. The loose webs caught the darkening sun, casting a red rainbow across the black hills surrounding the village. The air darkened even further with the tiny wriggling specks that were the spinners.

The world turned red and black in moments.

Then the wind took one of the children I had been practising with. Sooly was smaller than I was, one of the smallest children in the village for his age. I watched him go into the air, wrapped in webstuff so that he looked like a seed trailing its wind-catchers. I grabbed for his foot as he passed, clutched nothing but web, fell back as the wind grew around me.

I called out a warning to the other children. It was then that I realised the wind was louder than my voice, louder than I could shout. And its fingers, which only moments before had been playfully tugging at the ground, were now ripping large chunks of undergrowth into the air along with the walls and roofs of the nearby huts. A branch tore loose from the ground beside me and snapped upward. I fell aside, blood streaming from a leg scraped raw by its passing. The blood was caught up in the wind and whirled skyward. I fought to get closer to the ground, grabbing handfuls of dirt that crumbled between my fingers and was sucked away, trying to pull myself further down into the ground, trying to burrow into the ground the way the bark-skippers burrowed into trees.

I was big for my age, and heavy. Our family had eaten well because we were good hunters. And I was very strong. But there was nothing I could hold on to. The summer had been long this year, the ground was parched, the undergrowth stringy and easily broken.

Everything went up into the steadily darkening sky.

And then so did I.

It happened suddenly. One moment I was clinging to the ground, the next moment the ground had gone out from under me and I was holding nothing but crumbling dirt. In seconds even that was gone. I had a brief sensation of movement. I got dizzy and tried not to be sick. I stopped screaming when the air was sucked out of my lungs and I could no longer breathe. I struggled, kicking out against the sky that had eaten me, but struck nothing. Clinging folds of webstuff wrapped around me.

Wriggling spinners scrabbled through the web, crawling over me and biting me in the red-hazed darkness. My eyes were already shut. I felt the sting of poison run in my blood. I was hot and cold at once. My eyes pressed against the inside of my eyelids. I opened my mouth to scream for Father and a web-tree spinner crawled in and bit my tongue.

That spinner saved my life.

The inside of my cheek already swelling from the poison, my jaws clamped shut on the spinner, crushing it instantly. I felt sticky juices in my mouth. I was frantically tearing at the webstuff sealing my face when the poison made me go to sleep and darkness took me away.

I awoke in agony, hours later, I supposed. Something hard and jagged pressed into my back told me I was on the ground. I couldn't move. Or rather I couldn't control my body, which was jerking as the web-tree spinner's poison ran in my blood. Then I felt sudden coldness grip me. My body jerked upward, as panic set in. Cryuni. Cryuni had come for me!

I was not ready for the Sleep of Death. I remember screaming. I remember coughing up chunks of mashed web-tree spinner. I remember the crack of muscles only eight summers old as my arms and legs split the clinging webstuff around me. I remember the searing flush of poison, the agony as sunlight sought out my eyes like a hunter's blade and sank what felt like slivers of holy metal into my head.

And then I was
crying
screaming
breathing.

And darkness took me away again.

The next time I awoke I did not hurt so much. But I was very cold and very hungry. I was frightened to open my eyes so I felt around me with my arms and legs. I hurt wherever I touched the ground. My skin was sore and my chest hurt and my arm tingled strangely. I felt smashed branches, dusty webstuff, crushed animal bodies, jagged pieces of wood and stone.

That was all.

I opened my eyes.

Blinking away tears, I looked around me. I was lying head downward in a depression in the ground. A ruined landscape surrounded me, upside down. I tried to move. I managed to roll over on to my stomach. I was shaking. I tried to stand up, but wasn't strong enough. The sun, above me now, where it should be, was the same hot summer sun it had been – how long ago? Maybe a whole day. I didn't know and couldn't judge.

I grabbed the first thing I found that was solid enough to support me and pulled myself upright. I was in the jungle. Or, rather, I was where the jungle should have been.

The world had changed.

My life so far had been very well defined. The village was in the valley, the common land bordered the Beyond and the jungle surrounded everything. Beyond the jungle was the Black Wall and beyond that the Place of Tesh. Now most of the trees were gone. The landscape seemed to be made entirely of the smashed ruins of the very largest trees. I was clinging to the stump of one of these. I had struggled out of a deep bed of webstuff and dead animals. At the very limits of my shattered world was the endless Black Wall of the Tesh. My eyes couldn't look away from it. Light sank into it. It was nothing and everything.

I sank to my knees. I would never have looked away from the Wall if my head had not simply sunk downward through sheer exhaustion.

All around me not a living thing was moving. No people. No animals. Not even a web-tree spinner or bark-skipper.

Just me.

170

I fell against the tree, and even it was dead. I wanted to sleep. I think I cried out for Cryuni to take me but even the Guardian of the Sleep of Death ignored me. I wanted to sleep. I was too hungry. My belly ached and my back and my skin were covered in sores from the poisonous spinner bites.

I probably should have died then. But as I sank down into the soft bed of web my hand touched the furry body of a bark-skipper.

I had just enough strength to grasp the legs, tearing the body along its vulnerable underbelly. The meat was raw and tasted foul but I did not care. I ate until I was sick, then ate another. This one stayed down and I slept.

When I awoke I felt better. My head did not ache, my skin was not so sore, although my arm had swollen considerably, and I realised it must be if not broken, then badly sprained.

I stood, picking bark-skipper fur from my teeth, and began to walk back to the village.

I did not know where the village was, so I simply walked in the opposite direction to the Black Wall.

I walked for three days, eating dead animals and drinking their body fluids. Then it rained and the ground turned to slush. I drank rainwater and continued walking. When the water turned to flood I clung to a log and drifted with the current. A day later the floodwater was gone and I walked again, this time through mud. Finding food was harder now, but I managed it somehow, digging into the bark of trees for insects, ignoring the dead animals beached all around me. Their flesh was rank, the stench foul.

On the fifth day, I saw the mud in the middle distance explode outwards, splashed aside by invisible feet. As I watched, a tree stump was wrenched from the mud and held invisibly in midair, turned, examined, tossed carelessly aside. I crouched in the mud, just my nose and eyes showing, and watched the trail made by the Things from the Beyond pass within a man's height from me before moving away towards the Black Wall.

Touching my neck, left hip and left knee as I had been taught, I clambered from the mud and moved on.

Two days later I found some men and women from the village. They told me that the Black Wall had opened for a moment, long enough to emit the *Xaust* wind, which had destroyed a large portion of the jungle. They told me this was something that happened infrequently, about once in every generation. Nobody knew why, but some thought it was to keep the jungle clear of the Black Wall.

Eight days after the *Xaust* wind took me I was back with my parents and helping to rebuild the village in a new location several days, travel towards sunset.

The first thing my father did when he saw me was hug me. The second thing he did was cuff me around the face for losing his crossbow.

16
Landfall

I had not envisaged our arrival at Rapa Nui to be the most joyful of occasions. In truth it was a frightening thought to me. I would be going back to the past. I knew it would bring back pain – the pain of my abandonment of Alexander Richards – but I did not expect that it would also bring the pain of abandoning Leela and James Royston to the merciless clutches of the Pacific Ocean.

I stood at the bowsprit and watched the island glide closer to us across the water. At least, that was the illusion. The twist of rock and scattered vegetation curled up from the water towards a perfect sky. Cliffs. Waves. Bay. Nothing, it seemed, had changed in the three decades since I had last been here.

I found myself scanning the rocky skyline for indications of movement. Movement by objects that could not possibly move. I remembered that night so clearly. It had haunted my dreams and waking thoughts for thirty years, and it had not faded. I remembered the *rongo-rongo*. The chase. Seeing Tortorro succumb to madness and the stone *moai* walking. Now there was nothing. No sound to break the voice of waves and gulls, and no movement. Not even the movement of curious islanders watching us drop anchor in Anakena Bay.

I sensed a presence beside me at the cathead. Richards. Not the man I had abandoned. His sister. My nemesis. It was by no means the first time I had seen her on the voyage, but it was the first time she had deigned to engage me in conversation.

'A homecoming.' Her voice was quiet but emotion ran in deep currents within it.

'Hardly.' I did not want to speak to her. She stirred too many feelings within me I would rather have forgotten.

'Such a desolate rock, alone in all this wilderness of water. So silent and remote. Surely you feel something. I do and I have never been here before.'

She wanted the truth? Very well, she could have it. 'I feel... afraid.'

Her voice hardened. 'Imagine how my brother felt when you left him here.'

'That has been my cross to bear for three decades.'

'It's not enough!' A moment, then her temper passed, though her anger did not. 'Not nearly enough.'

She was right. A lifetime would not be enough to assuage the guilt I felt. It *hadn't* been.

I felt the ship rock beneath me as waves made shallow by reefs slapped against her storm-damaged hull. Richards moved aside to allow the men to take depth soundings as *Tweed* eased into the bay. I caught a glimpse of her face beneath the hood she wore with her cloak. Her face, lean and tanned by our passage, was expressionless.

'I remember your report to the Geographical Society. I have the last remaining transcript. It has been bedside reading for me for thirty years. I remember how you described that islander – Tortorro – I remember how you described his death. Speaking in tongues. Convulsing in madness on the ground, at the touch, no doubt, of some native poison administered by blowpipe in the darkness. I remember your fanciful stories of thirty-ton statues walking the length and breadth of the island. Of them chasing you.' I did not need to look to see her face twist with contempt. 'There's one part I shall never forget. The part where you describe my brother, Alexander, as your best friend, almost in the same breath as you describe abandoning him to his fate. The same fate as Tortorro. Do you remember that part, Horace?'

In truth I remembered every word of my report. 'If you seek to hurt me, you are wasting your time. Nothing can be as painful to me as the guilt I have suffered. Every night for the last thirty years I have lain awake, racked by dreams of him. I have cried out his name in the night. I have awoken sobbing and close to madness. I have driven more than twenty household staff from me in my guilt and madness.'

Now Richards turned on me, pulling back her hood to better view the man who had shaped her adult life. 'If you seek my sympathy *you* are wasting *your* time. My brother is dead. If it were not for the Doctor and his friendship with Captain Stuart you would be dead also. As it is, I live only to see your face at his grave, to see your madness grow and consume you. And then to kill you, if I can. I desire your death, Horace Stockwood, I desire it as some desire perfume or sweet appointments or love or life itself! Think on that as you conduct your studies and catalogue your artefacts. And think on this also: my time is *now*. Your time is done.' She turned then, went below decks and left me to my memories.

I did not move. I wondered, instead, if the similarities I perceived between us were the result of a madness in myself I could not judge. We had suffered together, for the same length of time and for the same reason. I agreed with her. I deserved every punishment she could heap upon me.

While I was wallowing in self-pity, the men dropped anchor and lowered the last remaining boat into the water. Captain Stuart invited me aboard. Ten minutes later the men jumped with a splash into the waves, dragged the boat up through the surf and beached her.

I got off, swaying drunkenly. I had not realised how much I had become used to shipboard life. Now the ground seemed strange – alien to my experience. The rocks and sand were immobile beneath my feet. I found myself swaying to compensate for the motion of a deck that no longer moved beneath me.

'It'll take y'a while t'find your land-legs agin, I'll wager,' Captain Stuart said, his voice confident with experience. 'Take a walk – but be careful. Here.' He offered me a pistol and a bag of powder. 'Don't try to shoot anyone with it. Run into trouble and loose a blast into the air. We'll hear it anywhere on the island.'

'I wish you'd had this much care in Portsmouth,' I said coldly, thereafter ignoring Stuart. But I took the pistol.

I moved across the beach, my feet growing used to the rocks, the clumps of sand between them. The bay spread out in a semicircle around us, encompassing perhaps two hundred degrees of arc. The cliffs sloped steeply upward from the beach. The cliffs were powdered with guano, reinforcing my first impression of thirty years ago that standing here was like standing at the bottom of a broken china cup some thousand yards from shoulder to shoulder. I shivered when I remembered that thought. Alexander had remarked that if Anakena was a cup then we should drink deeply from its archaeological and anthropological riches. I had agreed. A month later he was dead and I had begun another voyage – a life-changing one.

I moved up the beach, set my feet upon the rocky trail leading high up the cliffs and began to climb. A quarter of an hour passed before I stood at the summit. A line of four *moai* topped a nearby bluff, rough stone shadowed by high sun, weathered features dripping black shadows along mossy flanks. A fifth stone face ended the line with a cap of red stone perched upon its brow, some two storeys height from the ground. I looked at the monolithic faces and shivered, though the sun was cooled by only a hint of cloud shadow. Unable to bear what, to me, were accusing gazes, I turned away.

Rapa Nui lay spread out before me to the south, east and west, a green-brown lump of volcanic rock and scrub and bog. Rano Kao rose at the far end of the island, some eight miles to the south-west. The crater – largest on the island – blocked sight of jagged Motunui, the Bird Men's Island, further off the south-west point of the island. Ranu Raraku, home to many *moai,* lay four miles to the south-east. I remembered the moon shining down on the statues there, as Tortorro had succumbed to the inexplicable madness that had resulted in his death. Would the islanders remember me when they finally came out of hiding to greet us? I was thirty years older. The chances were most of the ones who were alive at the time of my previous expedition were now dead. I remembered Tortorro – his cheerful smile, his unflagging attempts to steal trinkets from us as gifts for his wife and son. I remembered how he had begged for – No. I put the memories aside. I did not want them. They were unwelcome visitors in a present that was torment enough already.

They – and another.

I turned at the sound of boots upon the trail from the beach and was in time to see the Doctor whirling his prodigious scarf as he strode over the ridge that marked the edge of the cliff. He cut a strange figure in his long coat, hat, and whirling scarf, framed by the sky and the sea. In this place of stark extremes he seemed to me both out of place and – curiously – perfectly at home. Beyond him the bay stretched out, a calm, cerulean plane speckled with reef shadows, cupped hands of stone holding *Tweed* in a sun-dappled puddle as if the seventeen-hundred-ton ship was nothing more than an intricate model.

Politely tipping his hat, the Doctor strode lightly on up the trail. He stopped beside the nearest *moai.* The great stone head dwarfed even the Doctor's lanky frame. As I watched, he immediately set about using his scarf to measure the circumference and shadow length of the stone head.

Unable to resist his unorthodox scientific methods, I walked slowly to join him. He did not look up, though I am sure he knew that I approached. Perhaps his behaviour was deliberate, designed to provoke my interest. I wondered why. If it were anyone else I would have assumed sympathy. Not the Doctor. That explanation seemed at once too simple and too complex. Simple because I knew the Doctor was a man of enormous intelligence and great capability but complex because, for all his worldly knowledge, he seemed at heart to embody the innocence of a child.

The Doctor had now rewrapped his scarf around his neck and pulled a black box from his pocket. The box was covered in knobs and dials, resembling the controls of an engine, only much, much smaller. I marvelled at the ingenuity that could construct such a device even as I wondered what on Earth its function could be.

'It's a molecular analyser.' The Doctor seemed to know I was going to ask the question.

'What does it analyse?'

'Oh, you know… anything.' he shrugged. 'Well – anything formed from molecules.' The Doctor waved the device at the *moai*. It bleeped and some of the lights flashed before he seemed ready to give any further amplification of his potentially revelatory statement.

'You have heard of the periodic table, I presume?' I waited for him to explain what he meant. 'Just out this year. All sorts of scientific revelations tied up with it, I understand.'

'It's been a long time since I walked in scientific circles, Doctor.'

'My dear fellow, anyone who claims to be a scientist and who hasn't heard of the periodic table is not so much walking as crawling – rather rapidly back into the Dark Ages.' I tried to keep my temper in check. This was after all the man who had financed the expedition.

The Doctor studied the flashing lights on his box for a moment, then switched the device off and jammed it back into his pocket. From another pocket he pulled a half-eaten apple. 'Care to join me in a spot of lunch, old fellow?' He noticed the apple core and threw it away. 'So sorry.' Trying another pocket he produced a flask and two china mugs. An expansive gesture reiterated the invitation.

Uncapping the flask he poured liquid into one of the mugs. I sniffed. 'Mushroom soup.'

'Mushroom and asparagus soup to be precise. Very nourishing. Lots of protein and very little fat.'

'And all made of *molecules*.' The Doctor refused to take my hint so I took the proffered mug and sipped instead. The Doctor replaced the flask and unused mug in his pocket. 'What were you doing with the machine? Your analyser.'

'Examining the *moai*. There are certain silicon-based life forms at large in the galaxy which fit your description of the walking stones and I wanted to make sure we were not dealing with something like that here. The Ogri insinuate themselves into primitive cultures, quite often masquerading as sacrificial stones. They don't move very quickly, you see. And they feed on human blood. Protective camouflage. Darwin was right, you see, and not just about this planet.'

I stared at the Doctor, soup momentarily forgotten, trying to fathom his words. Silicon life? Masquerading as stones? Protective camouflage? I added this to his earlier conversation and began to wonder – not for the first time – if he was quite sane. I finished my soup and handed back the mug. The Doctor cleaned it with a handful of sand and thrust it carelessly back into his pocket.

'But these stones are not Ogri. No, they're much more peculiar.'

I nodded. 'They walked. They hunted me.'

The Doctor adjusted his hat. 'Well, I don't know about walked, but they do have one very interesting property.'

'And what's that?'

'Their mass isn't constant. It's fluctuating.'

'That's impossible. Doctor, if you feel the need to poke fun I would be grateful if you wasted someone else's time.'

'My dear chap, every mass alters with time. The simple conversion of matter to energy which is the basic tenet of existence of everything in the universe ensures that. Everything from stars and galaxies to chickens and politicians follows the same rules. No exceptions.' He hesitated. 'Though of course some politicians might not entirely agree.'

'What exactly do you mean when you say "fluctuating", then?'

'Well, I should have thought it was quite obvious. I mean changing. Altering. Fluctuating. And if the mass of a thing is changing, then so is its energy state.'

'So the *moai* are giving off energy.'

'Or absorbing it. Or transmuting it. Or transferring it. Or any combination of.'

'But why?'

The Doctor fixed me with a perfect smile. 'My dear chap, that's the wonder of the universe, isn't it? To seek the answer to the fundamental question of everything.'

'You mean you don't know.'

'No. I don't.' The grin broadened. 'But I intend to find out.'

'With a scarf and a stage prop?'

'Eratosthenes worked out the curvature of the earth with a few sticks and some string.'

'Eratosthenes was a genius.'

'And who do you think taught him what he knew?'

I frowned. 'Surely you do not suggest that *you* taught *Eratosthenes* his craft?'

'Well, I can't claim all the credit. The Greeks were fairly intelligent chaps on the whole. Not particularly *open-minded*, mind you – look at the peremptory way in which they ejected me from the staff at the library of Alexandria – but, as I say, on the whole, largely intelligent. Wrote jolly good plays as well, as I recall.' He frowned. 'Wouldn't let me borrow any though. Suppose they didn't trust me after I misshelved the Dead Sea Scrolls. Oh well. Can't have everything in life, can we? Oh dear, that reminds me.' He suddenly took a fob watch from his jacket pocket and worriedly checked the time. 'Young Ptolemy's *Treatise on the Structure, Position and Medicinal Nature of Celestial Bodies*. It's two thousand and ninety-three years and four months overdue. I hate to think how much the fine will be.'

I tried to work out whether the Doctor required a response to his ramblings. I confess I found it hard to accept the fellow's sudden, radical changes of mood. I needed to focus on something. Something in the here and now. Something that didn't seem like the rantings of Verne or Poe or, worse, someone taking me for a gullible fool. I turned away from the Doctor, placing my hand flat against the *moai* which he had been examining. I looked at my hand. Stared at it, studied every mark and fold. Old, wrinkled skin, mottled with liver spots, the hairs turning grey even at my wrists. The last time I had touched stone like this the flesh had been smooth and muscular, a scientist's hands, an artist's: the hands of one who sculpted knowledge to show the truth. I think I may have suffered a minor revelation then. For the first time I found myself seriously considering the possibility that I had returned here to find not absolution but resolution. A final resolution. I wondered if I had returned to Rapa Nui to die.

I felt the Doctor beside me again. He moved quietly and quickly. His presence was… I couldn't find the right word for it. He seemed to fill the space wherever he was. My drawing room. A cabin on board ship. There was a lot of space out here on the cliff top but his presence seemed to fill it effortlessly.

I showed him my hands. 'How much blood is on these hands now? How many more deaths will occur because of my obsession?'

The Doctor tipped back his hat and looked upward. He seemed to be studying the sky. '*Quem di diligunt adulescens moritur.*'

The Doctor's glib quotation annoyed me. He had not left a friend to die on this island. 'Plautus, "He whom the gods favour dies young." You want to comfort me. I know it is well meant, but your gold is all I ever needed from you, Doctor. You can keep your absolution.'

'They're not dead, you know.' His voice was quiet. I knew he was referring to Leela and James, and that angered me further.

'How can they not be? You saw the seas! It has been a month or more. They had neither food, fresh water nor boat. They are dead, Doctor, both my friend and yours. And for that I am sorry. Leela had a good heart.'

'Her heart still beats.'

'How can you know that?'

'Because where Leela comes from the gods are real. And they do *not* favour her.' The Doctor hesitated. I sensed his words were as much a comfort to himself as me. If the ship's boats had not been so severely damaged during the cyclone he would surely have taken one and returned to find our companions. As it was he had spent almost two whole days petitioning the Captain to put about and search for them. I feel sure he would have led the crew to mutiny if there had been the remotest chance it would have succeeded, in order to rescue Leela and James. Now doubt showed on his face. I recognised it there because it was so like my own. 'She will live to be old and wise as you, Horace, if Plautus knew anything about anything. And if she is alive, you can bet James Royston is as well.'

'Do not offer me hope. I will not believe in it. I cannot believe in it.'

'"Hope is a good breakfast." Francis Bacon said that. Quite appropriate when you think about it.'

The image of someone named Bacon quoting hope as a breakfast was amusing. 'True enough Doctor. "A good breakfast – but a bad supper."'

The Doctor scowled. 'Quotes are tools, Horace. You don't have to get pedantic about them.'

'You are worried about Leela. And you use things to your own ends. Are you using me?'

Avoiding my question, the Doctor countered with one of his own. 'Do you know the Earth is my favourite planet in the whole galaxy and I've never been to Easter Island before?'

'Never?'

'Never. And I'm told that everyone should have at least one sea voyage in their armoury of experience.'

'Indeed.'

'Well, Columbus thought so and if ever there was a man whose judgement we should respect, young Christopher was he, don't you think?' I was on the point of observing Columbus to be a braggart and a scoundrel and nearly four centuries dead to boot, when the Doctor turned away from the *moai* with a characteristically abrupt movement. 'Shouldn't there be natives scurrying about and trying to steal things from us?'

On that matter at least, he was right. 'That is what happened the last time I was here.'

The Doctor began to walk inland, heading roughly south-east. Did he know Ranu Raraku lay in that direction? Was he deliberately trying to stir my memories?

'Why don't you tell me about your last expedition?'

I was right.'You know the end of it.'

'Then tell me the beginning.Tell me everything.'

'Everything?'

'Yes. Everything.'

I hesitated. I did not want to remember. Something about the Doctor's voice brought those first moments back to me. I had thought I remembered everything. How wrong I was. For now every last detail came back. I could recall with frightening clarity everything about the arrival at Rapa Nui of the Stockwood–Richards expedition.

'No one really knows the name of this island.The natives call it Rapa Nui. In their legend it is called *Te Pito o te Henua*, the Navel of the World. Even that may be more strictly poetry than a real description. Other names have included the Frontier of Heaven or the Eye Which Sees Heaven.The name Easter Island derives from its discovery by the Dutchman Roggeveen, on the afternoon of Easter Day in 1722.' I paused for a moment and we walked in silence over the tufted grass and hills of volcanic rock.The wind tumbled sand and grass seeds around us.A gull cried out from a great height above.

'I remember how quiet it was,' I continued at length. 'Even the gentle slap of waves and creak of timbers on the ship made the silence all the more perfect. It was night when we hove to. Heaven itself was our companion, the stars at our masthead whirling in eternal blackness above us. If not for that movement I should have thought time itself had come to a halt and we were beached on the shores of eternity, not some rocky knoll in mid-Pacific.

'Of the island we could see little in the starlight. Our

approach had been from the west so our first glimpse as the sun set behind us had been of a brazen shore, a jagged skyline broken by black dots that were the *moai* ranged along the island. Not a soul could I see anywhere on shore. The only movement was from the waves themselves, breaking against a line of lava blocks which formed the shore, as the setting sun drew night down around us like a cloak.'

The Doctor nodded. '"It was as though we had anchored with a hovering space-ship off the shore of an extinct world." Thor Heyerdahl wrote that a hundred years from now. The magic does not fade.'

I nodded, surprised at the depth of the Doctor's understanding. His image was perfect, even if his source was scarcely believable.

'Strictly speaking we should have announced our arrival. We thought it better to wait until morning. An arrival such as ours would herald one of the greatest moments of the year for the islanders. We did not want to disturb anyone at such an inconvenient time. We anchored under the lee of the cliffs and the next morning sailed around the island until we spotted a likely landing place in Anakena Bay.

'We were greeted almost before the anchor fell. Hordes of brown-skinned islanders swam out to meet the ship, swarming over the sides with more enthusiasm than sense, we felt. They wore little clothing, their bodies small and wiry. Their bodies were smothered with tattoos, principally of birds and strange figures which seemed to represent flying men. Some of their ears were... deformed, stretched by weights and by being fixed with thread to their shoulders until their length was prodigious. These people were lighter-skinned than the rest. Many had flame-red hair. All of them talked incessantly. Jabbered would be a more appropriate word. A Polynesian we had aboard translated for us. They were offering us things in trade: little wooden sculptures, bands and necklaces made of volcanic glass tied with dried grasses, trinkets of that nature. And every one of them was a thief of the most cunning skill I have yet laid eyes on. One man more persistent than the rest was shot and wounded before we realised what was happening. They gave back everything they had taken when we asked, only to steal it again at the first opportunity. One man of the crew had his pipe stolen and recovered no fewer than five times. It became a kind of game.

'We were greeted in person by the Mayor. We knew him to be such because he wore a cloak of bark cloth and what skin was visible was tattooed in a continuous pattern of birds and strange figures. He wore a crown of feathers on his head. His ears had been lengthened until the lobes hung about his shoulders. He wore pegs in them. Later we saw these pegs used to hold up the lobes as the islanders went about their daily work.

'The Mayor described the island as his personal possession. We did not choose to disabuse him of this fact. We asked for permission to explore the island and study the artefacts here. He granted permission at the exorbitant price of a bolt of cloth, two pouches of tobacco, and all the trade goods we could muster for bargaining per day. The Mayor introduced us to Tortorro, the islander who was to become my guide and friend over the next month.' I paused for a moment, lost in painful memories, then continued. 'A man I was to betray and whose death at the hands of his fellow villagers was my responsibility alone.

'Tortorro was a stout fellow. Small, brown as a nut, he was possessed, as were many of the islanders, of startling red hair. His fingers were nimble, his smile ready and his wife beautiful. He himself was as ugly as sin. I shall never know what a woman of such uncommon loveliness saw in him.'

'Perhaps he was a good provider.'

'Undoubtedly, judging by his skills as a thief.' I paused, not wanting to remember more, but unable now to halt the flow of words, memories. 'It was this skill which ultimately proved such a tragic misfortune. We had been on the island for a fortnight Richards and myself studying the island culture, Captain Farmer, First Mate Keable and the rest of the crew taking advantage of the famed Polynesian hospitality. The village in which we were made welcome consisted of a number of long, low, reed huts resembling upturned boats, carpeted with grass and containing no furniture save a stone which served as a pillow. The huts had no windows, and doors so low that it was a trial to gain entrance. Crops included bananas, sugar cane and sweet potatoes. The only animals on the island were fowl and a scattering of wild goats.

'It was as we turned our attention to the stone monoliths, the *moai,* that Tortorro's child grew ill with a fever. We learnt that many of the island's children had died from such a fever. Tortorro was heartstruck. He loved that child like no other I have seen. He promised me anything if I could use the white man's magic to help his son. I took the child to the ship's doctor and the man produced a remedy within hours. Without it, the child would surely have died. Tortorro was ecstatic. The villagers held a feast in our honour. During the feast I took Tortorro aside and began the sequence of events which was to end in such tragedy.

'I wanted to gain access to certain caves on the Bird Men's Island, a short journey by canoe off the southernmost point of Rapa Nui. I had heard talk of certain religious artefacts hidden in caves there. Ancient tablets with writing inscribed on their surfaces. Writing which might give clues as to the spread of the red-haired people through this part of the world. Clues which might ultimately determine the origin of the people living on this little island in the middle of nowhere. The first step in what I fully expected to be an impressive career.

'Of course Tortorro refused my request. The caves were holy. Transgression was punishable by madness and death, the method unspecific. I dismissed this as old wives' tales and insisted. After all, I had saved his son's life. At length, and with uncharacteristically bad grace, Tortorro relented. I persuaded Richards to come with us, to keep lookout for others. All I wanted to do was observe, perhaps sketch some of the glyphs I knew would be present on artefacts in the cave. I swear I wanted no more than that! But... when we were there... the sight of the tablets... the legacy they held... I'm afraid my scientific ambition got the better of me. I took one. I held it in my hands. The touch of it; the wood, so old, so intricately carved, it possessed me. It was lovely. It was more than lovely.

'And then they found us. The priests had missed us at the feast and come looking for their guests of honour. And where did they find us? Pillaging their holiest inner sanctum, a place no one outside the island culture had ever seen and which even the islanders themselves seldom visited.

'I ran. I feared their reprisals. I feared Tortorro was right and that I had brought madness and death upon us all. But I could not leave the *rongo-rongo*. That tablet of wood from ages past held me enthralled, mesmerised as though by a stage hypnotist. I took it and I ran. I dived into the ocean. I left Richards when he fell, I left Tortorro, I left them both to their fate at the hands of their fellow islanders.

'The rest you know. I have no explanation for the walking stones. I was quite mad with fear by then. At the time I considered myself lucky to escape with my life. Now... I wish I had died there. Or that I had never seen the wretched tablet. Or that Tortorro's son had died from the fever. Anything. Anything at all, rather than endure again the nightmare my life has become since that night.'

By the time I finished speaking the afternoon had drawn in around us, the sun moving across the sky to paint the island in shades of red ochre and grey. I looked around, realising our perambulations had brought us to Ranu Raraku, the crater in which I had seen Tortorro succumb to madness, and in which I had left Alexander to die.

I felt my gaze drawn to the many great *moai* scattered around the crater. Hewn from the native rock by the islanders over many generations, the statues stood or lay in disarray around us. Their abandonment was a terrible irony: to erect such vast tonnages of rock required wood for scaffolds, levers, rollers. Wood meant tree trunks. Over the generations, the islanders had denuded their land in order to situate the *moai*. With the trees gone the topsoil had begun to surrender to the wind. Now food was scarce and grazing was next to impossible. The islanders had sacrificed everything to whatever vision drove them to build these vast monoliths. But why?

I was on the point of asking the Doctor for his opinion when a sound like thunder rolled across the island. 'A storm?'

The Doctor looked up at the clear sky. 'That was no storm. That was cannon fire.'

I felt a surge of fear. '*Tweed* has no cannon.'

'I know. Come on.'

We turned and ran. The Doctor surged ahead. I struggled to keep up. I arrived some while later at the top of the cliffs overlooking Anakena Bay to see a new arrival there. Another ship. 'That's the Peruvian flag.'

'I know.' The Doctor drew me down among the scrubby grasses.

Cannon boomed again. Smoke blossomed on the Peruvian ship, halving the distance between itself and *Tweed* in seconds.

Water burst from the sea off the stern of the ship.

'They fired on the ship! Are they pirates?'

'I think it's worse than that, Horace.' The fury in the Doctor's voice was matched – even surpassed – by his expression. 'I think they're slavers.'

As we watched, another six vessels tacked about the point of the bay. All ran the Peruvian flag. All ran with cannon in the firing position. *Tweed* and everyone on her was trapped.

As I watched, *Tweed* ran up a white flag. Stuart, sensibly enough, had chosen to surrender rather than be sunk.

I hunched closer to the Doctor. 'If there are seven ships and they were anchored on the other side of the island, then that could mean –'

I stopped as harsh voices carried to us on the breeze. I risked a peek above the rocks of our makeshift hideout. Twenty Peruvian sailors were ambling across the rocks towards us. Though each was his own man, still they had several characteristics in common. For one they were weathered by a life at sea. Their skins were dark, bearded faces stained by the weather; their bodies contained no ounce of fat and their manner was that of assumed mastery of all they could kill or otherwise take for their own. Their clothing was rough and badly mismatched, with clashing colours and tarnished buckles. Shoulder harnesses held many pistols and bags of shot and powder, and each had a cutlass swinging arrogantly at the hip. All were shouting and laughing. Many held flasks of wine from which they drank, tossing the empty bottles aside to smash upon the rocks.

One of the men suddenly leapt into the air and loosed a barrage of pistol shots by way of warning. A second later he and three other sailors fell to the ground with throwing knives buried in their backs. The knife blades were black, the grips bound tightly with cloth. Obsidian. The islanders had finally shown themselves. They attacked as I watched, a group of thirty or more, charging across the rocks and screaming at the tops of their lungs.

I could see that carnage was about to take place. The Doctor put his hand on my shoulder. 'Stay here. If you get the chance, slip over the cliff, try to find a cave. This place should be riddled with them.' Before I could answer he stood up. He intended to stop the fighting, but how I did not know. There were forty men of two nationalities, and each side bent upon killing as many as they could of the other.

'I say, is this a private altercation or can anyone join in?' The Doctor's words were spoken jovially enough. He was simply ignored.

The fight had become bloody. The sailors took no more casualties. But of the islanders at least half were murdered, shot down in their tracks by the sailors. The Peruvians laughed as they killed. It was entertainment for them. Before too long had passed the remaining islanders were disarmed and herded together as captives.

The Doctor strode forward, hands raised, for another attempt at defusing the situation. 'Gentlemen. I see we have a communications problem here. Perhaps I can be of some help in facilitating –'

He got no further. One of the sailors turned and shot him down without a thought, before returning his attention gleefully to his new acquisitions, the captured islanders.

17
Dead City

Someone slapped me awake. I jerked into a sitting position, hand reaching for my dagger. It was not until the one who had touched me was on his back on the ground with my blade at his throat that I realised it was Stockwood. I mumbled something and put away my blade.

'I thought we were best friends,' he muttered, rubbing his neck.

I stood up and pulled him to his feet.

'You were unconscious, delirious – something about a childhood trauma. I thought you were going to die.'

I looked at Stockwood. He seemed exhausted.

'How long did I…?'

He smiled. 'Cryuni did not come for your soul. I watched you. You were just asleep.'

Beside us on the ground lay Royston. He was unconscious, as he had been before the sun ate us, but at least his fever had diminished. Had the *moai* healed him as Atani had claimed? Had the great god Vai-tarakai-ua spared his life in response to the prayer from the *rongo-rongo*? I did not know. All I knew was that he was breathing more easily and that now it was daytime, even though only moments before it had been night.

I examined Royston more closely. The wound inflicted by the pirate DaBraisse had opened in his side. More blood had seeped into his clothes, the shirt which the Doctor had used as a bandage. I touched the wound. 'This will need to be closed again.' I wiped away the blood and took the sailor's needle and gut from my pouch. There were a few flying-fish scales in there as well, but they were dried and shrivelled, and they stank. I threw them away.

I stitched the wound and looked around for something clean to cover it with. It was only then that I began to realise we were not on the island.

But where were we?

My first thought was that we were back in London, but a London that had grown old and died, and shrivelled as the dead fish scales had shrivelled. Then I looked again. This was not London. Even if the city had been alive, it would not have been anything like London.

There were many huts, more than I could count. They were tall, wide, round; their bases set close together upon a ground that seemed flat, though I could tell it was faintly curved. The nearest was an arm's length away. I touched it, withdrawing my hand immediately when I realised it was metal. All of the huts around me were metal. There were so many it was like being in a forest of thin, motionless trees. A mournful wind wound in between the huts, tugging every few moments at my skins. How many people lived here? Perhaps as many as had ever been born in the Land.

'How long has it been since the sun ate us?'

Stockwood looked puzzled. 'I'm not sure. I fell unconscious as well. I got an impression of travelling, of rushing through the darkness. I don't know how far.'

'The huts on the island are not like these.'

'That's true. Perhaps we've been ill. Perhaps a hole in the cave... blinded by sunlight, we could have fallen. Maybe we have been brought by clipper to another island and the others have gone to get help.'

I shook my head. 'This place does not smell like your land.'

'But still, another island...'

'I do not think so. It was night when the sun came out.'

'But –'

'No. The air here is dead. I have been in your land for many nine-days. I have seen many different places. The air did not smell like this anywhere I have been.'

'Well, what do you mean by "dead"?'

'It smells the way a corpse smells, long after it has died. No corruption, no rot. Just dust that was skin and muscle, organs and bone.'

'That's a horrible image.'

'It is the truth.'

Royston groaned. He stirred. For a moment I thought he would awake, but then he subsided into sleep again. Stockwood glanced at his friend. 'Will he live now?'

'I do not know. I am not a shaman. I do not know the healing ways like the Doctor. But he seems better than he was. I expect if he was going to die he would be dead by now.'

'That's hardly reassuring.'

'Then we must find out where we are. And if we can get help for him.' I stood up.

'You're just going to leave him here?'

'I told you, this land is dead. There is nothing here to threaten him.'

I began to walk, moving warily through the forest of metal huts. Each was about as round as the huts in my own village, but they were so tall I could not see the tops of them. But their shadows were strange – shaped almost like faces. I craned my neck upward to see more clearly and was reminded of something I had already seen. These huts were not huts at all – they were giant heads, like the *moai* on the island, only many times larger and made of the holy metal.

As we moved the slope of the ground increased. It was as if we were walking up the inside of a bowl, but one that had been carved by a giant's hand. As the ground increased in steepness, so the angle of the huts changed, too. They began to lie flatter against the ground. Or, rather, they stayed the same, pointing straight up at the sky, while the ground lifted around them. What kind of village was this? There was no common land, no room to farm or graze animals, no soil to grow vegetables, no windows or doors in the huts. I did not understand. I shivered.

'I do not like this place. It is full of death. Old death. We must be very careful.'

Stockwood nodded. Moving past me, he climbed higher up the sloping ground, pulling himself by wedging his feet and hands between the huts. I followed.

Then Stockwood gave a shout. 'My sainted aunt!'

I increased my speed, climbing faster until I could see him a few yards away among the huts.

'Leela, be careful!'

I felt his arm at my waist and thought it was no bad thing. Without that I would have fallen over the edge of the ground. For the huts had come suddenly to an end and with them the curved ground formed into a broad lip and then simply stopped. We were on the outside edge of the bowl – and I realised with some amazement that we were not in a village at all.

The bowl was located high in the air, perhaps at the top of a mountain or large hill. It felt very high, high enough for clouds or fog. There was nothing. Just the sky, stretching out above us, pale, like a pond-skimmer's eggs. Two huge moons and a dark, sullen sun hung there. They were like eyes and a mouth in the sky, a face passing judgement on us. Unsettled, I let my gaze fall towards the ground – and beyond. The mountain we were on was partially concealed by the lip of the ground, like the edge of a perfectly smooth cliff. I crawled carefully towards the edge and peered over. I gasped, I would have fallen if Stockwood had not grasped me again.

Neither of us had words to describe what we saw. For all around us the entire Land I could see that lay at the foot of the mountain was one vast village – a city, like London only much, much larger. I thought it must be at least as big as the entire distance we had travelled from England to Rapa Nui.

There was no sound except the moaning wind. No movement except the slow creep of dust. The huts – buildings – must have been as big as hills themselves, curving up out of the ground like the ribs of a corpse – of an army of corpses. Many of the buildings looked like faces. Giant, stretched faces, with huge noses and deeply shadowed eyes. They too looked like the stone *moai* on the island. Except these were many times taller than trees. Or would have been if there had been any trees here. Many of the buildings had fallen and now lay in tilted ruin between the more intact shapes. The ground rose between the buildings in dunes, crawling slowly at the insistence of the wind. It was as if the dust had smothered the city and was now picking clean its bones.

For everywhere I looked the city was deserted. Ruined.

Dead.

Only the great metal *moai* remained.

'Ranu Raraku,' Stockwood whispered, following the words up with a quiet murmur that even I could not hear. I think it was a prayer. My own thought was more sensible. 'We cannot stay here. We must either return to the island or go to the city.'

'We don't even know how we came here.'

'Then we have no choice. We must go to the city.'

'But how do we get there?' Stockwood's words came between breaths. I realised I was tired with the effort of breathing myself. 'We're so high up.'

I looked around, now gaining some idea of the shape of the place in which I had awoken. It was indeed shaped like a bowl

– a vast, shallow bowl tilted at an angle. And the metal huts stuck straight out from the bowl. They too were at an angle, pointing at a distant quarter of the sky, beyond the looming bulk of the larger moon. I thought about the slope of that angle. I wondered if the ground was lower on the other side. I said as much to Stockwood.

'I don't see any reason why not.'

'Then we must start now. It is a long way to the city.'

Stockwood agreed. We began to climb down through the forest of huts. We moved slowly and carefully. To fall here would be fatal. A broken limb would almost certainly mean abandonment and starvation.

As we moved I thought about Royston. Somehow we had to improvise a way of carrying him. Or one of us had to stay with him until he was able to move. Or we had to leave him here and hope he would be safe until we found help. I did not know how to answer these questions. There was nothing here we could make a stretcher out of and I did not know how long he would take to recover – or even if he would. I decided it would be best to think about these questions when we reached him again. But when we returned to the place where we had left Royston he was gone.

18
The Cave of the White Virgins

After the Doctor was shot I remember thinking that I must go to help him. My mind was willing but my body had ideas of its own. While my mind invented fantasies about sneaking out from cover, grabbing a pistol from one of the fallen pirates and fighting off the rest before freeing the Doctor and the captured islanders, my body was thoroughly occupied crawling as fast as possible into a hole in the cliff face which I had found some yards from our hiding place.

The hole led downward at a sharp angle. It was full of twists and turns. Head, down, I continued to crawl, whipping myself mentally for my cowardice. I did not even know if the Doctor was alive or dead. I had not even waited that long before retreating. Every stone which dug into my back, every breath of dirt reminded me of the man who might even now be lying bleeding on the rocks mere yards away.

I continued to crawl downward. I did not even bother to convince myself there was nothing I could do. That would have been too intellectual an argument. The simple fact was that I was terrified beyond rational thought – and principally for my own life. Later I would feel better about that: at least I had learnt that I had not come to Rapa Nui to die. And even if I had, then I had now changed my mind. The thought of the Doctor lying on the rocks only served to reinforce the preciousness of my own life.

Alexander, James, Leela, now the Doctor. Nothing, I was ashamed to observe, appeared to have changed over the last thirty years.

I stopped at the sound of movement beneath me. An animal? There were none bar goats, pigs and fowl on the island. So who was it crawling up the narrow tunnel to meet me?

Peruvians? Natives?

On my previous expedition I had persuaded Tortorro to show me a portion of the cave system. It was vast, with many caves, some enlarged by the islanders for use in time of war, connected by several miles of volcanic passages created when the island was born. I could not help reflecting that it was like a world in miniature, with cave cities connected by roads of lava tunnels. Like a world, the population would rise and fall, migrating from the surface to the tunnels and back again, with the exception of the young women kept down here to bleach their skins, and for whom the Cave of the White Virgins had been named.

I tried to tip my head upward, to get a better look further down the passage. The task would have been useless even if there had been enough light to see by.

The sounds came closer.

And breathing.

The touch of a knife at my throat brought me to my senses. I tried to back away but the movement was too little too late. My body was frozen, as motionless as my mind was a jagged frieze of memories, locked in a similar passage to that of thirty years before.

And then I realised: I was crawling down a bolt hole. We had seen no islanders because they were hiding from the Peruvian invaders. Now I was invading their retreat, crawling into their network of volcanic tunnels and caves. They thought I was one of the invaders!

I called out at once in the native Polynesian. There was a long moment of silence and then the knife was removed from my throat. The figure, of whom I could discern no details in the passage, retreated quickly from me, inviting me by tugging on my arm to follow.

Soon afterwards I began to see the glimmer of light from further along the passage. A moment later we had emerged into a large cave. A cave that, despite the thirty-year time lapse, I recognised.

The Cave of the White Virgins. My last stop before fleeing the island and leaving Alexander to his fate.

I stood, moaning aloud at cramp in my calves and a sharp pain which dug into my hip. I wondered whether the Peruvians, the islanders, Richards or arthritis would be my undoing the fastest.

I stretched, blinked, wiped dirt from my face and clothes. My hands came away from my face bloody from a number of scratches. I searched for a handkerchief but could not find it. I hesitated then, surprised at the effort it took, wiped my bloody hands on the breast of my jacket. Only then did I look around me.

The cave was lit by three torches. They guttered, sending a pall of smoke into the upper reaches of the cave. I wondered at the smoke, fearing it would find its way to the surface and be spotted by the Peruvians. The islanders did not seem worried, though. Perhaps it exited at a point far from the bay. The cave was full of people. They seemed to represent the same racial mix we had been so surprised by on first arriving here so long ago. Some were short, others tall, in excess of six foot. Some had Polynesian characteristics, others seemed almost European, with pale skin and red hair. The mix of women and men was equal, and there were many children. All were silent, crouching like ghosts in the smoky gloom.

Only one islander moved – the one who had preceded me from the passage. I perceived him to be a short fellow, brown-skinned and black-haired, naked except for what seemed to be an unbroken pattern of tattoos. His ears were of normal length, unlike those of others I could see in the cave. For his part the man was studying me as intently as I studied him – and with better reason, I should think. I represented the alien to his world – and so far the alien had brought only terror and death.

I ventured a few more words. The islanders showed neither surprise nor fear at my clumsy rendition of their language. But the man standing next to me tapped himself on the chest and uttered the word, 'Topeno', which I took to be his name.

In turn I introduced myself – as Horace rather than Stockwood, just in case.

I am not sure what I expected but I was certainly surprised when Topeno responded to my name by hunkering down in a darkened corner of the cave and proceeding to ignore me. With nothing else to do I sat as well. I made sure my movements were slow and non-threatening. Nobody responded. Even the children displayed a lack of curiosity I found disturbing.

We sat in this manner for some time – perhaps an hour. During the time I tried twice to make conversation. Nobody responded. Eventually I gave up. The silence was nerve-racking. And then the torches were extinguished. The sudden blackness was oppressive and frightening. I spent the next hours in a state of constant agitation, wondering whether Topeno would simply cut my throat in the darkness as I sat, unable to see to protect myself. In any event there was nothing I could do about it, so I had to endure it.

It was almost a relief when sounds of scrabbling hands and feet indicated another person approaching the cave. I wondered if it was the Doctor? I did not hear Topeno draw his dagger or move into the passage, though I knew he must have. There was a long moment of silence, then a shriek and a familiar voice cried out. A moment later the torches were relit in time for me to witness two figures accompany Topeno into the cave by a passage different from the one I had used. The figures were familiar. Jack Devitt, the ship's boy, and Jennifer Richards.

Even her face brought a sigh of pleasure to my lips, familiar as it was.

She stared at me contemptuously. 'Skulking like a coward in the darkness with savages, Horace? The boy here dealt more bravely with the Peruvians than you evidently have.'

Jack looked around nervously. I could see he was trying to hide his fear of the islanders. 'I done fer one of 'em with cook's carver, then the lady here an' me, we got ashore and hid in some caves.'

I licked my lips. 'Did you see the Doctor?'

'I did. I see'd 'im taken on the man o' war by them pirates. He was shot. Dunno if 'e was dead, though. S'pose not if they took 'im aboard. They got a load o' the islanders an all. Dunno 'ow many – more'n I can count. And the Cap'n and the rest o' the men. All locked in the black holds o' those devil ships, I shouldn't wonder, with who knows what mortal horrors.' Jack was silent for a moment. I could see him struggling with fear. He won out long enough to ask, 'What you reckon they gonna do with us, lady?'

'Sell us all into slavery I shouldn't wonder, at least that for the men. As for myself… well, I've heard tales… Let's just say that the first pirate who comes near me will feel the shot of my pistol in his gut. For I'll not be taken by those devils, mark me, boy.'

We fell quiet, silent as the islanders, who were all watching us by now. The passive curiosity they now displayed was as disturbing to me as their earlier indifference. I resolved to break the silence and, attracting Topeno's attention, bade him tell us what had transpired earlier upon the island. After consultation with a number of other men in the cave, Topeno told me a story I found all too believable.

The warships had arrived three days earlier. They had anchored in the bay. The islanders had swum and paddled out to meet the ship's crews, and had been delighted, when aboard, to be allowed to inscribe a few flourishes at the foot of a sheet of paper. Thereby they had signed a contract, I realised, to become slaves of the Peruvians. I imagined they were to be sold as labourers to the guano islands off the coast of Peru. Meanwhile the islanders were allowed free run of the ships. But when they wanted to leave they were coshed, bound and taken below decks.

Several hours later four boats put ashore with a pile of trade goods. Brightly coloured blankets, tobacco, seeds, trinkets of all descriptions. When several hundred more of the islanders came to examine these interesting things they, too, were attacked and captured. Now the Captain of the flotilla, a man named DaBraisse, but whom the islanders called the devil, issued instructions to the sailors, who came ashore with pistols and rope. Many more islanders were captured, hands bound, and taken to the boats, while those who tried to swim or run to safety were fired upon. As the last of the boats was ready to put off, DaBraisse discovered two islanders hiding in a cave near the beach. When he could not persuade them to go with him he shot them down.

Thus began a small war which, according to Topeno, had so far lasted three days and cost the islanders no fewer than seven hundred of their number – men, women and children.

And now they were waiting. Waiting for the Peruvians to find them. Waiting to fight, if necessary to die, to protect their families, their homes.

And now we were waiting with them.

19
Lost Worlds

I came close to panicking when we found James was gone. Leela held me together, her voice practical and harsh as ever. Leela saw signs in the dust and used her tracking skills to determine what happened: James must have recovered sufficiently to move on his own. There was only the one track so it seemed obvious that no one spirited him away. It was just a matter of following the trail in the dust.

This we did and a few moments later were puzzled to see that it terminated at the blank metal wall of one of the huge monoliths that so curiously resembled the *moai* of Rapa Nui.

Leela examined the wall. She was slow and cautious, but the moment her fingers brushed the surface something so strange happened that I can scarcely credit, let alone describe, it, for the truth is that what I saw defied all the comfortable laws of logic and science by which my life had previously been gauged.

The monolith became night.

Oh, I don't mean it turned black; I mean it became a three-dimensional, *moai*-shaped piece of night, standing impossibly four-square and real in the afternoon sun. Within the shape – for it had depth and perspective as if it were a three-dimensional window – I could see stars, a skyline, some vegetation, perhaps part of a city.

I walked around the piece of night. It was solid, rounded, and as I shifted position so my view through it shifted. I lost sight of Leela as I passed behind the object and caught sight of her again as I returned to my original starting point.

'It's real.' I think there must have been amazement in my

voice. I remember stammering, 'It's impossible.'

'If it were impossible it would not be here.' Leela observed succinctly. 'Obviously Royston entered here. We must follow.'

'Yes. Why, yes, of course. But how do we…?'

Leela stepped up to the impossible piece of night. I realised her eyes were shut. She kept on walking and simply became part of the view I could see. I rushed to join her before I lost my nerve. I lost my footing as I passed through the orifice and fell. When I regained my feet I felt heavier. Gravity was different here. My mind tried to grasp the truth: we were on yet another world. The second since leaving the island.

I spared a glance behind me: a *moai*-shaped piece of day stood impossibly behind me. Other monoliths stretched away in loose groups to every horizon.

Leela was already moving away. I hurried to catch up, staring around me as I went. Another great city rose before us, this one seemingly more conventionally formed. The buildings were tall, beautifully sculpted. Hovering platforms held what must once have been elegantly designed parks and gardens. The vegetation was now overgrown, spilling from the platforms and tethering them to each other and the ground in a three-dimensional maze which more resembled the artistic ramblings of Bosch than the creation of any city planner whose work I had witnessed. The garden platforms hovered even now, supported by machinery that had survived long after its creators had gone.

The sky above the city was dominated by two large moons, glowing ochre with reflected sunlight. Stars were splashed in a thick river across the heavens, so dense that their light rivalled that of the moons. The city was bathed in brown and silver. There were no other lights. No sign of movement. No sound. Just silence – the sound of growing things and the whisper of air. I realised this city was dead as well. As dead as the other we had seen.

As we followed Royston's trail closer to what had been the main centre of population, I began to smell something. Something rotten. I knew that here we would find bodies. Many bodies.

We stopped at the edge of a park drifting some yards beneath us. Royston's trail stopped at the edge of this section of pavement. I frowned. 'Are the sections moving?'

'No.' Her voice held certainty. 'Maybe once but not now.' She thought for a moment. In the lower section of park we could see a group of *moai* nestling among the overgrown trees. 'I can see where the foliage has been broken.'

And then she stepped off the edge.

I rushed forward, expecting her to fall. She didn't. She drifted gracefully as if gliding down the banister of an invisible staircase, and alighted at the bottom giggling. 'It's fun!'

I joined her, taking a deep breath and stepping from the edge. I too drifted down. The sensation was... well, there was no sensation – it was just like walking, except that I was moving without walking.

A few moments later we reached the group of monoliths.

Leela examined the ground. 'He entered this one.' She touched the surface – and immediately recoiled from a brilliant burst of sunlight. Allowing our eyes to adjust, we stepped through.

Gravity changed again. Now we were on a smaller world. My steps took us ten feet at a time – or would have if I had been able to get past my astonishment.

Allowing no time to observe my immediate surroundings, my gaze was captured immediately by the sky. The sun. It was small, a brilliant presence in the pale sky. Behind it was another sun – this one vast, a ruddy ochre globe blotched with darker patches. I could not help thinking of this pair as older and younger brothers. One youthful and the other entering its dotage. The crescents of moons and other planets drifted silently among the rarefied clouds scudding quickly through the thin air.

At last I lowered my eyes to the ground – only to find we were on a beach. Here the *moai* were less copiously distributed, framed by a dazzling green ocean with foaming whitecaps. The waves surged against the shore in caterpillar splendour. The sand was black, possibly volcanic in origin. It glittered like the obsidian blades the islanders used. Where rocks emerged from the shore I saw they held the classic sponge-structure of pumice – cooled lava. Other pumice islands drifted across the seascape. There were buildings there but, again, no sign of movement, no sign of life.

Royston's footsteps were fast being obscured by the tide, so we ran along the beach to the nearest monolith and passed through it.

I can only hint at the incredible journey that followed. A journey of awe and sadness – for, although we visited places without number and saw wonders of architecture that relegated the great cities of Europe to the status of crude experiments carried out by less than talented students of the craft, nowhere did we see a single sign of life in any form. No bird tipped its wing across the sterile moons and suns, no animal prowled among the parks and gardens, no fish swam in the ponds or oceans. Nothing. No life of any description, just corpses, many of them rotted almost to nothing in one or two cities.

I swiftly built up a picture of a world lost to time. Or rather worlds. For the journey we made through the worlds and their connecting *moai* doorways reminded me in a more spectacular way of the simple cave system located in the volcanic passages beneath Rapa Nui. I tried to imagine the worlds alive with the light and presence of people. I wondered what they sounded like, what they looked like. Perhaps their appearance had shaped the great stone heads that featured so heavily within their culture. I wondered if I would ever know.

I had my answer when we found the library.

I called it that because even from the outside it had the air of a building that served a function, a need. It was huge, with wide doorways and sweeping ramps which seemed to invite you to move further into its vaulted halls and chambers. And every chamber was in effect a view into the past, in the same way as the *moai* were views into the present – but these were views you could not interact with, only experience.

We found Royston collapsed on the floor of one of the chambers, his face clothed in tears. 'So beautiful.' His voice was a whisper. 'All of it. So beautiful.'

'What happened?'

'Watch,' he said.

It had been war of course.

Over the next minutes or hours or days, I wandered from chamber to chamber obsessively and, I must admit at first vicariously, discovering atrocity after historical atrocity. And not just discovering. For through some means unknown to me I actually *experienced* what it was like to stand on a world and witness the extinction of all life there. I felt the ruin of moons and whole planets. I watched a sun bullied by technology into premature age and imminent death. I saw so many people die that the word *extinction* became meaningless. It went on and on, the record apparently endless, the aggressor species ever voiceless, faceless, their reasons for this genocide – if they had reasons – never explained. I was sole witness to their thoroughness, their unswerving dedication to the end of all life not their own. They were without justification, reversal, compromise – and absolutely without mercy.

I realised I had slept when I became aware of someone shaking me awake.

'What does it mean?' Leela. Her face was haggard. She too had been experiencing the memories of a dead race.

'They died. They were killed.'

'I know. Why?'

'I don't know.'

Royston added, 'I've found something else.'

It was a small chamber which seemed to contain a record of industry. I recognised the planet on which we had first arrived, now revealed to be a moon of this planet. To my amazement the entire world was given over to the production of *moai* – so much so that it had been the ruin of it. An entire world strip-mined to manufacture these strange monoliths. And not just that. More worlds wrecked to provide a means of propelling the thousands of statues out into space.

I did not understand.

'They look like Vai-tarakai-ua – the god in the cave which brought us here.' Leela was right. I had a sudden gleam of – not understanding exactly but – *connection*. I saw the islanders stripping their own world as these great ones had ransacked their own, in emulation of the *moai* which did not originate in their own culture.

The islanders had copied what happened here – unwittingly, history had repeated itself.

I felt a great sadness inside. That so much should have come to so little. And for no reason that I could see.

There was a sudden noise. Footsteps.

'Hello? I say, is anyone there?' The Doctor.

We turned away from the history lesson in time to see him enter carrying the unconscious body of Jennifer Richards, her blouse and jacket soaked with blood.

Leela leapt up joyfully. 'How did you find us?'

The Doctor pointed to a set of strange carvings on the floor and grinned. 'Ever been on the London Underground? "You are here." All this is child's play by comparison. Now – who wants to find out what all this really means?'

20
Man o' War

Earth. It's my favourite planet. I can't imagine why. I've been hurt here more times than I can recall. I've seen friends and companions injured or die here. I died here twice myself.

Thankfully I was nowhere near death at the moment. I was recovering from a pistol wound to my chest in the hold of the man o' war. With me were about a hundred islanders. They were terrified, agitated, violent. Their anger was in the main part directed at myself, as the only white-skinned foreigner present. I suppose I was lucky they did not try to cut out my heart. Double redundancy goes only so far, and my right heart had already suffered minor damage when I was shot. Fortunately, that was healing now. I would have to expel the bullet but I could do that at any time, assuming no major artery was nicked beforehand.

I observed my surroundings as a way of passing time while I healed. The hold of the ship was a terrible place to languish. Filthy, bloody, it stank of the salt-water-and-vinegar solution with which it was infrequently washed down. Rats scuttled among the islanders. Cockroaches scuttled among the slops. Several of the islanders were wounded, one quite badly. Moans rumbled through the darkness. I made a mental note to take the Captain to task regarding the hygiene of his vessel. Perhaps I could bargain for the release of the islanders with an offer of my lemon-juice-cordial scurvy remedy. Then again maybe they had already looted the medical supplies from *Tweed*. That made me think of Stuart and the rest of the men, incarcerated in the hold of their own ship. I tried to think what I could do to help them. For the moment, beyond trying to heal, I was forced to accept that I could do nothing at all.

Instead I concentrated on my wound.

A lifetime ago and many hundred years in the past my dear friend the Master Padmasambhava had taught me the healing ways of his people in return for my helping to ward off Chinese bandits intent on ransacking the monastery and killing the monks, the beginning of a political and religious rout that was not to end for centuries. My mind slipped back to Tibet as I wove a healing trance around myself.

For a time, time itself became fluid. I was simultaneously here, in the hold of a Peruvian man o' war, and *then* in the monastery of the monks of Det Sen, high in the Himalayas.

And then I felt something give inside my chest. A blood vessel. I was aware of blood gushing out into my chest cavity. I shut down conscious thought and let *then* and *now* become one, as *then* I fought Chinese swords with holy prayer as *now* I fought myocardial infarction and shock with meditation as *then* I fought the political infection taking root in the country as *now* I fought the biological infection taking root in my body as *then* I was wounded while defending Padmasambhava's life as *now* I was shot while trying to save the islanders as *then* I lay dying on sunlit snow as now I lay dying in the stinking hold, a bandit sword buried in my heart pirate lead buried in my heart, and *then* at the moment of death

Padmasambhava

touched me and

healed me and

now I remember fleeing from the Chinese and *then* I remember being given the holy *ghanta* for safekeeping and *then* I remember the blood gushing from my body and *now* I remember the promise I made to return it and *then* I remember the healing touch of his hands and *now* I remember the healing touch of his mind and *now* I remember and I remember and

time returns to normal.

I sat up, taking cautious deep breaths, grinning when nothing hurt. I wiped blood from my chest. The wound was gone. I performed a few experimental sit-ups and a bit of running on the spot. Blood routing normal. Bruising minimal. Adrenaline level minimal, Artron energy at optimal. All systems very definitely go.

'Just like riding a bike.' I realised I had spoken aloud when a hundred pairs of eyes turned to look at me with fear. And I knew what they had seen: a man on the point of death rising to life, brushing aside what for them would be a mortal injury as if it were no more than a bedsheet.

Well – it would be something for them to tell their grandchildren about.

I stood. I stretched. And then I beamed. With the healing meditation had come a fresh bloom of insight. The *moai*. The islanders. The slavers. The *rongo-rongo*. The reason for everything.

I looked at the islanders. Some were cowering in fear, others were making aggressive noises and looking around for weapons, presumably to use on me. I poked my finger through the charred bullet hole in my shirt and wriggled it happily at the islanders.

'Nothing like a good myocardial infarction to hoover away the cobwebs. Now,' I added in Polynesian, while buttoning my shirt, wrapping my scarf around my neck and tapping my hat firmly into place, 'who wants to know a really good plan for getting out of here?'

No one wanted to know the plan. About ten of the men jumped on me at once, screaming invocations to their gods, denouncing me as the devil while trying to strangle me with my own scarf.

My belief in self-determination was only mildly shaken when – with perfect timing – a handful of armed Peruvians descended into the hold, kicked aside the islanders trying to kill me and dragged me up on deck to meet the Captain.

DaBraisse was a tall man, rake-thin and spare of movement. He was dressed, unlike the rest of his men, with some dignity. His clothes were of impeccable quality and his beard was neatly trimmed. His sun-darkened skin bore many scars, the price of the life he had chosen. His black eyes sparkled with cold intelligence. He stood at the port deck rail, one hand resting lightly upon it, the other at his breast, fingering the engraved barrel of a silver-plated pistol which rested in a harness there. His head made tiny, precise movements as he followed the sounds of fighting and distant gunfire rolling off the shore.

'Do you hear them screaming, man of the cloth?' When he spoke his voice was like a breath of wind curling gently from an iceberg. 'We have started this day upon a profitable venture.'

'I compliment you.' I made no effort to keep the irony from my voice. 'You are a perfect example of evolution in action.'

He did not turn from his view of the island, did not so much as clench his fist upon the deck rail. 'I thank you for your compliment, though I have no doubt you did not mean it as such. I pride myself on efficiency, man of the cloth. The most return for the least effort, that is my motto.'

'And you expect to make a profit from today's atrocities?'

'You have already heard me say that I do. A handsome profit.'

'You are a man of some intelligence. This island is small, isolated, defenceless. Surely you see if you continue on this course the population here will be decimated; it will never be the same again.'

DaBraisse turned at this, his eyes hungry for my words. I had only a slim hope he could be convinced. 'Your effort here will be wasted. Your government will release those you take as slaves – but by that time over nine hundred will be dead. The rest will die from smallpox after being returned to the island. You, DaBraisse, will be personally responsible for destroying an entire culture.'

'What kind of man of the cloth are you that you can see things to come with such certainty?' DaBraisse lifted his hand from the deck rail and ran one elegantly manicured fingernail along an old scar running beside his right eye. 'Tell me, man of the cloth, has your Church learnt to predict the future yet?'

'All religions make that claim.'

'You have a penchant for imprecision and avoidance.' He smiled. 'Word games. It seems the province of religion does not change no matter who the god in question.' He turned at the sound of many guns firing simultaneously. 'The religions of these savages also make many claims. To the future, the past. Who is to say if they are right or wrong?'

'You hunt them with superior weaponry and superior force and yet you call *them* savages?'

'There is no virtue in honour when death is the result. The only honour is in winning. That and profit. I am a man of intelligence, Doctor. I can turn that which is valueless into that which is worth much.'

'As a man of cloth –' I touched my scarf for luck and hoped I would not have to be specific about *which* cloth, exactly – 'I demand their release.'

'I have not come all the way here to forgo my cargo.'

'I have money. Diamonds. I could buy them from you.'

DaBraisse turned, interested by the mention of his own god. 'You have diamonds, you say?'

At gunpoint I removed a leather bag from my pocket and offered it to DaBraisse, who took it, weighed it and tucked it into his purse.

'Well, man of the cloth. Now you don't have any diamonds any more, do you?'

I sighed. 'You don't understand. These are a peaceful people. They have no weapons.'

'Who then would be better to attack?'

'But they have nothing of value.'

'Their work is their value. They will make excellent slaves. So you see, I am after all able to convert valueless human life into precious stones. The medieval necromancers could have learnt from my skill, don't you think? Turning lead into gold would be easy by comparison.'

'From the disposition of your men and the conditions of your prisoners I should have thought the Inquisition could have learnt from your skills.'

The Captain did not reply straight away. When he did his voice did not change inflection one iota. 'Indeed. Your sympathies reside with the Spanish. How unfortunate for you. As you are a man of the cloth – albeit of somewhat uncommon dress – and of obvious intelligence, I was prepared to be magnanimous towards you. Instead I find I must now treat you with the utmost contempt due to an enemy of my people.' He spoke over his shoulder to the men holding me. 'Empty his pockets and then take him back to the hold. Later he will perform for our amusement upon the plank.' My last sight of DaBraisse as I was taken below decks was of his head jerking back and forth to the sounds of fighting, as if he were keeping time to a beautiful piece of music.

21
Rosetta Stone

I do not know what happened to me. One moment I was quite clearly dying, carried through a night filled with screams and cannon fire to a miserable cave full of chanting islanders by the man whom I had betrayed; the next, the night had turned to day – a kind of dull, hazy, summer afternoon – and the pain from my wounds had severely diminished.

I remember drifting in and out of consciousness as I was carried across a place which made a nonsense of my experiences of travel in Europe. There seemed to be two suns. And many different moons. And a plethora of great cities which seemed to me to be larger and more beautiful than any I had ever visited.

But there was no sound. Not a sound anywhere save for the even breathing of the Doctor as he carried me, and his strange double heartbeat, which seemed to vibrate through my body and fill it with every pumping double thud. It was by listening to the hypnotic quality of this sound, and being rocked by the motion of his steps, that my senses were robbed by a deep and dream-troubled sleep.

When I awoke I found myself in a building. Stockwood was there. And Leela. And Royston. We were five. I learnt the world was dead and I overheard the many theories and conjectures put forward by the Doctor as he examined the various recordings held within the library, as he called this place.

I found the experience disturbing. I was reminded of a time in my youth when, delirious with fever, I had visited the tropical rainforest, spoken with fairies at the bottom of my garden, and flown naked across the surface of the moon. All were fantasies, the ramblings of a girl brought to the point of death by illness and later burnt from her by ridicule and practical motherly concern.

I had recovered of course, and put these ridiculous imaginings from my mind. The world was far too unforgiving a place to indulge such fancies, particularly – as my mother insisted many times – when you were a girl in the bloom of her womanhood, with marriage to a good husband and a good station in life the possible sacrifice for ever listening to your dreams.

At the age of eighteen my efforts at dismissal were finally – and horrifyingly – vindicated when my elder brother Alexander failed to return from his expedition to the Pacific. He had been twenty-four. He had followed his dreams and they had led him to his death. I vowed never to repeat his folly, to waste the life God had given him. Dreams were for the sleeping world, not the waking.

Now, as the library showed the others views of the people and worlds of this place I gathered my strength. Stockwood was here. He would not always be protected by his tame lioness. Though I had been forced to surrender the *rongo-rongo* to the Doctor to help him understand the language of this world and, therefore, more properly translate the images of the library, I still had the knife I had taken from Stump after leaving Portsmouth. It was small and had remained concealed at every step of my journey so far. I had been saving the knife. I would await my chance and, when the time was right, I would take it.

And I would kill Horace Stockwood.

22
Face from the Past

I do not know how long we waited in the cave. Certainly long enough to grow hungry and thirsty. No one apart from Topeno spoke a single word to Richards, Jack or myself the entire time.

That was the situation when – some time later – another islander crawled into the cave. He seemed most agitated. He conferred with Topeno for a few moments in speech too rapid for me to follow. Then both men crossed to me. They indicated that I should follow them through the passages. Richards and Jack were made to come as well. I wondered if we were being taken off to be killed, or given to the Peruvians as bargaining chips in order to save the islanders taken captive. If this was the case there was nothing I could do. I was simply too sick to my soul to protest.

We followed Topeno and his friend, crawling for what seemed like miles through the maze of volcanic tunnels, until eventually we emerged into an even larger cave. By now my clothes were filthy and beginning to tear. Of us all Jack seemed the most spry. As we emerged into the cave, I realised it was full of islanders. They were deliberating in agitated voices. I caught enough phrases to realise they were holding a council of war. But it was the speaker whose voice I was drawn to in the darkness.

'If you do not fight you will die. Do you want to die in the caves like animals? Where is your pride? Where is your fighting spirit? This place is your home! Will you allow it to be invaded? I say no! In my Place of Land, if another tribe attacked then the Sevateem fought back with every weapon and every man, woman and child until either the attackers were dead or we were. And we live! All the while one of you remains free and unbowed your people will live. They can take your people. They can kill your people. They have better weapons. But they are few and you are many. And you have stealth. And you have guile.' She saw me entering the cave and smiled. 'And you have me.'

'Hello, Leela,' I said quietly.

'Hello, Stockwood, my best friend. We are at council of war.' Her voice raised exultantly. 'And I say we kill the enemy! Kill them now! Slay them and make playthings of their bones for the children!'

The islanders responded with a few cries. The cries grew into chanting. The chanting into a unified, rhythmic shout.

Someone beside me spoke. The voice was husky, exhausted, but familiar. 'Look at her, Horace. Anyone who could whip up a thousand savages whose language she did not speak only last week into a killing frenzy within hours of arrival half dead on their shore deserves at least one term of political office, don't you think?'

I turned. 'James! By all that's merciful, you're alive!'

He managed a smile. And as the council of war continued, he told me what had befallen himself and Leela, during their many days at sea. I learnt about the whale, the sharks, the amazing journey through the waterspout with the whale, and then the even more amazing escape from the inside of the whale as it sank after being flung clear of the tornado. I learnt how they had remained adrift clinging to the wreckage salvaged from *Tweed* before finally being spotted by a Polynesian fishing party out in canoes. They had been picked up and taken to one of the French Polynesian islands, where they had been fed and their wounds were treated. After much discussion there a group of islanders had brought them across the intervening ocean in a tiny fleet of fishing canoes. The journey had taken many days but this time they were prepared and provisioned. The Polynesians were expert sailors and their tiny ships virtually unsinkable. 'I never realised what a rare delicacy turtle meat was until I had the opportunity to eat some as an alternative to fish,' James said, seemingly overwhelmed by his adventures. I didn't blame him. 'I tell you, Horace, if I never see a plate of breaded prawns again it will be two weeks too soon.'

Despite our circumstances, I found myself grinning like an idiot as the tale unfolded. 'I can't believe you're alive,' I said, rather unnecessarily, as James finished speaking.

'I wouldn't be if not for Leela. I've never met anyone like her.' I nodded in heartfelt agreement. 'And now we have arrived here, it seems, only to step from the frying pan into the fire. Peruvian slavers, I understand.'

I nodded. 'They arrived here three days ago and invaded without warning. They attacked the clipper, imprisoned Stuart and the crew. They have taken several hundred islanders captive. And they shot the Doctor.'

'Shot the Doctor? Is he dead?'

'I hope not.'

'I wonder if we can buy them off with gold,' James mused.

I shook my head firmly. 'They would take your gold and kill you without a moment's thought. They are blaggards and scoundrels. I watched them shoot down a party of islanders in cold blood. They laughed. It was like sport to them.'

James's response was interrupted by a minor commotion some distance from us. I saw two of the men arguing with an old woman. I realised with a sudden shock that she was pointing at us. At me. It was clear she recognised me. The inevitable had happened at last. I had been discovered. By now a significant number of the men had become involved in the fracas. Leela's council of war had stopped to allow the matter to be dealt with.

I watched as the men brought the old woman closer, surprised at how calm I was. James sensed the hostility of the group and tried to interpose himself between us. I pushed him aside. 'This is my responsibility,' I told him. I saw Richards keeping to one side. She was watching intently. I saw the islanders draw their obsidian knives. Was Richards to get the grandstand view of my death, which she craved so much?

I suppose I should have run, protested, struggled, something. In truth I found the strength to stand, enough to meet the old woman's accusations with some dignity. Perhaps humility would have been better. I could not summon that much strength. And they did not realise how much I had already punished myself over the matter of the *rongo-rongo*. Nothing they could do to me now would match the suffering I had inflicted upon myself. The worst they could do was kill me – and then at least the punishment would be over.

The woman – whose name seemed to be Atani – broke from the group of islanders and ran towards me. She stopped within an arm's length. She was ancient, her skin warped tightly across prominent bones. Her face was tattooed and her ears stretched to her shoulders. They had been pegged back but one had broken loose as she ran towards me. Now she stood before me and pointed in accusation.

'He is the one. He is the one who stole the *rongo-rongo*. He is the one responsible for my brother's death. Tortorro trusted you and befriended you and you betrayed him.'

'I saved his son's life.'

The woman spat at me. 'His son is dead, killed by the Peruvians. So all you did was delay what was meant to be.'

I searched for something to say. I could find nothing. I tried to conjure an image of the tiny child I had saved so many years ago. At that precise moment I couldn't even remember what colour his hair had been. Atani was right. The only difference my involvement had made was to enable us to blackmail Tortorro into getting us to Bird Man's Island and stealing the *rongo-rongo*. To my left I could see Richards watching silently. Her face showed no emotion at the woman's accusation.

By now the cave was silent.

Topeno came forward and stood beside the woman. 'You are Stockwood who stole the *rongo-rongo*?'

I nodded miserably. 'Yes. Yes, I am. And I know I was wrong, and I know there's no excuse for what I did. So why don't you just kill me now and get on with it? Get it over with! Come on! Use one of your damn knives or strangle me or turn me insane with some poison if you must, only do it now before I go quite mad with impatience!'

I felt James's hands upon my shoulders. 'Hysteria serves no one, Horace.' His voice was quiet, calm. Amazingly so under the circumstances.

I took deep breaths, waited for judgement.

A moment passed. No one spoke.

And then there was movement. Slow, deliberate movement. The islanders parted to allow another through into the clearing which had grown around me. It was a man. Tall, a shock of pure white hair crowned a face gone to age and madness. The skin was paper-thin and pale from lack of sun, stretched across a skull which seemed to be trying to escape from the body with every change of expression. The body jerked, as if movement was unfamiliar, lurching towards me, arms outstretched in senile greeting.

And I recoiled from the arms raised in greeting as I recoiled from the mummified smile as I recoiled from the recognition boiling up like hot bile within me.

'Hello... old... friend.'

The voice was like a scratched gramophone, a distorted

version of that which I remembered so well. 'Alex...
Alexander?'

'Welcome to... Rapa Nui,' he said in cracked tones. 'I am your
punishment.'

I staggered, my head whirling, grabbed the wall of the cave
for support. 'Alex? Alex Richards?'

He had stopped, his arms drifting like withered leaves until
they were motionless at his sides. His skin was chalk-white,
creased with age, starkly naked when compared with the
tattooed islanders.

'Alex, I... I...'

'You have returned,' he said in a voice like razors moving
across a sharpening stone. 'The sun will shine in the night. The
dead will live again. I am your punishment.'

I took a step forward, all thought gone. My friend whom I
thought dead was alive. Alive! I had no thought for the wasted
years. My redemption was at hand. He was alive! I would take
him away from here, take him back to London. James would
help. His madness could be treated, cured. My friend! Alive! 'Oh
Alex...'

And then she moved. The old woman moved. She produced
an obsidian knife from her belt and laid it across his throat. I
stuttered, pointed. Nobody moved. Topeno and the other
islanders seemed content to merely watch. Alexander did not
even move. It was as though his every response had been
choreographed, like a dance or a play.

'Tell him who you are,' the old woman hissed.

'I am your punishment,' Alex said as she slit his throat from
ear to ear.

23
Voice from the Future

Five minds, interconnected; memories like struggling insects trapped in eternity's web. Myself, Horace, Leela, the Doctor and Richards. Five minds, thinking as one. A chorus of thoughts and memories. The past become present. A litany for the future.

And

the Fathers of the Tribe of Sevateem were sent forth by Xoanon to seek Paradise

And

the Members of the Geographical Society have voted to sponsor the Stockwood–Richards Pacific Expedition

And

we must launch the moai *into space. Like seeds they will land on other worlds. Our DNA will be encoded by retrovirus into that of the local dominant life form. We will die but our race will remain hidden from those who would destroy us. In time we will return through the* moai *gateways and the dead will live again*

And

while the Tribe of Sevateem searched for Paradise the Tribe of Tesh, who remained at the Place of Land, betrayed our Fathers

And

Horace Stockwood, hear me, for I curse you for a coward if you leave me here to die with these savages

And

the new arrivals carry our death within them. A genetic corruption. An alien virus. We are all infected now. We have

227

no defence

And

the Tesh made a pact with the Evil One and Xoanon turned his face from us

And

the blank eyes of the moai, *and the accusing screams of Alexander Richards follow me for months back to England and a lifetime beyond*

And

so that's what happened to the thousands of islanders that have vanished over the generations: used as carrier pigeons for an alien amino-acid chain

And

the Evil One raised the Tower and defended it with the Black Wall

And

I have cried out his name in the night. I have awoken sobbing and close to madness

And

Stockwood took the rongo-rongo, *and with it the operating instructions for an Einstein–Rosen Bridge*

And

the Tribe of Tesh, who stand between the Tribe of Sevateem and Xoanon, God of their Fathers, must be killed

And

I live only to see your face at his grave, to see your madness grow and consume you, and then to kill you, if I can

And

the face of the enemy is upon us and it shows no mercy only death

And

now is the time when the Tribe of Sevateem shall rise in their wrath and kill the Evil One

And

I desire your death, Horace Stockwood, I desire it as some desire perfume or sweet appointments or love or life itself!

And

and I see worlds destroyed, life eradicated. I see the rape of hope and the annihilation of truth and beauty. I see it all and the horror is more than I can bear

And

the library takes me and shows me and I know. The gods help me I know. *I know how it ends. I know how it begins.*

I know everything.

24
Firefight

The islanders washed Stockwood in the blood of his friend whom they had killed. I watched Richards while they did this. I knew she would try to kill him. Revenge. But she was in the waking sleep – her mind robbed by shock. She sat in one corner and a number of islanders comforted her as she descended even further into madness. I knew the islanders would take care of Stockwood now. They had punished him. Now they would welcome him into their tribe. So, leaving Stockwood and Richards to deal with the death of Alexander, I led an attack on the pirates.

There were three Peruvian sailors keeping watch over the island from the top of the cliffs overlooking Anakena Bay. They were passing a bottle between themselves, drinking and laughing. Occasionally they would loose shots at a rodent or fowl. We waited until they were drunk before moving, then Topeno and another islander called Tenini slit the throats of two and I gutted another, pushing him to the ground and covering his mouth to prevent warning screams as I took his heart.

Royston, who had followed us, was appalled at our actions. 'Leela! What do you think you are doing?'

'Winning,' I told him softly. 'Now be quiet. I still do not trust you.'

Armed with an assortment of pistols and daggers, in addition to our knives, we made our way to the beach, moving quietly and checking for other sentries. There were none. Three guards for seven ships. This DaBraisse was a stupid man. I wondered if all men on this planet were as stupid. Topeno signalled to the others and we slipped into the water. More than a hundred islanders followed us. We did not make directly for the pirate ships. Instead we swam quietly out to *Tweed* and, even more quietly, climbed the bow ropes on to deck. There were more pirates here. A lot more. They were busy looting the various cabins and drinking the liquor they found or had brought with them. One pirate was throwing his knife repeatedly into the corpse of one of the men from *Tweed* who had been tied to the mizzenmast. His astonished look when the knife he had been throwing was returned, apparently by a dead man, to bury itself in his throat and take his own life, was most satisfying.

After making sure the pirate was dead and lowering his body over the side to avoid its accidental discovery, Topeno and I opened the quarterdeck hatch and slipped quietly down the ladder to the lower decks. Checking the companionway was clear, we made directly for the Captain's cabin. Five pirates were busy inside, rifling through the Captain's sea chest. It was the work of moments to kill them all. I regretted the blood that would spoil the beautiful carpet but spared no thought for the lives we took. The pirates had forfeited their right to life when they had first killed. Though Royston would not admit it I knew the truth. We were at war. To lose was to die. There were nine more pirates on the ship. Topeno and I hunted them silently through the decks and cabins. In ten minutes they were all dead.

When there were no more pirates left alive we went directly to the hold and opened the hatch. I called down into the darkness. 'Captain Stuart!'

His voice answered at once. 'Leela? By the heavens, is that you?'

'Yes. I have come to free you so that we may kill the pirates and free the islanders and the Doctor. Come with me. Bring your men. And guns.'

Now we had a hundred and fifty men armed with pistols and swords, some armed with the pirates' own weapons. Cook was first on deck. He wore a cutlass and a pistol, and carried a meat cleaver and a large pepperpot. 'Time to chop cutlets, lads.' His voice was even. He did not smile.

By now there were nearly two hundred people on *Tweed*. I turned to Captain Stuart. 'Keep them quiet. Follow the swimmers in boats when you are able. Your job is to take one of the pirate ships. We must use their weapons against them. Do you understand?'

'Oh, I understand all right. And so will they – when I get my hands on their cannon.'

'Good.' Topeno and I climbed back over the side of the ship and slipped into the water. We swam slowly and silently for the leading Peruvian ship. It was running low in the water with the weight of its cargo of islanders. That made it all the easier to slip aboard. I climbed over the stern deckrail and crouched dripping on the deck. Topeno followed me. There seemed to be no one nearby. But I could hear singing and clapping from the direction of the bowsprit. The moon was a thin crescent, barely topping the rocky hills of the island, and it cast scant light. The stars were bright, though, so we would have to be careful. I moved along the deck, crouching beside the deckrail and making sure I remained in shadow. Lamps were strung up along the spars. They threw an oily yellow light barred with black shadows on to the ship.

The singing got louder as we moved forward. The pirates were obviously drunk on wine or brandy. This was going to be very easy.

Then I saw the Doctor.

He was perched upon a plank which projected out from the

side of the ship. The plank swayed with every movement of the ship. The Doctor's ankles and wrists were tied with rope. Heavy chains had been looped around his ankles and these were attached to what looked like a badly cracked cannon casing. Another rope was looped tightly around his neck. This rope was tied to a high spar. Every movement of the ship threatened to pitch the Doctor from the plank, so that he would either drown or break his neck. Many pirates were gathered on the deck and more clung to the rigging. Most of them were laughing. Some were taking bets on how the Doctor would die. Every so often someone would fire a shot into the sky. The catcalls and sounds of drunken mayhem were loud and constant.

I crouched beside the mid-deck hatch, shrouded in darkness, and studied the positioning of the pirates that I could see.

The man nearest the ship end of the plank was the most important. He held a cutlass and was taunting the Doctor with it.

Reaching out beside me I found Topeno's hand in the yellow gloom and took his knife. I checked the balance for throwing. I could not afford to miss.

I took one last look around me, gauged the distance, stood, threw Topeno's knife and immediately crouched back into the shadows. The knife flashed once in the yellow light as the blade bit into the spar an inch from the rope secured to the Doctor's neck.

I had missed.

I already had the second knife ready for throwing in case I had been seen. I was lucky. The knife was small and the black obsidian blade was not seen in the gloom.

My heart banging in my chest I prepared to make the second throw. I waited for the ship to come to an even keel, stood and threw again. The knife bit into the rope at the precise moment the man with the cutlass jabbed the Doctor in the back. The Doctor wobbled, swaying as the ship continued to roll with the waves, trying to regain his balance. The men gave a mighty shout of glee as it looked like the Doctor would fall after all. Then three things happened at once. The Doctor regained his balance, the rope fell clear of the spar, and from somewhere nearby came the boom of a cannon.

Captain Stuart.

In seconds there was chaos. The cannon blast had snapped the mizzenmast at the height of the second spar. Sails, rigging mast, spars and all came smashing down into the deck, the wreckage bringing about thirty men with it. Most were knocked senseless; some fell into the water. In another moment a hundred islanders had scrambled aboard the ship, obsidian knives held in gleaming teeth, and the deck was awash with blood.

But the movement of the ship had caused the Doctor to lose his balance. He fell from the plank. Then, amazingly, he stopped, hanging suspended in midair. Like Jack and me in the cyclone, the Doctor was prevented from falling by the chains and weight, which had fallen from the other side of the plank and now acted as a balance to keep him from falling. He swung upside down from the plank – I thought I made out a bemused shout of surprise.

Then I saw the sailor with the cutlass make for the ropes securing the plank to the deck. If he cut those the plank would fall, taking the Doctor with it to his death.

I ran for the pirate, who swung to face me, cutlass outstretched. I drew my blade and threw it with one motion. The pirate fell, the cutlass scraping the deck before jamming against the rail. I retrieved my knife and scooped up the cutlass. Such a long blade was unfamiliar, but its reach would be useful.

The ship was now in an uproar. There were shouts and the sound of pistols firing. Screams lifted into the night. Another cannon blast sounded. This time the ship took the blast broadside at the waterline. Smashed planking erupted into the air in a burst of flame and smoke. I saw three men impaled by smashed railing – two Peruvians and an islander. At the same time yellow flame gushed upward from the quarterdeck as the oil lamps which had been fixed to the smashed mizzenmast set light to the fallen shrouds.

I turned to the Doctor and ran out along the plank.

'Do you know, Leela,' he called from beneath me. 'I really hate hanging about like this. It's awfully boring. Can you get me free?'

'No.' I could not cut the chains. If I pushed them free of the plank the Doctor would fall. There was no way to free him without killing him. Worse, my weight on the plank was bending it towards the sea. And the combined weight of the Doctor and the cannon barrel was dragging the chains in juddering movements along the plank. They were about two feet from the end. And the further they got the more the plank bent.

I heard the Doctor call, 'The chains are secured by locks. DaBraisse has the keys. Get the keys, Leela! It's the only way to free me.'

Without answering I leapt from the plank on to the deck, which by now was covered with fighting pirates and islanders. I looked around for DaBraisse, seeing nothing but flashing steel and puffs of smoke and flames. The cannon sounded again. I crouched, expecting the ship to roll as before, but there was no movement. The cannon were obviously being aimed at another ship. In confirmation I heard a massive explosion to starboard. The fighting stopped momentarily as everyone turned to witness a nearby ship burst into flames.

'– hit the magazine –'

'– down she's going to –'

The ship took another broadside at the waterline and exploded violently, a vision whose light dwarfed the crescent moon easily. Her masts snapped, her sails blazing in the night, a rain of smoke and burning debris smashing into the water and the other ships anchored nearby. Above my head, debris slashed a trail of sparks and smoke through the mainmast rigging. The shrouds caught and the air was full of smoke. I turned as a pirate swung towards me, and threw the cutlass. It turned in midair, striking the man and knocking him over. I leapt forward and cut his throat, moving on quickly before anyone else could attack me.

By now the fighting had renewed, with the added complication that men were leaping off the side to avoid the flames prowling like starving animals across everything that would burn. I wanted very much to join the fleeing men but could not. If I saved myself the Doctor would die. I had to find the key. And that meant finding DaBraisse. But how was I to do that? I could see only one chance.

I turned towards the foremast and began to climb the rigging. I knew my only chance of finding the pirate Captain was to try for a better view. I gained the first spar and tried to peer through the smoke and flames. I saw cook on the port beam throw a handful of pepper in a pirate's face and then bury his cleaver in the man's skull while he was trying to claw the stuff from his eyes. He waved to me as he pulled the cleaver free.

Then a shout from the starboard beam caught my attention. Someone was on the plank with the Doctor, pushing the chains along the plank so that he would fall off. At the same time I caught sight of a man moving with some purpose through the screaming sailors, cutlass flashing and pistol spitting flame as he strode untouched through the smoke. This fellow wore clothes of a finer quality than the rest. And he moved as if he knew what he was doing. He had not succumbed to the panic aboard ship. It must be DaBraisse. But he was on the mid-deck and making for the port side. If I went to help the Doctor he would escape. And if I tried to get the keys to free the Doctor the pirate working on his chains would have the time he needed to drop the Doctor over the side. The man working at the Doctor's chains was too far away for me to throw a knife at. There was only one chance.

I ran lightly along the burning spar on which I was perched, cut away a long length of furling rope, lashed it to the end of the spar and threw myself off the mast. I screamed as I swung down from the spar, felt smoke rush into my lungs and scorch them. I screamed to get the attention of the man working to kill the Doctor. If I could distract him for just a second I would hit him and knock him off the plank. The man looked up as I hoped he would. His mouth opened in surprise as I flew through the air, past him, round in a big arc out over the water and back again, kicking him with both feet soundly in the head as I passed, knocking him from the plank before spinning back across a deck now burning fiercely to smash against another pirate at the exact moment the spar from which my rope hung burnt through and smashed into the deck.

Clinging to the pirate I fell to the deck with enough force to knock the breath from me. I lost my grip on my knife, which skittered away across the deck. The pirate was on his feet in an instant, pistol levelled. I was staring at death. I knew what it was like to be shot and I wasn't looking forward to it happening again. But there was nothing I could do about it. I had no weapon.

I heard the shot before I felt it. In fact – I did not feel the impact at all. I stood quite still, waiting to fall, waiting to die.

Nothing. Instead the pirate froze, an expression of astonishment crossing his face before he fell, to reveal Royston, holding a small pistol. 'You see, Leela?' He called with a grin. 'I told you you could –' he stopped suddenly, coughed blood and fell to the deck – 'trust –' He blinked, rolled on to his side, and kicked feebly.

I saw the dagger emerging from Royston's side at the same time I saw the pirate captain staring at me. At the same time as the foremast top spar began to fall, burning, to the deck.

DaBraisse. Pistol levelled. At me.

I moved fast, rolling across the deck as the spar fell, to smash into the deck between us. I heard the pistol discharge but once again felt no shot. I dived over the burning wreckage and wrapped my arms around DaBraisse's waist, and we both crashed to the deck. We rolled in flames. My skin screamed. I felt his hands about my neck. But I wasn't trying to kill him. That could come later. I wanted the keys I had seen jangling at his belt.

I grabbed the keys, whipped them backwards into his face as his grip tightened about my throat. He screamed and rolled away from me. Scrabbling for a weapon, he fell through a gap in the deckrail and vanished overboard.

Wasting no more time, I hurled myself through a wall of flame and on to the port deck. The Doctor was hanging, feet uppermost, at the very edge of the plank, which was cracking from the heat even as I ran along it. The ship's movement made footing treacherous. As I reached the Doctor one of the chains slipped over the edge. He fell an arm's length closer to the water before jerking to a halt. I stretched downward to cut the ropes binding his arms and then reached for the locks holding the chains tight around the Doctor's ankles. I had the key in the lock when the boat rocked with another explosion and the chains slipped again. Now the Doctor was hanging upside down, his head under water and the locks at his ankles well out of my reach. In a few moments he would drown. But I couldn't reach the locks.

Desperately, I wound the loose chain around my own ankle and lowered myself head first from the creaking plank. It took me three tries to get the key in the lock, and each second our combined weight dragged the cannon upward and lowered us further into the water.

Then the lock sprang open with a rusty click and the Doctor plunged into the water. At the same time, freed of its balancing weight, the cannon fell from the other side of the plank, dragging me back upward and over the top with it.

Now I was hanging from the plank with the chain wrapped around my ankle, the cannon a muscle-cracking weight at my feet, a moment away from drowning myself.

Desperately I kicked my way clear of the chain and hauled myself back up on to the plank – just as it cracked through and began to fall.

I scrambled on to the burning deck as first the cannon and then the plank followed the Doctor into the bay.

I got up and tried to find a way across the deck. I had been wrong about Royston. He had saved my life. If there was the slightest chance he was alive I was going to save his in return.

The deck was almost completely burnt through and the ship was listing badly. The foremast was creaking dangerously above me as I used another rope to swing across to the port beam. Royston was where I had left him, tucked into a corner of the mid-hatch coaming. I could see much blood – but he was moving. I ran to him and scooped him up. He groaned. Good. If he had the strength to protest he had a chance at life.

Holding Royston, I turned towards the port rail – it was on fire. There was no way off the ship there. The front of the ship was now a wall of flame and the deck was collapsing beneath my feet. I ran towards the stern of the ship, trying to find a way off. The deck was a maze of burning wreckage; the remains of the mid- and mizzenmast, the spars, burning shrouds, the dead bodies of islanders and pirates alike. I ran towards the stern. As I passed the mid-deck hatch it blew into the air atop a fountain of flame. Part of the deck followed almost immediately. Burning debris peppered my back and hair. The ship's magazine had caught fire. I remembered the other ship exploding and ran faster, flames licking at my heels, the deck shaking and tipping under my feet so that I was running uphill, the smoking wreckage of spars and timbers and ropes falling around me like a burning spinner's web, until the stern rail appeared through the flames and, clutching Royston as if both our lives depended on it, I threw myself over the stern.

The ship exploded while we were still falling, the blast of scorching air lifting us further away from the ship. I remember seeing, while upside down, the mid-deck dissolve into flame. The remaining mast toppled, burning, smashing through the weakened deck and slicing the ship in half, allowing more air in to mix with the burning gunpowder.

A storm of wreckage erupted into the air as we hit the water.

Taking hold of Royston, I dived as a deadly rain of burning timber smashed into the water all around us.

We now had one chance at life – and that depended on how long both of us could hold our breath.

25
Virus

The Doctor explained what the Llibrary had shown us.

'There were aliens who influenced the development of the culture on Easter Island. But they only did it by accident. They lived in a solar system – this system – many light years away, and were fighting their own great war at the time.

'Losing the fight to their aggressors, they decided to preserve their race by launching great quantities of their own DNA into space, preserved within support mechanisms controlled by intelligent machines. On arrival at a suitable world, the DNA would be introduced into a group of host organisms. This DNA would then attach itself to the host species' DNA and remain dormant there, hidden from any inquisitive glance by the aggressor species.

'The DNA would remain hidden as long as it took for the aggressors to leave the original system. When this happened a signal would be sent to the intelligent machines, now spread randomly throughout the galaxy. The machines would use subsidiary extensions – what you know as the walking stones – to open and stabilise the negative mass of an Einstein–Rosen Bridge – a kind of tunnel through space – and the individual members of the host species carrying the dormant DNA would be returned through the bridge to the original home system, where automatic systems would reactivate the dormant DNA and re-create the original species from the host individuals.

Obviously this would take thousands of individuals – so many of the intelligent machines were launched into space. One came to Earth – to Rapa Nui – and influenced the culture there over the generations that it remained dormant. Hence stripping the island to build the *moai* – a reaction to a buried race memory which may have slipped back into the islanders' cultural patterns over the generations.' The Doctor thought for a moment and then added, 'So that's what happened to the thousands of islanders that have vanished over the generations: used as carrier pigeons for an alien amino-acid chain.'

I frowned. This was beginning to sound more than ever like the ramblings of a tortured mind. 'Doctor, I am a medical man, a man of science. I hear your words but I do not understand them. What is "DNA"? What is an "amino-acid chain"? And what has it got to do with carrier pigeons? How can an individual be transformed into another? Surely that is akin to alchemy – and we all know how ridiculous that idea is.'

Now it was the Doctor's turn to frown. 'Yes, of course, stupid of me. We're about a century too early for DNA, aren't we?' He thought for a moment. 'All right, think of it like this: you're fighting a war and you want to send important messages to your men at the front.'

'Yes.'

'But you can't send them in plain English because your enemy can read English.'

'Yes.'

'So what do you do?'

'Why, send them in code of course!' The moment the words passed my lips I understood the Doctor's analogy.

The Doctor beamed. 'It's so simple. The aliens had encoded *themselves*. The islanders were their message. The *rongo-rongo* was the cipher wheel used to encrypt the message and the *moai* the means of transmitting it.'

I looked at Horace. He was smiling – he understood, too. Even Richards's expression showed a dawning realisation.

Only Leela seemed puzzled. 'If they were so clever, why are

they still dead?'

The Doctor began to pace. 'A good question. Anyone know the answer? James?'

I hazarded a guess. 'Either the encryption details were lost or the message became corrupt.'

The Doctor nodded, displaying the absent-minded pleasure a schoolteacher might take in a promising pupil. 'Or the encrypted message was re-encrypted.'

'I don't understand.'

'The library mentions a plague. And it seems clear to me that the surviving structures within this culture are not as old as the culture itself. Someone must have been alive to build or maintain them.'

'But who?'

'Well, it's my guess that the plan worked and many thousands of carrier organisms were returned through various wormholes from many different planets to this system. Enough to begin reseeding the race. Then disaster struck: one carrier organism returned with an additional virus – one unknown and lethal to the original species. A plague. One which wiped them all out for a second time, leaving just the intact structures and cultural remnants we've all seen, the oldest site being the factory world where the original *moai* were built and launched into space.'

There was a moment's silence as we all considered the Doctor's tragic hypothesis.

'But which of the thousands of host organisms carried the virus?' Horace asked in a whisper.

'According to the library, the last host organisms arrived here about thirty years ago – and originated from Earth.'

Horace said quietly, 'You mean *we* killed them?'

The Doctor nodded.

I said, 'The Polynesians are an isolated culture – those on

Rapa Nui even more so than most. It's possible they have not been exposed to certain diseases. Visitors to the island could have brought anything from measles to smallpox – any one of which might have been lethal to the islanders or carried in a dormant form when they returned here. Do you remember telling me Tortorro's son suffered from a fever? Well, that might have been given to him by one of the men on your ship – someone who displayed no symptoms of the disease himself.'

'I see.' Horace's voice seemed to shrink. He licked his lips. 'I think I'm going to go for a walk if you don't mind. I think I need some air.'

The Doctor said sympathetically, 'Of course, my dear fellow, but don't wander too far, will you?'

'Don't worry. I've seen how easy it is to get lost here.'

He walked out of the library and into the daylight.

The rest of us were silent for quite a while longer.

'Do you think they'll ever come back again?' I asked. 'It would be such a shame if all this were to be… well, wasted.'

'Shame?' The Doctor frowned. 'That has to be the understatement of the millennium. It would be a tragedy beyond even biblical proportions.'

'But… there were thousands of *moai* abandoned on the factory world. They must have sent millions into space.'

'Even millions isn't that many. Consider the sycamore tree – that releases thousands of seeds every year. Over the lifespan of the tree that probably adds up to millions. How many seeds come to fruition? How many fall on stony ground or are eaten by animals or killed by cold or radiation or any of a hundred other natural controls?'

'I see what you mean.' I thought for a moment. The wound in my side was aching and I too felt like sitting down. 'In other words… these islanders… they could be this culture's last hope of survival.'

He nodded. 'But they're still carrying the virus. Whatever it is.'

Another thought had been worrying me. I voiced it now while I struggled to understand the Doctor's words. 'I've been thinking about something else. Can you explain how it is that I still live? As a student of the human anatomy I'm quite aware that the wound DaBraisse inflicted was terminal.'

The Doctor shrugged. 'That I don't know. Perhaps the transport system has some kind of biological stabilising subroutine built into it – something to minimise or control physical trauma to emergent returnees.'

I thought about that. 'If there was, wouldn't it prevent the islanders from bringing a plague here?'

'Possibly. Perhaps they never thought of that. I imagine they were in something of a hurry. And perhaps they were just unlucky. The chances of a host virus being able to affect the originator species are probably millions to one against. Think of animals – most diseases that affect dogs don't affect people. Those that can be transmitted across species are rare.'

'Not being a veterinarian, I'll take your word for that.'

'Good. An open mind is the sign of true forward thinking.'

I studied the Doctor intently. I shivered, and not just with the cold. I watched him has he glanced around the library, touching the walls and floor with his eyes and mind, caressing the structures – and more than that, reaching backwards in time to the people who had built them. 'You want to bring them back, don't you?' It wasn't a great leap of imagination.

'I want to do a very great many things before I grow old.' His voice – and his expression – hinted at awe for the ingenuity of this alien species.

For myself I was in two minds. Although the victims in this situation were only Polynesians, still they were humans. On the one hand I could see how the Doctor might be impressed. On the other, as a member of the species who might have been affected by their actions, I felt only outrage.

The Doctor moved to one side and placed his hand flat against the curved wall of the library. 'The DNA hidden from your enemies inside another species, the wormholes to bring the DNA carriers back. It was a good plan. It should have worked. It deserved to have worked. All we have to do to make it work is work out why it didn't.'

'So we're back to the plague again?'

'Yes.'

'Something to which the islanders are immune but which is lethal to the species whose DNA they carry?'

'Yes.'

'And which wiped out the previous colonists when brought here by the islanders decades ago?'

'That's it exactly.'

'Well… as a doctor I have to say there are any number of possibilities. Measles, mumps, chickenpox, scarlet fever, whooping cough, polio, the common cold.'

The Doctor nodded glumly. 'A list as long as my scarf.'

I looked at the prodigious item of apparel and frowned. 'I do hope not.'

'I wonder if a broad-spectrum antibiotic would –'

'A what?'

'Never mind. I don't suppose you've heard of penicillin?'

I frowned.

'Or got any? I had some, you see, been keeping it for a rainy day. But DaBraisse, he went through my pockets while I was a prisoner on the man o' war. I made the mistake of telling him I had diamonds. He took everything. Even my yo-yo.'

'I see.'

He thought further. 'You know, I get the feeling I'm missing something. Do you ever get that feeling? That there's something right there, perched on the end of your nose, but you can't see it?'

'Not unless you're talking about a pair of spectacles.'

'Dr Royston, this is no time to be obtuse. We need answers.'

I considered. 'I suppose we could synthesise a serum from my blood, or from Horace's or Miss Richards's. We'd be immune to or inoculated against some of those diseases.'

He sighed. 'It's no good. We need to hit all of them at once. And that means you'd have to be inoculated against them all, and that's impossible, unless you were from –'

Leela interrupted warningly. 'Doctor, Something is wrong, I feel it –' But the Doctor wasn't listening. He had turned, slowly, to stare at his companion.

'– the future!' He finished, suddenly slapping himself on the head. 'Oh! I'm a dunce! I'm an utter nitwit! A nincompoop of prodigious proportions!' Picking Leela up as if she were a child's doll, the Doctor whirled her around in a kind of madcap dance. Clouds of dust erupted at every step.

'Doctor, what –' Leela protested.

'Leela, I've said it before and I'll say it again: you're a genius!'

'Oh good. What's a genius?'

'It doesn't matter. What does matter is that you're from the future! Hundreds of generations in the future. Those on Earth now are your ancestors. Why, Dr Royston here might be your great-great-great-great-great-great… er, where was I? Oh yes, great-great-grandfather.'

'And?'

'Well, medical advances being what they are I should think you're immune to everything and the common cold. I mean, why else send starships out looking for new planets to colonise unless the population growth on good old Terra Firma had been raised to bursting point by advances in medical knowledge and techniques?'

'Er…' Leela bounced helplessly in the Doctor's arms.

'I don't know.'

'Know? Of course you don't know! Not in your head, not in your experience. But in your genes, Leela. Your DNA. Because immunity factors can be conferred and transferred and bottled and labelled and… ooh, you are a clever savage, did I ever tell you that?'

'You said I was a genius.'

'Did I? Oh good.' The Doctor abruptly deposited Leela on her feet, where she swayed dizzily for a moment, beaming happily. 'Now we must cross back over the Einstein-Rosen Bridge. Go back to the island. You must get whatever medical supplies and equipment you can and then we can take some of Leela's blood and we can inoculate the islanders so they won't carry whatever disease it was that killed the last lot of returnees, and then, when they are ready, they can come back again. To their home. And the dead can live again. Just like in the prophecy. Across the sea of night to shores where dreams are real.' He beamed, and his smile seemed to warm this cold land for a moment, as if in preparation for new arrivals.

'Now doesn't that sound like a good idea?'

I had to agree.

The Doctor seemed about to expound even further upon the subject when Leela suddenly looked around in alarm. 'Did you hear that?'

'What?'

'A cry! The sound of death!' Her expression hardened. 'Where is Richards?'

I looked around. She had gone, slipped out, I presumed, while we were talking. And then it hit me. She had followed Horace. Could it be she intended him harm?

Leela obviously thought so. 'I said I felt something!'

Dagger drawn, Leela ran from the library. The Doctor and I followed.

We found Stockwood and Richards huddled together on the ground, motionless. Blood seeped out from beneath their bodies; I could not tell whose.

'I warned Stockwood about her. I said we should have killed her. Now it is too late!'

I was about to move close to examine them when Leela gave a sudden shout – not a word, an utterance. A noise that seemed more akin to an animal than any person. I looked at her in surprise. She staggered backward, sat abruptly on the ramp. Her face was alight with dumb shock, pointed upward into the sky. I followed her gaze.

'*The sun. Something has poisoned the sun!*'

26
The Cave of the Sun's Inclination

All I really wanted to do was sleep. At this moment I would have traded every penny I ever owned for one night's sleep. One night with the dreams of childhood, of innocence. One night with fantasies of the French tutor mother had once arranged for summer holidays, one night with memories of my mint-julep-sodden fifth Christmas, one night with dreams of bullying or football or inadequacy. Anything. Anything at all. Anything rather than face Alex for this last time.

But my dreams had vanished years ago into a past long clouded by doubt and guilt and nightmares. And now I was here, on the southern slopes of Ranu Raraku, in sight of the stone devils that had hounded me from a secure and confident youth into a dubious future; here with the funeral bier of my old friend with visions of whose death I had tortured myself for thirty years, never once realising what the awful, ironic truth of his actual death would finally be, or how much more it would hurt than all my life's fevered imaginings.

And so I stood with my friend in the star-shadowed darkness of the crater, the moon gone, and I laid my hand upon his cold brow, lined in madness, now smoothed in death, and I bawled like a child and screamed and stamped and kicked the nearest stone monolith and cursed it to move and punched it with what feeble strength I possessed until finally, spent, aching in every joint, the skin of my knuckles rubbed agonisingly raw, I sank to the ground beside the bier and let the chill of the ground and the sky and his death seep into every bone and fibre of my being and mind.

And I knew he was gone.

And he *was* gone.

But I was not alone. *She* was here as well. I saw her cloak outlined against the stars. A void darker than the night sky shaped like a woman. She walked slowly across the grassy stones of the crater to stand beside us. 'I have only to close my eyes for a moment in exhaustion or grief and, in my head, he is alive.' Her voice was a whisper, loaded with grief.

I nodded silently. 'His skin warm, his face creased in concentration or laughter; the insignificant movements of and relationships between the facial features that signify the ongoing processes taking place within the controlling mind.' Processes which I knew had now stopped.

I heard surprise in her voice. 'You understand.'

'How could I not?'

'I don't know what to do. I stand here and look at him and my heart tells me this husk is not my brother. It is not how I remember him. It is not my brother.'

'It is. Oh, Lord, save us, for it *is* he.'

And now she turned away from the bier, turned to face me, the grief replaced by anger. By rage. 'Get up, you snivelling wretch. Show some pride and manhood before the man your arrogance destroyed!'

I let my head sink on to my chest. Truly I was a wretched specimen. I could not respond, could not argue, could not even speak to this woman whose grief I understood at least as clearly as my own.

'And don't think you understand what I am feeling. You do not!' Her voice was a whip in the darkness, cracking about my body. 'You men. You go off on your adventuring. You live your dream and in some cases you die for it. And that's enough for you. Well, it isn't enough for me! None of you ever think of the women who love you. The women you leave behind. The women you judge too frail or stupid to accompany you into life's great adventure. A woman would – *could* – never do that. She would never leave family or loved ones, not for all the scientific knowledge, nor the acclaim or fortune it brings, nor all the tea in China!' Her voice broke then and she began to sob. 'I do not understand you and I hope to God in heaven I never will.'

Another voice spoke harshly in the darkness. Leela. I had not heard her arrive. That wasn't surprising. She moved like a shadow. 'Hear me, Richards, sister of Alexander, who is dead. My name is Leela and I am a warrior of the Sevateem. Where I come from I am a hunter and a provider. I have saved the lives of many and taken the lives of many to do so. I have loved ones and I have left them. I came here to this land to understand myself and my ancestors. The Doctor tells me that by learning we change ourselves. He invokes the Prayer of Uncertainty by the Priest Heisenberg: "That which we study and learn from, we also change." This I do not understand. But I know this: all things can be understood by those with the will. All things. And I will keep my love for my father and mother and sister, though my father is dead and my sister was killed before I was born, and I will hold their faces and their love like holy metal within my head and I will *still* go open-eyed into the world – because if you do not learn then you are no better than an animal: just mindless meat waiting to become somebody's food. Hear me, Richards, and hear this: if the women in your land do not learn and travel and take control of the ties that bind them, then *they are already dead*. Rejoice, Richards. Offer thanks that the death of your brother has brought you life, as the death of my sister brought me life.'

Leela fell silent. I wondered if she had gone as quietly as she came. Probably not. I had a feeling she was there not to argue with Richards as much as to protect me from her wrath. But

255

Leela had made a telling point. Life was what was important. I had life. How much of it had I wasted on guilt for a death that had not occurred?

I began to get to my feet. I was cold and my legs were getting cramped. I needed to take a few paces to restore the circulation. As I moved so did Richards. She moved towards me, as if to help me rise.

Leela spoke at the same time, her voice even harsher than before. 'Hear me, Richards. Put down the knife. Attempt to take Stockwood's life and you will lose your own.'

Richards froze. So did I, half risen from the ground. The starlight painted us all in a dim tableau.

And I saw the knife Richards was holding. Had been holding, I now realised, all the while.

'You were going to kill me?'

Richards's voice cracked with emotion. 'I promised you that much. Your pet animal saved you this time. But she won't always be around.' Richards turned and walked away from us across the crater. I thought I heard sobs as she went. They, at least, must be genuine.

Leela helped me to my feet and we watched her go.

'I can't believe she had a knife on me the whole time.'

'I would not have let her kill you.'

I kicked frustratedly at some loose rocks. 'But don't you think she is right? Don't you think I deserve to die?'

'No.' Her response was stark, immediate, completed by a single qualification. 'If I thought that I would kill you myself.'

My face tried for a smile without my permission. 'You are a strange woman, Leela.'

'Why?'

I hesitated. 'That wasn't the answer I expected.'

'You should expect the unexpected. That way you will live longer.'

'I suppose so.' I looked up at the stars. They were clear and bright, no hint of cloud shadow. The moon had dipped beneath the hills. It seemed that we alone existed in all of space and all of time. For a moment I found myself imagining a set of cosmic scales. One where Alex weighed in for Death and Leela contributed her mass to Life, and the stars above coldly observed the difference. Where did that leave me? A symbol for humanity, caught, as ever, in the brief moment of balance? A child species brimful of speculations and tribulations, fears, hopes and dreams, for ever changed by the moment of observation? I did not know. But I might learn. If I took the control about which Leela spoke. If I added my weight to Life and abandoned my friend a final time to Death. It was a decision I could not make immediately. I opted for an interim step. 'Tell me what happened in the attack.'

'I would rather kill Richards.'

'Leave her. She won't hurt anyone.'

'If an animal has gone mad you must kill it before it kills you.'

'She's not mad. Only with grief.'

'She is right, Stockwood. You do not understand her.'

I sighed. 'Don't you all gang up on me. Tell me about the attack.'

'We took one of their ships. Two were destroyed. The rest escaped.'

'Four against two. That's better odds than before, anyway.'

'You are wrong. The ship we captured was badly damaged by cannon fire. And *Tweed* has no weapons. Captain Stuart is transferring some of the undamaged cannon to his ship now in case DaBraisse comes back.'

'DaBraisse?'

'The pirate leader. He got away.'

'Oh. Was anyone else hurt?'

Now it was Leela's turn to hesitate. 'Royston was injured

saving my life. I did not trust him. I was wrong. The Doctor is with him now, trying to save his life.'

I felt the ground lurch beneath my feet. 'Why didn't you tell me?'

'I have told you now.'

'I have to go to him.'

'There is nothing you can do.'

'I can pray.'

I found the Doctor and Royston in the village, in a hut, surrounded by islanders and a few squawking chickens. My friend lay on a bed of grass, bare to the waist so the Doctor could examine his wound. It did not look bad: a thin strip of inflamed flesh with a slit in the middle of it. But it ran deeply into his side. When he breathed I heard a faint gurgle. There was blood in his lungs. His brow was fevered, his skin waxy. Though unconscious, he jerked and thrashed. A number of islanders held him to the ground.

The Doctor straightened from his examination. 'It's not good news, I'm afraid. The wound is deep. The lungs have been penetrated. And there was some poison involved.'

'Can you save him?'

The Doctor hesitated. 'I'm sorry, Horace. The most I can do is make him comfortable. It won't be for long.'

'I don't believe you! I saw you shot in the chest! You healed yourself, now heal my friend!'

The Doctor spread his hands sorrowfully. 'Horace, listen to me carefully. I was not born on this world. The technique I used on myself owes part of its effectiveness to that and part to a three-hundred-year-old Tibetan philosophy in which I am but a novice. I cannot save your friend.'

I felt anger inflame me. 'You speak of aliens and three-hundred-year-old monks and my friend is dying! You mock me, sir! I will not have it!'

I ran forward and aimed a punch at the Doctor. Leela caught my arm before the movement was half over. 'Listen to his words. He speaks the truth.'

'His words are nonsense.'

The Doctor took Leela by the shoulders and gently moved her aside. He took my head and laid it against his chest. 'Listen.'

I struggled. His grip allowed no movement.

'Do you hear the heartbeat?'

'Yes! Now let me –'

He moved my head to the other side of his chest. 'Tell me what you hear!'

I froze. It was impossible. My mind reeled. 'I hear… another… it's impossible!'

He let me go. 'Listen to me, Stockwood. If there was a way I could use one of my hearts to save your friend I would. This is not fantasy. I cannot save him. I am sorry.'

I stuttered something, I do not remember the words. I felt my mind reeling. Too much. It was too much. The shock. I felt my heart hammer in my chest. I heard the thump of blood in my ears. My eyes saw nothing but whirling shapes. I struggled for breath.

'I know how to save him.'

The words were like a slap, a bucket of icy water across my face. I turned. Facing me was the woman who had recognised me. The woman who had killed Alex. 'Get her away from me! I'll kill her! I swear I'll –'

I lurched forward towards the woman. I felt hands grab me. In truth it did not take many to hold me fast.

The Doctor spoke softly. 'I think you'd better explain, Atani.'

The woman gazed peculiarly at the Doctor, her eyes moving from one side of his chest to the other. I thought about the double heartbeat I had heard and was silent. 'If you want to save your friend take him to Vai-tarakai-ua – the *moai* in the elder's cave, the Cave of the Sun's Inclination.'

Leela said scathingly, 'How can a statue save Royston?'

'Stockwood took the *rongo-rongo* from us. Now he is returned. Take Royston to the cave and speak the healing prayer inscribed on the *rongo-rongo* and Vai-tarakai-ua will save him.' The woman turned to leave, then looked back and added one more thing. 'It has been many, many years since the *moai* have walked on this land – now the *rongo-rongo* has returned, perhaps they will walk again. Then the sun will shine in the night and the dead will live again. And we may go to join our ancestors.' Atani pushed through the villagers and out of the hut.

For a moment there was silence.

'This is sheer nonsense!' I spluttered.

The Doctor glanced at me. 'I thought you were a scientist. An anthropologist. Do you never listen to the people you study?'

I fell silent, ashamed. He waited for a reply. 'Of course.'

'Then let's listen to what she said.' The Doctor turned to Topeno, standing nearby wearing an angry expression. 'Is there truth in Atani's words?'

Topeno frowned. 'She is old. Age does not always bring wisdom.'

'Don't avoid the question. I didn't ask if she was wise, I asked if she spoke the truth.'

Topeno licked his lips. Others among the islanders were stirring, their voices muttering uneasily. 'Once her words would have been truth.'

The Doctor nodded. He began to mumble to himself. '*Moai*. Fluctuating mass. *Rongo-rongo*. Missing. Returned. Once she would have spoken the truth. Spoken. Speaking. Speak the prayer of healing.' He nodded. 'We have to get Royston to the Cave of the Sun's Inclination. Now!'

The Doctor scooped my friend off the mat of grass on which

he lay as if he were a child. 'Topeno.' It was not a request. The islander led us from the village.

'And you, Stockwood.'

Leela in tow, I followed the little entourage along a path from the village into the hills. There we descended into a small cave, the Doctor still managing to carry James even though he was bent almost double.

Minutes passed in dusty silence. Then we emerged into a space I could tell from the echoes was very large. Islanders lit torches. And I gaped in astonishment. The cave was huge – perhaps a hundred yards high and twice that wide. Every piece of rock was covered with painted inscriptions and diagrams. There were figures of birds and men and the curious bird-man hybrid that had captured my attention so thoroughly on my first visit. But the object to which my gaze was inexorably drawn was a *moai* – this one fully twice the height of the others I had seen, which completely filled the middle of the cave. Its monolithic features gleamed dead black in the torchlight, with no hint of tools or markings to show how it was made. The red cap upon its head scraped the roof of the cave. Its eyes, darkened by shadows thrown up from the high cheeks, seemed to glare arrogantly around the cave, to fasten with undeniable eagerness upon my own.

I remembered to breathe.

'Vai-tarakai-ua.' The name was no more than a breath of sound from Topeno's lips. The islanders knelt before the monolith.

The Doctor laid Royston at the place where its chest entered the ground. He cast a quick glance across the planes and angles of the metal face. 'Not so much a god as a voice-activated computer.'

'A what?'

'Never mind. Give me the *rongo-rongo*.'

'The tablet?' I felt a cold sensation rush across my stomach. 'I thought you knew. Richards took it from me shortly after we left Portsmouth. I don't have it.'

The Doctor stared at me impatiently. 'We only need the inscription. Can you remember it?'

'No.' I reached into my pocket. 'But I took a rubbing. It's a few years old now and it may not be accurate but –'

The Doctor snatched the paper from me and smoothed it out. He turned to Topeno. 'Can you read this?'

Topeno studied the paper. 'Of course.'

'Then please do so now.'

Topeno hesitated. 'There are rituals. We must observe the proper respect for Vai-tarakai-ua.'

The Doctor sighed. 'Listen.'

We did so. Even deep underground we could hear the distant thunder of cannon. DaBraisse. The pirates had returned – and renewed their attack.

'Computers do not require respect. If we wait Royston will die. Now read the inscription.'

Still Topeno hesitated. The Doctor sighed. 'Horace, Leela, come here and hold Royston. Topeno, give me that rubbing.'

Leela and I moved forward and took hold of James. The Doctor took the rubbing from Topeno.

'I didn't know you could read Polynesian.'

'It's not Polynesian.' The Doctor began to read.

The sound of cannon fire increased. Topeno and the islanders fled the cave. I heard the clash of steel and the discharge of pistols. Screams. I felt Royston stir beneath my hands.

The Doctor finished the incantation.

And the sun came out.

27
Across the Sea of Night

I gazed up at the sun. Normally dark and sullen, blotched with darker patches, now the sun was brighter, the light harsher. And it was smaller. Shrinking as we watched.

I tore my eyes away from the dying sun, turning my gaze to the ground – where my friend Horace lay, his body entwined in death with the one who had killed him.

No – I looked again. There was movement. Horace groaned and managed to struggle up on to one elbow. Leela knelt beside him and gently examined him. 'You are injured.'

His voice was weak. 'She crept up on me… she went mad… stabbed me… she began to cry… then she took her own life. Why did she do that? She took her own life… and she… spoke not a single word… the whole time.' With a groan, Horace collapsed again, his words draining the last of his dwindling energy.

Leela went to the Doctor, who was staring mesmerised up at the shrinking sun. 'Stockwood is dying.'

The Doctor seemed to ignore Leela. 'Suns don't do that. Not this fast. Something's causing it. But what? Some kind of berserker probe… a fail-safe… a last weapon… in case they came back… But they haven't come back.'

Leela tugged the Doctor's sleeve impatiently. 'They have not come back *but we have*.'

The Doctor slapped himself on the forehead. 'Of course. Any life would trigger it. Any movement, any activity.'

I shook my head. 'No. If the aggressor species left a last booby trap for anyone returning here, it would have been tripped half a century ago – even before the islanders brought the plague here.'

The Doctor frowned. 'You're right. You're right. But then I don't understand....What could be making the sun go –'

Leela interrupted angrily, 'If we wait to work this out then not only this world will die but Stockwood will as well. We cannot save a sun. We can save a man.'

The Doctor suddenly jumped. 'What?' He turned his eyes to the ground. He saw Stockwood, gasping on the ground, Richards lying dead by her own hand beside him – and then he seemed to come to a realisation.

'I must be getting slow! It's not the aggressors – if they'd wanted to destroy the system by blowing up the sun they would simply have done it the first time round. No! Oh, it's still a trap, still responding to our presence, but it's the *originator species who set it*!' He thought for a second, then added, 'Yes, yes, of course, it all makes sense. If you send a million Einstein–Rosen Bridges out across the galaxy you don't want them to be used by just anybody. And if you're as paranoid as a large interstellar war would make anyone then I doubt you'd want your world to fall into the hands of the enemy. So you'd simply build a doomsday weapon and program it to detonate the sun if anyone not carrying dormant originator DNA returned through the wormhole.'

He waited, evidently expecting questions. There were none.

Leela scooped Horace up from the ground. He groaned and lapsed into unconsciousness. 'If we take him back through the *moai* to Rapa Nui he will be healed – like Royston was healed.' It was not a question.

'Yes. Yes, that's logical. At the same time, if we leave the system, then hopefully the booby trap will recognise that and be able to return the sun to normality.' The Doctor spun round. We were faced with at least a hundred clusters of *moai* at various distances from the library. 'Do you remember the way? Can you retrace your steps?'

'I am a hunter.'

'Then run, Leela, run for all our lives! And everyone else –' there was only me – 'be sure and keep up! Now,' he added in a tremendous shout whose echoes rolled to every horizon, and might possibly be the last sound this world would ever hear, '"*Further up and further in!*"'

And with that he scooped up Richards's dead body and together we ran for the first of the many gates in the sequence that would take us back to Rapa Nui and – hopefully – save not only Horace's life but an entire solar system as well.

28
Stone Walking

I was watching three stars burning in Anakena Bay and thinking how good it would feel to take the life of the man who had killed my brother when the *moai* walked.

The stars were Peruvian ships under fire from *Tweed* and the captured pirate vessel. As I watched, one of the ships took a broadside at the waterline and burst spectacularly into flame. The magazine caught fire and it exploded, showering a rain of burning debris for many hundred yards around. A moment later the sound reached me, a concussion rolling like summer thunder across the scrubby hills of the island. I wondered if the ship was under Stuart's or DaBraisse's command. Not that it would make much difference now. More shots were exchanged. More cannon fired.

And then, all around me in the darkness, I felt a storm of energy gathering. My hair prickled. My skin itched. Above, the stars seemed to ripple as cloud drifted inward from every horizon to gather above the island. And then I heard noises. The chanting of islanders. Singing voices. Screams and cries and the sounds of pistol fire and clash of steel were an ugly counterpoint to this primitive but somehow stirring noise.

And then I heard the relentless grind of stone upon stone.

I felt the ground shake. I wondered if the volcanoes here were going to erupt. Then something moved along the cliff top. A wall of stone drifted past me, its passing leaving no trace in the earth. I saw earth and small creatures dragged from the ground and seemingly sucked into its surface. I felt the pressure of wind tugging at me and fought against it. I caught a glimpse of monolithic features in the dim starlight and then it was gone. But its presence lingered. I fell to the ground shaking. This could not be happening! Stone could not walk. *Stone did not walk!*

But I had seen it. And the *moai* had been moving. I had not been dreaming, though the Lord alone knew I had suffered enough shocks to see an army of scientists to their graves.

But I was here. I had seen it. Stockwood was right. The *moai* had walked.

I blinked. The feeling of expectation, of electricity, gathered around me, pulling in the night like a smothering blanket. The very air I breathed seemed charged with energy. I sensed, then saw, other movement about the island. Great shapes moving with purpose in the darkness. Above me clouds had whirled into a vortex, thickening to form an impenetrable ceiling which roofed over the island. Lightning flashed within the cloud.

And then, as one, the movement of stone upon the island halted – as if each monolithic monument had its own place and had now reached it, as if some sleeping giant had awoken briefly from his slumber and turned once beneath the earth before returning to full wakefulness.

The feeling of energy grew. The cloud gathered. Lightning cracked. I felt the air pressing tightly about me.

And then I could not breathe. Everything was moving again, this time in a way I could not describe, let alone understand. It was as if everything on the island – every piece of rock, every animal, every human, every *part* of every rock, animal, and human – was at once splitting apart and rushing together in a colossal explosion of light and noise.

And then – for a moment in the cloud-darkened night – the sun came out.

It was huge, dark and sullen, hovering low to the ground above the volcanic crater of Ranu Raraku. There were two moons. I saw clouds drifting in front of them, clouds from another sky, an impossible world, somehow superimposed upon the real world; alien from the world in which I had been born and lived.

The vision was too much. I felt on the very edge of madness, as if walking a slippery cliff from which one wrong step would send me plummeting into an uncertain future. I screamed but heard no voice. I did not even feel the passage of air in my throat which would have signified making a sound. Everything was suddenly motionless. The light, the clouds above, the fighting, the smoke from cannon in the bay, frozen as if by a painter's eye, and transcribed on to canvas.

In that moment I remembered ice dripping from ferns at the edge of a pond where I had played with my brother as a child, the only movement his excited form skittering across the frozen surface on wellington boots three sizes too large to avoid cracking the ice.

Jenny, hurry, come and look at this! See how the ice remains frozen, the movement stilled? A perfect encapsulation of a particle of time!

I remembered his arms waving excitedly, his hands blue with cold as he touched the frozen ferns. I remember his voice, how it shook, the joy of discovery in it; the moment of dawning when he knew the path his life would follow, and I suddenly burst into tears. He was gone. My brother was *gone*! Thirty years I had grieved when I could have come here at any time and brought him home, and all it would have cost was money. And now it was too late. Because of Stockwood.

I vowed to kill the man who had brought my brother to his ruin – and in that moment the sun went out, taking its impossible world with it into storm-tossed oblivion.

The island was dark again. Above, the clouds shredded as if torn apart by a giant's breath. I could breathe. I could scream. I could hear gunfire and shouts and

people there were people coming up the cliff path and
there were pirates. DaBraisse and his men. Come to take us all to perdition.

I turned to run, found another figure behind me, this one made of flesh and blood and righteous anger but still as impressive as any *moai*.

'Give me the *rongo-rongo*,' said the Doctor.

'I can't do that.'

'"The sun will come out at night. The dead will live again." Your brother knew the truth.'

'And died for it!'

'And how many more must die because of you? I understand your grief. I understand your anger. You have to let them go. There are larger issues at stake.'

I laughed contemptuously, remembering Alex's words as he left with Stockwood so many years ago, remembering Stockwood's words when he returned without my brother. 'I do not care about scientific truth. I do not care about alien cultures. I do not care about destiny. I want to kill Stockwood. That is all. After that my life has no meaning.'

'He's gone. The bridge exists. You saw it. You saw the sun come out at night. You saw the sky of another world!'

'Ridiculous!'

'Give me the tablet! The inscription we have is incomplete. With the tablet the islanders can fulfil their destiny. Rejoin their ancestors. *Become* their ancestors.'

Before I could answer, a man's voice said, 'The time for games is over, Doctor.' DaBraisse. 'Miss Richards, you will give the *rongo-rongo* to me.'

Half a dozen men bearing cutlasses and pistols emerged on to the cliff above Anakena Bay. They stood behind their leader, weapons drawn, faces set in violent anticipation. The newly reappeared stars painted them with a cold, inhuman light.

I ran to stand beside DaBraisse.

The Doctor looked at me. Compassion. Pity. Curiosity. I shrugged off the look. I did not care what he thought, what anyone thought. DaBraisse would get me what I wanted. He would kill Stockwood and anyone else who got between us. I did not care if everyone on the island was slaughtered so long as Stockwood died. If the *rongo-rongo* was the price of that co-operation I would not hesitate to pay it. 'Your friend Leela gave me some good advice. I have now taken it.'

'And sold out to the enemy.'

'I am not your enemy, Doctor.' DaBraisse's voice was soft but it carried easily on the cool night air.

'That's an odd way of describing a man who tried to make me walk the plank.'

The pirate laughed. 'I am your death!' He drew his cutlass and advanced towards the Doctor.

The Doctor jumped backwards. 'You would attack an unarmed man?'

DaBraisse laughed. 'Oh, you English, you are so parochial. Of course I would attack an unarmed man. And now I will.' Sword arm extended, he leapt forward.

The Doctor whirled, looped his scarf around a jut of rock and leapt out from the cliff. He spun out over the bay, so far below, whirled around DaBraisse and landed lightly behind the pirate on the cliff path. The other men were too astonished to react. Before they could so much as even gasp in surprise, the Doctor had grasped a cutlass from the belt of one and jumped again from the path, where he swung, suspended again over three hundred feet of empty air, before landing back on the other side of DaBraisse, just as the pirate finished turning around to face his men.

'Here I am, DaBraisse! You want to play games? Very well. I say let us play catch as catch can!' The Doctor ran backwards along the cliff path. I waited for him to fall. He did not. I cursed Stump's inability to kill the man in Portsmouth. 'DaBraisse, he is playing with you! All my gold if you kill him!'

DaBraisse glanced back at me just once. I had a moment to realise my mistake as he spoke. 'Your gold is in England or on the boat. Either way I do not need you.' To the men he added, 'Kill her!'

In a moment I was held. I had no time to scream. I felt a freezing pain pierce my side. A knife. I sank to the path. I could not breathe. I could not scream. I could not see.

I waited to die. I waited for the blow or shot that would finish me.

Neither came.

I felt the rocks writhe underneath me – no, it was I who was writhing, jerking with the need to live, the body's reaction to the shock of the wound I knew must be mortal.

I heard voices. Islanders. Screams. I felt hands lift me, burning where they touched so that I gasped. My vision cleared for a moment as I rose, parting like clouds just long enough to see the duel between the Doctor and DaBraisse, which I had started, come to its inevitable conclusion.

I surrendered to the pain of death, knowing at last that with DaBraisse's long fall from the cliff top had gone my last chance to see Stockwood dead. The Doctor lived. And now I would die.

I watched him approach. He took me from the islanders.

His voice echoed as if from a long way away. 'The Cave of the Sun's Inclination. We must take her there. Now.'

A voice I recognised dimly through the pain as Topeno said, 'Her life is not important.'

The Doctor's voice was furious. 'Every life is important, Topeno. Do you hear me? *Every life!*'

And holding that life – my life – in his hands, he began to run.

Epilogue
The Eye Which Sees Heaven

December 1902

'Old and young, we are all on our last cruise.'

Robert Louis Stevenson,
'Crabbed Age and Youth'

The great *moai* are walking.

They shape the night and day of this microcosm we men call Rapa Nui – Easter Island. Named for the resurrection of Christ, it is now the source of resurrection for an alien species whose name I have never known.

Thirty years have passed since the Doctor and Leela departed Rapa Nui with naturalist and painter Marie Anne North on the first leg of their journey to India. I often wonder what adventures befell them there. James Royston has gone, too, with his own burden of experiences, carried once again by Captain Stuart on his wonderful vessel *Tweed*. Richards we buried beside her brother upon our return to the island. Of those who left England, only I have remained upon this island, which shaped so much of my life. It is my belief that the people here deserve a protector, someone to guard against other men of the sword such as DaBraisse – as well as men of knowledge such as I once was myself.

It is a good life, if a trifle lacking in the basics. I miss shampoo most of all. That and Chocolate Surprise.

Every year the *moai* walk. Every year the island's population grows less. I have watched the numbers fall from twenty thousand to less than two hundred in a matter of years. In the days and years to come others will puzzle over this. They will suggest sickness or deforestation or slavery to be the cause. But I know the truth. Here in my last year of life I will see it again, one final time. I will travel with the last of those returning to their home circling another star – perhaps one which, even as I write this missive, pours its cold light down upon my lonely Pacific island – and my work here will be done.

And so once again I'll see the sun come out in the night. And I'll see the dead live again, as my dear friend Alexander predicted. And I'll see such scientific wonders as you who may one day read my words cannot possibly imagine.

Closing my eyes in anticipation, I see a galactic Easter. A world reborn. And who could ask for a better epitaph than that? Some may think me cursed, but I am blessed. For mine is the eye which has seen heaven.

Soon now, I will see it again.

Horace Stockwood, MRGS
Easter Island, Earth
December 1902

Author's Note: Invasion of the B-Movie

No. I haven't got religion. True, *Eternity Weeps* and *Eye of Heaven* both contain rather large gobbets of religious symbology. This is more, I think, to do with the saturation of religion into modern society than it is an indication of my (somewhat odd at the best of times) world-view. Then again, it does provide some spankingly cool imagery. And, I guess, it's something you can fall back on, like the ubiquitous 'Destruction of the Universe' or the infamous 'It's a Million-to-One Shot but It Might Just Work' syndrome, which seems to have sleazed its way into the annals of current literature, TV and film with equally terrifying thoroughness. As far as I'm concerned, if there is a god, then God is capricious. I asked for two miracles in my life. One got you these books. The other, the most important swap I ever wanted… Well, I guess God had something better to do: Dad got to keep his brain tumour and I got to live to write this. Them's the breaks, I guess.

Also guilty of providing inspiration for some of the imagery in this book are various pieces of literature, one exceedingly cool novel and two classic children's novels from the misbegotten days of my primary-school youth, together with a couple of classic vids. And they are: *Aku-Aku*, Thor Heyerdahl; *Portsmouth in the Past*, William G. Gates; *Classic Sailing Ships*, Kenneth Giggal and Cornelius de Vries; *The Clipper Line*, Francis Chichester; *Deep Time*, David Darling; *Whale Adventure*, Willard Price; *Contact*, Carl Sagan; *The Last Battle*, C.S. Lewis; *The Face of Evil*, Chris Boucher (ta for the spot-on review of *Decalog 5*, by the way); and the wonderful *Marco Polo* by John Lucarotti. Cheesy Movie of the Week award goes to Jan du Bont's *Twister*. Best TV Mini Series in the History of the Universe award goes with a vengeance to *Tales from a Parallel Universe*. Check it out: it's awesome, and then some (and then some more).

A luvverly 'ello guv'nor to the usual suspects: Jo (!!!???satisfied???!!!) and Steve, Jop and Andrea, Mum and Dad, Andy and Sue, Trees, Timbo, and Kurt, Thomas and Gizmo, Brandy, Caffreys, and Bess (remember: wallpaper-paste cocktails are not cool), Allan, Roger, Miles, Steve, and Phyl, Jon, Alison, and Zak, and all the etceteraz, whachamacallitz, oojamaflipz and howzyerfatherz. Cheers to Alan and Alis for supplying invaluable reference material, and a big nod for Trees's dad, who supplied the most perfect book about Portsmouth in the precise decade I needed information about, on less than no notice, when the best work of reference I could find in *the whole of Bristol* in *an entire month of looking* was twenty words on the back of a Brook Bond PG Tips card. Oh yeah: hi to Dave Owen and Leon Vincent (ta for the cool reviews) and Steve (*whipping noises* – 'I don't have the manuscript, I assume you're down the post office posting it now!') Cole, my editor, menacing whisperer and long-suffering answerphone demon.

SPECIAL MESSAGE: Help! I'm going through a mad retro phase. I need LEGO™. I need it *now*. If everyone who buys this book sends me just one brick I'll have twenty thousand bricks – and suddenly that awe-inspiringly realistic, rotating, illuminated, auctioned-for-charity, contributors-get-to-name-a-character-in-the-next-book, six-foot-long *Babylon 5* model starts to become terrifyingly real. *Doesn't it?* Address in the back of *Eternity Weeps*. Thank you, I love you, you're gorgeous.

EXTRA-SPECIAL MESSAGE: Stop press! Nakula's getting married and moving to Ireland. Ace or wot?

A word of warning: never let your buddies buy you glow-in-the-dark Space Mucus. Take a postcard instead. Take a used banana skin. In fact take *anything*. Trust me on this.

And finally, in anticipation of twenty more episodes of *Sex, Insects and More Sex*, I bid you adieu and I'm

Outtahere –

Jimbo